2/15

EVERYTHING
BURNS

OTHER NOVELS BY VINCENT ZANDRI

The Remains

The Concrete Pearl

Scream Catcher

Lost Grace

Permanence

THE CHASE BAKER SERIES

The Shroud Key

THE JACK MARCONI PI NOVELS

The Innocent

Godchild

The Guilty

THE DICK MOONLIGHT PI NOVELS

Moonlight Falls

Moonlight Mafia

Moonlight Rises

Blue Moonlight

Full Moonlight

Murder by Moonlight

Moonlight Sonata

Moonlight Breaks Bad

Moonlight Weeps

EVERYTHING BURNS

VINCENT ZANDRI

 THOMAS & MERCER

For Laura

"Fire! Fire!" says the Town Crier;
"Where? Where?" says Goody Blaire;
"Down the town," says Goody Brown;
"I'll go and see't!" says Goody Fleet;
"So will I," says Goody Fry;
"Burn! Burn!" says Goody Stern. "Burn her! Burn him!"

—Nursery Rhyme, circa 1920

"When life gives you lemons, you put the lemons down and go burn down a building."

—Unidentified Pyromaniac

Prologue

The boy wakes to smoke and fire.

The thick black smoke chokes his ten-year-old lungs as if he were swallowing dirt. It makes his eyes water and sting. Makes the darkness that fills his small second-floor corner bedroom even darker.

Then there's the heat.

A heat like he's never felt before. But that's not right. He's felt this kind of heat on other occasions, under far different circumstances. When his father, after a long day's work, would build fires in the fireplace he built himself out of fieldstone in the downstairs living room. Sometimes, after coming in from playing out in the cold and the snow, the boy would warm himself by the fire. He would sit on the stone ledge only inches away from the dry wood–fed flames until he could feel the heat seeping through layers of thick clothing. If he sat there for too long, the heat would penetrate the layers and burn his skin until it stung. The fire brought him pain then, but it was a good pain.

That's the kind of heat he's feeling now. Only thing is, the pain that comes with it is not good.

Some of the heat is making its way through the wall that separates his bedroom from his parents' master bedroom. More heat is blowing in from the hallway, where the fire burns and creeps. When he looks over his shoulder, he can make out the flashes of firelight that break through the thick darkness out in the hall. The fire gives the hall a strange, flickering glow. Like candlelight dancing against the walls, only bigger, hotter, deadlier. His heart pounds and his smoke-filled lungs ache. He coughs and chokes. He's just a boy, but he knows that this should not be happening in the upstairs of his home in the night.

Then comes a scream.

The scream is louder than the fire and pierces his flesh and bone like a sharp knife. The scream belongs to his mother.

She keeps screaming.

Her screams are high-pitched and filled with suffering, like she's trapped in hell. He knows she's in pain. He closes his eyes, tries to convince himself that what's happening is a nightmare, and that if he closes his eyes tight he'll go back to sleep. If he closes his eyes now, he'll wake up to sunshine leaking in through his windows in the morning and everything will be okay. His mother won't be screaming anymore. She'll be downstairs in the kitchen wrapped in her old blue terry-cloth robe, making pancakes while the first cigarette of the day dangles from her lips. His two older brothers will be dressed and fighting over who gets to drive the pickup truck to high school that day. His father will already be off to work.

His mother's screams strike a new, fiercer pitch, jarring his eyes back open.

This scream is followed by a kind of guttural moan, and then, nothing. The boy lies on his back, his eyes wide open, feeling the wetness from the tears flowing down his smooth cheeks. Even in all his despair he's a little surprised because the tears dry up as fast as they pour out of his eyes. The heat has become that intense, the flames that close.

Suddenly the figure of a man appears in his doorway. It's the boy's father.

"We have to get the hell out of here, Reece!" his father shouts in between lung-choking coughs.

"Dad," Reece cries above the roar of a flame that is eating away the walls, "are we going to die?"

His father enters into the bedroom, wraps his red, white, and blue Superman comforter tightly around him, and lifts his youngest son from the bed. He then cradles Reece in his big arms, presses the boy's face into his chest to protect him from the fire that is sure to come.

"Listen to me, Reece," his father says. "We have to make a run through the fire. You are not to inhale a breath. You understand? When I tell you to, I want you to close your mouth and your eyes and don't breathe. You got it? Do not take a breath."

Reece tries to say something while his face is stuffed against his dad's chest, yet it's impossible for him to utter a single word. But then, what difference does it make? He's far too afraid to speak anyway.

Turning for the door, his father grips him so tightly, Reece feels like his bones might break. "Ready?" his father shouts above the roar of the flame. "Close your eyes and your mouth. Do it now."

Reece does it. At the same time, he feels himself being propelled out the open bedroom door, then down a hallway that is hellishly hot and deafeningly loud. He feels as if he's been tossed into a furnace, the iron door slammed shut behind him. He hears his father do something he's never heard him do before. His father screams. The voice is piercing and filled with pain, just like his mother's voice sounded only a split second before her shrieks suddenly stopped.

Then he feels himself descending the stairs. Still clutched in his father's arms, he's falling fast, until he feels his father's feet land square and flat onto the stone vestibule floor. The front door is wrenched open and slammed against the interior brick wall, the big opaque glass panel embedded inside it shattering into a million pieces, and just like that, a wave of cool air slaps his exposed head along with the small portion of his face that's no longer stuffed into his father's chest.

His father runs out onto the lawn with Reece now bouncing in his arms, until he drops the boy onto the damp lawn and begins roughly *rolling him back and forth, as if they are playing a summertime game of roll-down-the-hill-on-your-side. But this is not a game. It doesn't take long for Reece to realize his comforter is on fire and if it should burn through the fabric, it will scorch his skin.*

All it takes for the fire to go out is a couple of rolls on the dew-soaked lawn.

"Breathe now, boy," his father says from down on his knees, his voice having gone from panicked and loud to an exasperated whisper. "Breathe."

Reece opens his eyes and inhales a mouthful of sweet night air. But the sweetness lasts only as long as it takes his eyes to focus on a house that is entirely engulfed in red-orange flame. Emerging from out of the darkness now is a team of firemen who carry hoses and axes. Their faces are covered by translucent oxygen masks, their thick shoulders bearing the weight of heavy oxygen tanks. There's a squad of fire trucks, police cruisers, and EMS vans parked up on the lawn, their rooftop flashers beaming red, white, and blue light throughout the neighborhood. A never-still light that reflects off the vinyl siding of the cookie-cutter ranches and colonials.

"What about Mom?" Reece cries out while sitting up, touching a painful place on his head where his hair caught fire. "What about Tommy? And Patrick?"

He locks his eyes onto his father and is shocked to see what's become of him. The dark hair on the man's head is partially burned away, and his right ear and cheek are blackened and blistered like a hamburger patty that's been left out on the grill for far too long. A long blister has formed on his right arm where the sleeve of his pajamas has burned off. The blister runs the length of the arm. It makes the boy's back teeth hurt just to look at it.

"They're gone, Reece," his father says as he begins to sob.

"What do you mean, Dad? How are they gone?"

"I couldn't get to them in time. It was just too hot. Your mother . . . I warned her about smoking in bed. I told her what would happen."

"Did Mom start the fire? Did she burn my brothers?"

"She didn't mean to start it, Reece," he cries. "But now she's killed them all."

Reece watches his father cry. Watches the man bury his face in his burned hands as the ashes from the fire rise up into the night and disappear into an eternal darkness. His eyes might be glued to his father, but in his head he sees his mother and his brothers burning in their beds. He sees their skin on fire, burning, sizzling, charring.

Reece listens to his father's sobs and it makes his heart burn with a sadness so profound, he feels as if his body will melt into the earth. The destruction is all around him. It has become a part of him now and of who he will become tomorrow, and the day after that and the day after that.

He is haunted by fire.

BOOK I

Chapter 1

October, present day
Albany, New York
___

"You're sure that going under the knife all by your lonesome is a good idea?" I say as my frantic ex-wife, Lisa, grabs her overnight bag and slings it over her shoulder, careful not to catch her long, lush, dark brown hair under the thick leather strap. "What if something goes catastrophically wrong?"

Lisa shoots me a look that's part smile, part smirk.

"I think it's you who's nervous about being left alone," she says. Then, "Here's an idea: Why don't you call Blood and have him stay with you?"

Blood is my part-time research assistant. A tall, formidable former Green Haven Prison inmate, the muscular black man is one of the smartest and most loyal friends I have in the city. It also so happens that I saved his life one late summer afternoon when we were crossing Lark Street in downtown Albany immediately following some research conducted at our favorite wine bar.

"Can you imagine my asking Blood to babysit me?" I say after a prolonged beat. "He'd probably tell me to go out and buy a pair of big-boy panties."

"You saved him from getting mashed by that car outside the Laundromat," Lisa says. "He feels he owes you."

"That doesn't mean he has to watch over me like I'm a five-year-old. My dad raised me better than that. He taught me to be self-reliant."

"You go with that, Mr. Independence," she says. "Your dad raised you on his own. He had no choice but to make you independent." She shifts her head so that she's now facing the single-story ranch home's one long corridor. "Anna, let's get a move on!"

Then, her eyes back on me, "Okay, I get it, macho man. No Blood. But the question remains: Are you going to be all right staying here alone? This is the first time you'll be all alone overnight in my house in the two months we've been back together." Leaning into me, to whisper in my ear. "No rummaging through my underwear drawer, big fella." She takes me by surprise by cupping her hand gently but still alarmingly around my unmentionables.

"Yikes," I blurt out, but as she removes her hand, I grab for it. "Hey, don't stop now."

Her hand escapes me.

"You'll have to take care of that yourself," she laughs. "I'll be out of commission for a few days."

"Coming, Mommy," I hear from the direction of Anna's room. Eight years and two months old but going on thirty, Anna is our only child together. A self-proclaimed fashionista, the tall-for-her-years, slim third-grader is always late getting out the door for anything, be it the school bus or friends wanting to ride bikes around the neighborhood. After all, she can't go out in public with long hair that's not highlighted with yellow and red streaks or clipped up in a crazy 'do that mimics Selena Gomez or Hannah Montana. Although, if I were to mention any of these names to her, she would no doubt stick her index finger in her mouth and, while fake-gagging, retort with something like "Ummm, I don't think so, Reecey Pieces. Hannah Montana is like soooo long gone."

"Maybe Anna should stay here with me, Leese," I say, fingering the inch-long scar that I earned on the day my childhood home burned to the ground. "We can make homemade pizza for dinner. I promise not to burn it this time. In fact, why don't you change your mind and stay home tonight."

But she shakes her head while going through the pockets on her long brown suede coat, the one we picked up at the leather market in Florence on our honeymoon ten years ago. Searching for her keys or Ray-Ban aviator sunglasses or iPhone or wallet or lipstick or some combination thereof, she shoots me a look with her extra-wide brown eyes. Eyes that still send a wave of warmth up and down my backbone when I peer into them.

"Reece," she says, her tone stern, "are you really willing to give up two full days of writing to take care of me? I'm having my tear ducts fixed. That means I'm going to be partially blinded by ice packs for forty-eight hours. Do you have any idea what that means?"

"Means you can't see me," I say, stuffing my hands into the pockets of my jeans. It's what I do when I'm nervous or feeling guilty or both, which is precisely the case right now. Years ago, I might have lit a few matches, one after the other, in order to calm myself down. At the very least, I would have flicked the flame on a Bic lighter I might store in my pants pocket just like some people might keep a rabbit's foot or a lucky coin. But now that I'm over the power of fire, I just satisfy myself with keeping my hands busy in other ways.

"I can't see you. Brilliant response." Lisa faux-smiles. "You should be a best-selling novelist. But there's more to it. I'll be on my back for hours at a time. Aside from the icing, I must remain perfectly still, or so the doctor tells me." She finally finds her car keys and her aviators in her coat pocket. She slips on the sunglasses. They make her look as young and beautiful as the day we met at a local Starbucks fifteen years ago. "Plus you'll have to look after

Anna. I know it pains your artistic heart to know that my parents can do a far better job of it. But they can." She purses her lips, takes a glance at them in a mirror that hangs on the wall beside the closet, but then quickly shifts her focus to her watch. "Anna, now!"

"Coming, Mommy. You don't have to shout."

I catch a quick glimpse of my salt-and-pepper–stubbled face in the mirror as Anna emerges from her bedroom like a rock star taking the stage. She's wearing high heels, orange tights, a pleather mini-skirt, and a blue zipper sweatshirt that has the word "PINK" printed on it across the chest in hot pink lettering. Her hair defies gravity from one of those red plastic alligator clips, and it's going a dozen different directions on purpose. Covering her eyes is a pair of bright yellow cat-eye sunglasses Lisa picked up for her in the dollar bin at the local Target. Strapped over her shoulder is a cloth bag that's filled with the DVDs and CDs that will amuse her while she's doing time at her grandparents' house. I can't see it, but I'm sure her fire-engine red mini PSP video game player is stuffed somewhere in there too.

Lisa and I lock our collective eyes on our spawn.

"She's eight years old," I say. "That outfit would be perfect on Forty-Second Street circa 1978."

Lisa shakes her head, says, "I don't have time for her to change. Anyway, she'll be locked in the house with my dad while my mother stays with me for the operation."

A car horn honks from out on the driveway.

"Oh dear God," I say, eyes wide with alarm. "It's your mother. Quick, where do I hide?"

"Funny," Lisa says.

Frankie, our two-year-old Italian greyhound and Chihuahua mix, comes storming into the living room, leaps onto the couch, and starts barking up a storm like she actually poses a threat to any-one who might think of intruding. But in all reality, the ten-pound, black-and-white spotted pooch is more pussycat than dog.

"Easy, Frank," I say. "It's just Vickie. It's me she hates."

"Cut it out, Reece," Lisa snaps.

The doorbell rings. Lisa unlocks the deadbolt, opens the main wood door and then the screen door to reveal a small woman in her early seventies but who might easily pass for fifty. Like her daughter, her hair is dark brown and thick, and they both share the same lips and perfect nose. She's wearing a short, fall-weight wool skirt over matching tights and tall black Italian boots similar to the ones Lisa's wearing. Parked in the driveway is her brand new Volvo station wagon, the engine still idling.

"Ready to go?" She smiles at the females while shooting me an eyes-at-half-mast look that cuts through me like flame through tissue paper. Truth is, Lisa's mother is not so crazy about seeing me. Never has been since Lisa and I divorced eight years back. But she's even more unhappy to see me now that her daughter and I decided to give the relationship one more try two months ago.

But then, thinking back on it, Vickie was never crazy about Lisa marrying a writer in the first place. Especially a broke writer unknowingly entering into what would become a seemingly incurable bout of writer's block. Lisa's parents had always hoped she'd hook up with an accountant or a doctor or even a big-time CEO of a major law firm, like her dad. But when Lisa sets her sights on something or someone, there's no talking her out of it, no matter the consequences. Even though they've threatened to yank her monthly trust fund allowance over my return, it hasn't happened yet.

"And a good morning to you, Victoria," I say in my best Eddie Haskell. "You look positively ravishing this morning."

"Can it, Reece," she says, along with a pronounced roll of her dark eyes. "How's your new novel going? It must be keeping you very busy to keep you from bringing Lisa for her eye surgery."

"Mom, we went over this," Lisa interjects. "Reece has to work."

I nod emphatically. "Yes, I'm very busy, Vic. Fact is, a true artist's work is never done, merely abandoned. Guess you can't say that about the lawyering profession, can you?"

"Well, I sure hope we're making money this time around," she says in a mock singsongy voice.

"That's enough, you two," Lisa says, buttoning up her coat. "I'll be right out, Mom." Then, "Anna, go with Vickie, please."

"Hi, Vickie," Anna sings, preferring to call her grandma by her given name. Something Grandma doesn't seem to mind in the least. "Can I sit in the front seat?"

"No you may not, Anna," Victoria informs the child, bending down in a way that allows Anna the chance to kiss her politely on the cheek, not on the lips.

The front screen door opens and our eight-year-old would-be pop star steps out onto the concrete landing.

"That's some outfit you have on, young lady," Victoria comments, holding the door open for my daughter.

Raising the fingers on my right hand to my lips, I shoot Anna a kiss.

"Be good, Acid Queen," I say.

"Please don't call her that," Lisa jumps in.

"Good-bye, Reecey Pieces," Anna says.

"When are you going to call me Dad?"

"You ain't my dad, silly."

"Very funny, Anna banana," I say, seeing myself holding her in my arms only seconds after she was born. She bore a full head of dark hair, and I swear she was smiling. My dad was standing by my side, slightly taller than me, his thick black hair having thinned and turned white ages ago.

"You sure you want to name the little angel after your mother?" he said. I remember nodding, feeling my eyes fill with tears.

"Yes," I said. "Lisa and I can't imagine naming her anything else." I remember the sad smile he assumed as he reached out with his fire-scarred hand and touched her cheek.

"Give my best to Alexander, Victoria," I call after them.

"I'll leave that up to you," my former mother-in-law grouses, allowing the screen door to close on its own. For those not in the know, Alexander is Victoria's rather serious and very strict husband of fifty or so years. Like his wife, Alexander was never crazy about my career choice and is even less crazy about it now that I've reentered the family fold, as it were. Taking hold of Anna's hand, Victoria begins accompanying the little girl to the car. As the two disappear from view, I can't help but hear Anna's words resonating in my head.

"You ain't my dad, silly."

The words may be said all in fun, but they still sting me, burn me. Worse than the fire that took away my mother and brothers all those years ago, leaving my dad and me to fend for ourselves. In the back of my mind, I can't help but ask the question *What if it were true? What if it were to turn out that Anna is truly not my daughter?* But these are the questions of a fiction writer with an overactive imagination, and therefore they are questions best left ignored.

With Frankie having resumed her near-perpetual curled-up sleeping position on the floor in the playroom, which is just off the dining room at the back of the house, the joint grows ominously silent. But then the silence is broken by Lisa's cell phone, which blares out a tune from Lady Gaga. Pulling the phone from her pocket, she looks at the digital ID readout. Her lips grow tight while she whispers, "I'll call him back later."

Call him back. Call who back?

Then, as she returns the phone to her pocket, "Do you and my mother always have to bicker?"

"I wasn't bickering. I thought I was being nice . . . And who is the *him* you need to call back?"

"You know, Reece, if it weren't for my parents, Anna and I would've had no way of getting by all these years while you were building your writing career. And forgive me for bringing it up, but when you got sick after we split up, it was me who took care of the hospital bill."

Just the mention of my writer's block–induced nervous breakdown, which occurred only weeks after we broke up in September of 2006, and the resulting hospitalization and electroshock therapy, sends a chill throughout my body. Lisa is correct in that she did foot the bill for the stay. But it was worth every penny since the therapy finally resulted in breaking down my block, which, truth be told, had actually begun to crumble ever so slowly almost from the minute I walked out of Lisa's life, as if she had somehow been the cause of it all along. In any case, the therapy, when combined with my new single status, would eventually pave the way for the completion of my first novel, *The Damned*.

"Okay, I surrender," I say, a sly smile now painting my face. "You're right. Your parents have been kind. They did buy you this house. And you did pay for my stay at Four Winds Psychiatric Facility, which is the same as saying Vickie and Alex paid for it. But believe me, electroshock therapy is no holiday."

Lisa pinches my stubble-covered cheek. "You got me there, Reecey Pieces," she says. "I'm being a tad insensitive. But allow me to pose a question regarding my parents' generous financial gifts: Would you rather I worked a full-time job while Anna was tossed into day care, day in and day out? You know how many of those kids wet their beds every night?"

A wave of warm remorse washes over me.

"I couldn't really afford you guys until recently." It sounds strange coming from my mouth. But it's the truth, and sometimes the truth sounds far stranger than fiction.

She lowers her hand.

"You've done well for yourself, Reece," she says. "I'm proud of you. I love you. I know you haven't had it easy. But you still have a few things to learn in the parenting department. Important things."

"It's true," I have to admit. "Life's easier when all you're looking after is yourself."

"I'm glad you're back," she says, gently kissing me on the mouth.

Whenever Lisa kisses me I feel like I'm levitating. It's a feeling I was never able to forget when we were apart and something I will never get sick of for as long as I live. Maybe even longer.

The car horn honks once more.

"I really should go," she says, once again reaching into her coat pockets, this time coming back out with her car keys. "Vickie is already wound tighter than a snare drum this morning." She holds the key ring out for me.

"You don't want to take your keys? What if you need them to get into your folks' house?"

"I'll be half-blind, and my mother will be with me, remember?"

I stare down at the packed ring of keys. There's a full set for the locks on her house she had changed at my insistence immediately after she and her ex-boyfriend, David, broke up. There are keys to her parents' house, to her Volkswagen, and to the red Ford Escape I inherited from my dad after he died. Plus a plastic swipe card for the gym and yet another one for a VIP cost-saving membership at the supermarket up the road. I can't help but notice something written in blue ballpoint on the supermarket card. A five-digit number.

"What's this?" I say, holding up the plastic swipe card while the many keys dangle off the metal ring.

She gazes at the keys while pulling her coat collar up. "That's Dad's house alarm code."

"You keep it on your Price Chopper card? Jeez, what if it gets stolen?"

"It's just a random set of numbers, and it won't get stolen."

"Here's an idea: memorize it."

"Are you kidding? I can't remember my PIN number for my debit card or my Facebook password. The digital age sucks sometimes."

"Yeah, but if not for Facebook you wouldn't have hooked up with David."

"Leave him out of this, please. David, and everything that happened between us, is now the very distant past."

Like I said, David is the boyfriend and lover Lisa took on almost immediately after we split up eight years, one month, and five days ago. It was a love that lasted the entire time we were apart and that no doubt had been brewing while we were still together. The newly formed pit in my chest reminds me of the phone call she ignored moments ago.

Another honk from an overanxious and over-annoyed Victoria.

"Really, Reece, I've got to go."

Setting the ring of keys on the rail of the small bench that's been built into the vestibule wall, I take my ex-wife into my arms, hug her tightly. At five feet ten inches she's a full inch taller than me. When she wears thick-soled boots, she's even taller. It forces me to gaze slightly upward into her sunglass-covered eyes before I kiss her mouth.

"Good luck, baby. You know, your eyes are perfect just the way they are, even if they do tear up too much."

"I'm forty-two," she says. "Trust me. I'm at the age when the body parts start wearing out and sinking. Next year I'm having a tummy tuck."

"So what you're saying is I *missed out* on your prime time while David *lucked out.*"

"Oh for God's sakes, Reece, get over him already. Besides, you won't even want me in a year."

"Bite your tongue. I didn't get you back just to let you slip through my fingers again."

"I'll let you bite my naked butt when I get home on Wednesday afternoon, big boy. How does that sound?"

I feel a twinge in my stomach when she says it.

She turns, opens the screen door, steps on out. I'm not sure why, but just looking at the black Volvo pulled up in the driveway reminds me of something else. Something not very pleasant. Something I'd rather forget. I see another vehicle that was parked in that very spot, night after night, year after year. A brown four-wheel-drive Honda CR-V hatchback that belonged to David Bourenhem, the man who stole Lisa's heart at a time in my life when I'd become impossible to live with due to my writer's block. Weird thing was, David was a writer like me. According to Lisa, I'd met him once before when he came to the house to show me his manuscript, back when the two former high school friends had gotten reacquainted on Facebook sometime back in the late spring or summer of 2005. This wasn't all that long before Lisa got pregnant with Anna. Later on, when I left the house and Lisa started seeing him for real, she continued to insist that I had met him and even talked writing with him. But for the life of me, I could not place him. Even when I looked up his scruffy face on Facebook, I still could not remember him. But then, since my most recent bout of electroshock therapy, I tended to not remember certain things all that well. Or maybe the therapy simply made it easier for me to forget instances and people I'd rather not remember, which is more likely the case. Maybe I just didn't want to remember the face of the man who was lying beside my wife every night in my place. We don't talk a whole lot about it, but Lisa claims that my reentering her life has not sat well with David, for obvious reasons. To make matters worse, my gut has been telling me that he's been e-mailing, texting, and calling Lisa again. But whenever I ask her about it, she denies it.

I'll call him back later . . .

From the open front door, I watch my ex-wife and present lover descend the few steps down the landing to the short walk that leads to the driveway.

I can't help myself. I have to know.

"Lisa," I call out. "That was him, wasn't it? David."

I feel the weight of the screen door resting against my shoulder.

Lisa stops, turns, shakes her head. "It wasn't him, Reece. It was my doctor, if you must know . . . if you insist on not trusting me."

"I trust you."

"Okay, maybe you trust me, but you don't trust David. Don't trust our breakup. You're letting him get to you, Reece. Let it go. David's as docile as a puppy. His feelings are hurt. That's all. He's not calling me."

"His feelings are hurt because I got you back, or because I'm a best-selling author and he's the wannabe?"

She laughs, but it's not a happy laugh.

"You really are a tool, you know that, Reece?" The horn honks yet again, startling Lisa. She shoots her mother a look to kill. Then, turning back to me, she smiles. "But a cute tool. Promise me you won't get all paranoid while I'm not home for a couple of days. Keep yourself occupied. If it's too much for you to stay in the house alone, go to your writing studio or at the very least, text Blood, tell him to come over. Okay? Promise me?"

"I'll be okay, Lisa," I say, knowing it could very well be a lie. "I'm better now. No more anxieties. No more writer's block. No more benders. No more fires. Just good stuff to look forward to."

She kisses her hand and tosses the kiss to me. I return the favor. I watch her graceful body as it jogs to the car, the black mini-skirt she's wearing over black tights accentuating the muscles in her heart-shaped bottom.

"I'm a lucky, healthy man," I whisper as she gets into the car, closing the door behind her. As the car backs out, Frankie trots into the living room, jumps up onto the couch. I close the door behind me, lock the deadbolt. "I'm a lucky, healthy, happy, best-selling author. Isn't that right, Frank?"

Frankie just looks at me like I'm still nuts.

"I'm a lucky, healthy, happy, best-selling author who is fine with the fact that the one woman in the world he's ever obsessed over has been fucking another man for a whole bunch of years."

Feeling a surge of warm adrenaline fill my brain, I head into the kitchen and spot the cordless phone sitting out on the counter. Let's not call it paranoia. Let's call it writer's intuition. But something tells me that Lisa is lying and that David has indeed been calling again.

I pick up the phone.

Chapter 2

I see my dad. See him as clearly as if he's really standing there, only a couple of feet away from me in the vestibule of Lisa's house. He's wearing his usual uniform of pressed khaki pants and a short-sleeve, button-down shirt that exposes a burn scar that runs almost the entire length of his arm.

Don't even start, Reece, he says. *Ignore the voice inside your head that's telling you to search the list of called numbers on that phone, to turn the whole joint upside down. Ignore the tightness in your stomach and the pit in your chest that tells you Lisa can't be trusted. It's not worth it, Son.*

You see, he says, *it's* you *who can't be trusted.*

It's you who spent two months in the nuthouse for lighting that fire on the back deck of her house only weeks after walking out on her. The fire that would have killed them all if the flame had taken. But that was a long time ago. And you're all better now. You have a stellar career, you have your health, you have some scratch in your pocket, and most of all, you have Lisa to call your own again. You both made mistakes along the way and you succeeded in hurting one another. But now you've agreed to look beyond the mistakes of the past and to try one final time. If not for you both, then for Anna's sake. So why take a chance on screwing that all up for a second time?

Focus on something else.

Get out of the house. Go for a run. Go out for breakfast. Go to the Starbucks and write. Go away for the night. Go see your agent in the city. Or call Blood. Go drinking with him. Just don't start searching the house for something you do not want to find. Lisa has taken you back. She wants to give it another try, even after all the crap that went down the first time around. Isn't that enough to tell you she loves you? Wants you? Forgives you? Forgives herself?

Don't do it.

Don't dig too deep, don't think too hard. There are things about you and Lisa and the past that you are just not going to want to remember. You hear me, Reece? Some things are better off forgotten. Don't open that lid, Son. Because once you pry it off, you'll never get it back on.

Just. Don't. Do. It.

Here's what I do instead: I set the phone back down onto the counter, go to the junk drawer, dig around in the very back behind all the junk. I find the little pack of wood matches that I've stored there for just such an emergency, when my anxiety begins to get the best of me. Stuffing the matches into my jeans pocket, I head out the back sliding glass door, then out through the gate in the fence to the left of the deck. I follow the fence line until I come to a dirt road that leads to the edge of Little's Lake State Park, which abuts Lisa's property.

The park is protected by a chain-link fence, which I can easily scale. Jumping down onto its opposite side, I head through the weeds and bushes until I come to the park. Set directly before me is Little's Lake, which is more like a very large, kidney-shaped pond. To my right is the swamp and beyond that, a small patch of woods consisting mostly of tall pines. To my left is a picnic area that also serves as a small, sandy beach. Several garbage cans made of heavy concrete and metal are situated throughout the picnic area beside some black metal charcoal grills that beer-drinking teenagers use for burning wood during the cool weekend nights.

I go to the first can that's facing me, look inside it. It's filled with paper cartons, old newspapers, and other junk.

Perfect . . .

Looking one way and then the other, I grab hold of a chunk of newspaper and roll it into a tight, one-foot length of paper pipe. Then, reaching into my pocket, I pull out the matches and take one from the box. I strike the match and bring the orange flame to the tip of the dry newspaper. The paper takes the fire like it's been waiting for it. As it rapidly combusts, giving off its heat, I feel the calmness that envelops my insides. It's a feeling that can only be duplicated by sex, and even then, sex can be hit or miss sometimes. But fire? Well, fire always performs because after all, everything burns.

Dropping the paper into the can, it only takes a few seconds for the entire container to light up so that the flame shoots out of the top round opening like a volcano that's just erupted. I can't help but recall an old nursery rhyme my mom used to recite when I was just a little boy. It helped to calm me down at night when I couldn't sleep.

"Fire! Fire!" says the Town Crier.

"Where? Where?" says Goody Blaire.

"'Burn! Burn!" says Goody Stern. "Burn her! Burn him!"

Once more I look over both shoulders, knowing that if I get caught, I'm being carted away to jail. Now that my dad is dead, I'll have no choice but to track down Blood to bail me out.

Okay, maybe I lied a little. Maybe I'm not over fire.

Maybe I never will be.

But lighting these garbage cans on fire every now and again is better than lighting someone's home on fire. At least that's what I keep on telling myself as I turn tail and head back to Lisa's house.

Chapter 3

When I slip back inside the house through the sliding glass doors, I can see that Frankie is lapping water from her dish. When she's done, she turns, looks up at me with her big black eyes.

"You're giving me that look again, Frank," I say, my eyes shifting from the dog to the phone and back again. "You know, the look that says you're worried about me. Well, let me reassure you that I am in total control of my situation . . . my *alone* situation."

I'm picturing the garbage container and the fire that is no doubt still burning strong. I listen for the sound of fire engines, but I don't hear a thing other than my heart pounding in my chest.

"What is it with writers?" says Frankie. Or should I say, it's what I imagine she would say, if only she could talk. "You can't stand having people around you, but then you go completely nuts when you're left all alone."

I consider this while pursing my lips.

"We usually end up shooting ourselves," I say. "Or hanging from the rafters. Or, in my case anyway, burning things down. At the very least, we sometimes engage in imaginary conversations with dogs."

I can't help but imagine what my older brothers would have done if they saw me conversing with one of the dogs that used to roam our neighborhood back in the seventies. Tommy, a thickly black-haired, mature seventeen-year-old and the weight lifter of the family, probably would have tossed his big arm around my neck and put me in a chokehold until I swore I would never talk to another dog again. Patrick, the younger at sixteen, and whose freckled face and red hair made us wonder where he came from, would have laughed his ass off and poked fun at me until I cried. But when the tears finally came they'd both take me out for ice cream.

In my mind, they are both still teenagers, and both still watching out for me even while busting my chops.

"And what an imagination you have," Frankie says. "Being a human must suck. But being a human *and* a paranoid artist must double-suck."

The dog engages in a full-body shake that actually lifts her four paws off the floor, like a wind-up dog you buy at Kmart. Then she turns her back on me and heads down into the playroom for a nap.

"Yeah, I love you too, Frankie."

Turning back to the counter, I once more lock eyes on the house phone that's just sitting there. It's lying on its side on the white Formica-covered counter beside a sink filled with dirty breakfast dishes, as if Lisa either didn't have time to place it back on the cradle in the playroom or, in her rush to get out of here, absentmindedly tossed it onto the counter and forgot about it.

Don't do it. Don't touch the phone.

For the second time that morning, I pick the phone up. Just gripping it with my right hand makes my stomach grow tight while that pit in my chest gets bigger. Maybe it has something to do with the newness of my relationship with Lisa. My second-go-round relationship, that is. You would think that by now, I would know Lisa inside and out. But then, we've spent the better part of the last decade apart, much of that time occupied with other lovers. Like I said, people change.

As much as I think I still know her, a major part of Lisa seems like a stranger to me now. What's different? It's not easy to put my finger on it. But she seems more confident. Like the life she's experienced without me has somehow affected her in ways she and I both never would have imagined. Her life experiences with David, that is.

Example: I've seen it in our lovemaking.

What used to be the typical heavy-petting foreplay followed by the few minutes of missionary-position sex has now become something much more complicated, for lack of a better word. Lisa talks now, for one thing. Lying on her back in bed, she'll ask me to do things to her that, years ago, never would have crossed her mind. Things that involve the tying of limbs, or blindfolding, or simply watching or being watched. She's even asked me to recount for her in detail my sexual escapades with other women during our separation, especially the sex I had with Rachael, the woman who became my lover for three years. The more accurately I recount the sex, the more turned on she seems to get. It's an entirely new experience for me, and it can be as exciting as it can be disturbing.

Lisa has changed. There's no denying it. Nothing unusual about that.

But I can't wrap my head around the fact that David is entirely responsible for changing her. He's the only man she shared a bed with after I left. Or so she's assured me. Her relationship with him lasted far longer than our marriage. Sometimes I can't help but think that David is still changing her. That this mystery man, David Bourenhem, the man who replaced me in Lisa's bed, is forever going to be in her life, whether I like it or not.

Holding the phone in my hand, I stare down at the black-on-white digital push-button numbers, at the clear electronic readout, at the green "Talk" button, and the red "End" button. Located in the center of the phone is a push-button command application that allows you to access a list of incoming calls or a list of outgoing calls.

I feel the cold, hard plastic of the phone resting in the hot, perspiring palm of my hand, and I thumb the command for incoming calls. The first call that appears is the most recent. The date on the light-up display is today. The time is eight thirty in the morning. The caller ID reads "Vickie." Lisa's mother.

I thumb to the next caller.

It says "Olga," and it's from last night. Olga is one of Lisa's neighborhood "mom" friends, even if the fortysomething woman is childless and recently divorced. She lives all by herself just a few houses down from Lisa.

Next person on the list is Blood. Although he would never lower himself to leave an actual message, I know he's returning my call from last week regarding the novel I'm presently writing and some research I'm in need of. I make a mental note to call him back.

Next caller. It's a 1-800 number. A cold caller looking to sell something.

I thumb the device for the next number. My heart beats a paradiddle in my chest. It's as if my gut knows exactly who the next caller will be even before I press the button. The name "David" appears. He called yesterday afternoon, when I would have been at the gym. Three o'clock on the dime. As if the call were planned that way.

My heart goes from beating to pounding.

I thumb through the rest of the numbers. David's number shows up three more times over the course of five days. Each one of the calls is scheduled for a time when I can be counted on not to be home. Times that match my daily routine precisely. Times when I am either at the gym, or outside jogging, or at my writing studio in the city.

Shifting my thumb, I check the outgoing messages. Lisa has called David only once. Just five minutes after he called her yesterday afternoon. Calling him back rather than choosing to ignore him.

My mouth goes dry as I further scroll down to a directive that will allow me to listen to caller messages. But when I press "Listen," the electronic prerecorded voice tells me that there are no new messages. If David left a message, Lisa has already erased it.

Placing the phone back down on the counter, I feel my body begin to enter into a slow burn. Questions: Should I call Lisa, expose her lie, and demand an explanation? Should I ask her point-blank why she is scheduling calls with her ex for when I am not going to be around? Should I press her on why she continues to communicate with him now that they are broken up? And why lie about it?

I draw a deep breath, exhale it slowly. To be truthful, I feel like running back to the park and lighting another garbage can on fire. But that would be stupid. The cops might be prowling the place now, searching for the crazy pyro who keeps lighting up the cans.

I've got to get my shit together and look at the phone calls for what they are. Just phone calls. What harm can they do? Maybe if Lisa didn't tell me about them, it's for my own good. Why start unnecessary trouble? Maybe Frankie is right when she says I'm being paranoid. Maybe Dad is right when he insists that keeping the lid sealed on this Pandora's box is my only option. I have no reason to believe that anything bad is happening behind my back. Anything devious. Sure, Lisa has changed since our first go-round together. But she's always been the most trustworthy woman I know. That was the constant bond we shared. No matter what happened between us. My writer's block, my inability to support my family, my drinking, my breakdowns, my need for fire . . . no matter what happened, we could always count on one another for one thing: trust.

Or perhaps I just wanted to believe I could trust her.

Lisa lied when she said David hasn't been calling.

That's her fault.

But what's not her fault is that he will not go away.

Chapter 4

I check the time.

Nine o'clock.

I should get back to work on the new novel. But then, I'm not feeling very creative right now. Better if I do something physical, like head out for an early run, in the opposite direction of Little's Lake, just to play it safe. After that, I can hit the gym. A little exercise will clear my head, take my mind off things. Later, after I've showered, I'll see things in a new light. I'll see that I'm just being the jealous ex-husband.

But first, I need to do something.

I shove my right hand into my pants pocket, locate the pack of wood matches with my fingers. Sliding back a cardboard top that sports a picture of Smokey the Bear wearing a park ranger's hat, I pull out a single match and stare at it like a pack-a-day smoker who's just decided to quit quitting.

I shoot a glance over my right shoulder, spot Frankie looking up at me from where she's lying on the sofa.

"Not a word of this to Lisa or Anna, you understand, Frank?"

"What's in it for me, Reecey Pieces?"

"Extra dog treats. Bacon Bits. I swear it."

"Knock yourself out. My lips are sealed."

I've done my research. The striker on a matchbox is constructed of 25 percent powdered glass, 50 percent red phosphorus, and some other things like black carbon. Most people give it little thought, but matchbox construction is a science all its own.

I strike the match and it happens: the rapid oxidation of an exothermal reaction that results in instantaneous combustion and the release of light and heat. A beautiful red-orange glow. As the fire burns, I feel my heart rest and my breathing grow easy. *Easier*, anyway. It's not quite the almost sexual sensation I get from torching those garbage cans, but for a *legal* quick fix, it will have to do.

I breathe in the acrid smell of burnt powder, charcoal, and wood and it makes me happy. I allow the matchstick fire to burn right down to the tips of my fingers. I take the pain delivered by five hundred degrees Fahrenheit until the fingertips begin to sizzle and blister, and I can't take it anymore. Only then do I toss the still-lit match into the sink, where it falls into a coffee cup still partially filled with coffee. The matchstick dies with a gentle hiss, like its fiery soul has left its body.

I shoot another glance at Frankie. "Okay, so what do you want from me? I've never fully gotten over fire."

The dog raises up her head from the couch just a little. "Now who's the liar?" she says.

Canine's got a point.

"I guess the fire is never far from my mind, Frank," I say.

I wait for a response which, thankfully, doesn't come.

Chapter 5

In the master bedroom, I dig out my running clothes, which are stuffed into the bottom of an old backpack I've owned for going on twenty years now. You find something that works, you stick with it. Reece the practical.

I've yet to be allocated my own chest of drawers at Lisa's new house. Things take time. I was, however, granted a key to the place just a couple of weeks back. A major life-move Lisa didn't take the least bit lightly. It's important to take things slow and steady in these matters. What's the rush? We've been apart for nearly a decade. What difference is a few more months of living separate, but together, going to make in the grand scheme of things?

I pull out my running shorts, a plain cotton T-shirt, and my running shoes. But no matter how much I search the backpack I can't find any socks. Lisa must have tossed them in the wash. As much as she's changed over the years, there's one thing that hasn't: Lisa's near-obsessive hatred for even the slightest accumulation of soiled clothing. If it were up to me, I'd use a single pair of jogging socks for three or four days before I changed them. My dad used to do the same thing when we were living together way back when. A dedicated gym rat, and my weight-lifting big brother Tommy's hero, he'd wear the same workout clothes for two or three days before switching up to some clean ones. "What the hell," he used to say, not without a smile, "they're only going to get sweaty again."

I'm not running without socks. I go to Lisa's chest of drawers and open the top right-hand drawer. It's filled with sweaters of all makes and colors. Wrong drawer. I check the one below that. Jeans and pants. Then, the one below that. T-shirts and sweatshirts. Shifting over to the left-hand side, I pull open the second drawer down.

Socks. I shuffle through them until I find a pair of black peds. Perfect. I should stop right there and get back to dressing for my run.

But I don't. I can't.

I move up to the top left-hand drawer and slide it open.

It's Lisa's underwear drawer.

Okay, sure, I knew it was her underwear drawer even before opening it. But this is the first time I've been alone in the house for an extended time, and this is the first time I've had the drawer all to myself.

Setting the black socks on top of the chest of drawers, I begin to sift through the soft cotton lace and silk panties. I can't help but recall, back when we were married, how Lisa preferred to wear plain underwear. Nothing special. Usually black cotton bikinis from the Gap. But now I can see that she's changed her undergarment habit. Not that I haven't noticed it already during the few times we've undressed before one another and made love. It's just that I never really made the connection until now.

The panties are accompanied by several pairs of black, thigh-high stockings. There's even a garter belt to go with them. And behind that, three or four lace push-up bras from, you guessed it: Victoria's Secret. Sexy stuff Lisa would have laughed at when we first got together.

But then I find something else.

A clear plastic freezer bag. Pulling the bag out, I don't need to open it in order to see what the bag contains. There's a vibrator inside. A blue, translucent vibrator.

My heart is beating rapidly again, and if I didn't know for certain that Lisa was about to undergo pre-op for an eye operation at nearly this very moment, I would swear she was just about to walk into the bedroom and snag me going through her most personal and intimate possessions. How would I explain myself? It's perfectly within Lisa's right to own this stuff. She has a life all her own now. Who am I to judge what she does for fun? Or, more accurately, what she and David used to do for fun?

I quickly return the bag to the drawer, stuffing it back in the very same place I found it. That's when my hand brushes up against something else. A manila envelope. I slide the envelope out, my fingers trembling as I pull back the metal clasps and peel back the flap. The package contains maybe three or four eight-by-ten color glossies.

I pull them out and examine them, one by one.

The pictures are full-color proof positive that the Lisa I once knew and loved as my lawfully wedded wife is no longer the Lisa I have come to know once again.

Chapter 6

Then, the pitter-patter of little feet. Paws, actually. Frankie, standing in the open bedroom doorway, looking up at me.

"Oh my God," she says. "You're going through Lisa's junk."

"She told me to go through it, remember?"

"I believe her words were 'Don't be going through my underwear drawer, big boy.'"

"You heard her whisper that from all the way in the living room?"

"I'm a dog. I have big ears. I can hear shit coming from across the river in Troy. You know, where your old girlfriend, Rachael, lives. You remember Rachael, don't you? She'll put a knife in your back you ever come within spitting distance of her again."

"I'm trying to forget Rachael and her threats," I say, picturing the very attractive but very angry blue-eyed, blonde-haired woman. "So back to the reason I'm going through Lisa's underwear drawer. In humanspeak, when someone whispers seductively in your ear not to do something like Lisa told me not to do something, it's actually an open invitation to go do it. Get it?"

Frankie just gives me that blank, million-mile stare. "You know something, Reece? You're an all-around good egg. But you sure have some quirky habits. Like having pretend conversations with dogs, for instance. If only your big brothers were around to witness it."

"Frankie," I say, imagining the beating and tongue-lashing I'd have no choice but to endure, "you have no idea."

The dog wags her tail, about-faces, and heads back out of the bedroom.

Finally, it's just me and the photographs. Again.

I decide to examine them further. Study them. Slower, more methodically this time.

In the first picture, Lisa is standing at the foot of the bed. She's wearing black stockings, which are supported by the matching silk garters and belt I just found inside the drawer. She's wearing one of the black Vic Secret push-up bras and on her feet, black pumps. She's not wearing any panties. I can't help but notice that her pubic hair has been trimmed to perfection, the baby-blue cherub tattoo she acquired soon after college plainly visible directly beside it.

She's smiling slyly, her hands planted firmly against her hips, like she's posing for *Playboy*. Her luscious lips have been painted red and her long, thick hair has been parted just above her left eye. The way it drapes her tan face causes her big brown eyes to take on a sort of playful glow. She's clearly having fun.

Next picture.

Lisa is still dressed in the same sexy outfit, but this time she's laid out on the bed on her flat stomach like a pinup girl. She's wearing black pumps even on the bed, one leg bent at the knee at a ninety-degree angle, the other positioned straight, her perfectly shaped glutes a feast for sorry eyes. She's still smiling slyly for the camera and her hair has shifted sexily so that half her left eye is hidden behind it, while the other half is exposed and glowing in burning candlelight.

Third and final photo.

This one robs me of my breath. Lisa is sitting back against the headboard. Her legs are spread and she's gently touching herself. She's no longer smiling but instead appears to be drowning in a fiery pit of sexual pleasure. I can only imagine that the person behind the camera is David and that no pleasure is lost on him either.

As I return the photos to the envelope, I feel myself getting dizzy. My hands tremble and my stomach feels like it's filled up with bricks. I'm also ashamed to admit it, but I'm as hard as a rock. It's all I can do to resist the urge to relieve myself on the spot. How strange to be turned on by Lisa's private photo collection on one hand but, at the same time, be shattered by it. Maybe it will help if I keep trying to convince myself that Lisa has a life. Or *had* a life with another man once. That what I've just witnessed in her telltale underwear drawer is perfectly normal.

Or is it?

Lisa and I are together again. Been together for weeks. Months.

She should have gotten rid of these pictures by now. Destroyed them. Hell, burned them. Maybe she should have tossed out the vibrator and hit up the Gap for new undies. And why is David Bourenhem calling incessantly? Calling when I'm not home?

Closing up the underwear drawer, I go back into the kitchen and light another match. After it's burned down to my fingertips, I toss the remaining flame into the sink. Again, I get that familiar, satisfying hiss when the lit matchstick touches liquid.

"Fire! Fire!" says the Town Crier . . .

My eyes shift to Frankie, who's asleep on the couch.

"I promise you, Frank, I am not crazy."

I see the phone on the counter. I pick it up. Pre-op or no pre-op, I'm about to get to the bottom of what's going on between Lisa and her former lover.

Chapter 7

She answers after the third ring.

"Reece," she says, "is everything all right?"

My throat constricts at the mere sound of her low, smooth-as-silk voice.

"Yes," I answer. "Or, well, no."

She giggles, telling me they've already begun sedating her.

"Well, which is it, Reece? I haven't got all day. The lovely handsome doctor will be back in a minute and this time he will put me out for good."

I clear my throat. "I checked the house phone, Lisa," I say as my face fills with hot blood. "The son of a bitch has called three times over the past three days."

"Who's called, Reece? Who's the son of a bitch this time?"

There's anger in her voice, despite the sedation. I need to take it easy.

"David." I dry swallow.

She exhales. "Okay, Reece, I'm going to level with you. David *has* been calling again."

I feel my legs melting. Like my body is about to form a giant puddle on the kitchen floor.

"Thanks for the truth."

"Listen, I'm sorry for keeping it a secret. But trust me when I say there's no deception here. He just calls to say hello, and that's it. It wasn't worth letting you know and going through all the trouble."

"Calls to say hello," I repeat, like I'm not buying her story.

"Yes, just hello. Come on, Reece, if I was so concerned about keeping his phone calls a secret, I would have made sure to erase the caller ID before I left."

"But I asked you this morning if he was calling again and you denied it."

"Calm down, honey. It's not what you think."

"Lisa, he calls when I'm not home."

Her pause is as weighty as her sigh.

"I can't possibly control the times he calls. If he's called when you're not home, it's purely by coincidence."

"You might ask him never to call again. I see you've called him back. Do you speak with him when he calls? Carry on a conversation? Have phone sex?"

Another giggle. Not the answer I want.

"Jeez, Reece, I spent almost eight full years with the man. He's really a nice guy. It just didn't work out between us. He loves your books. Truth is, he wishes he had your talent, your ability to be so productive and prolific, so that he didn't have to work public relations for some second-rate community college."

"At least he's got a gig. It's more than I had when we were married."

"Don't you remember meeting him before you and I split up to discuss his manuscript? He's not the enemy. You're just being paranoid, honey."

Lisa keeps telling me I've met him before. Back before we split up and I finally broke through my writer's block in order to start on the novel that would become *The Damned*. My first best seller. I've racked and racked my brain, but for the life of me, I cannot remember meeting him. If not for Facebook, I wouldn't even know what he looks like. The black-framed eyeglasses, the thick black hair, the scruffy face. But then an image of him taking pictures of a naked Lisa pops into my overheated brain. My throat constricts. My heart pounds.

"I appreciate your telling me all this, Leese. Maybe I'll give him some free fiction-writing lessons just to show what a sport I am. You can join us. We can have a threesome."

"You're being mean and stupid. He's a nice, sweet, gentle man who wouldn't hurt a fly."

"You used to fuck him and do God knows what else with him, Lisa, and now he's calling again."

Another sigh. "Tell you what, Reece. If David is upsetting you that much . . . if you don't *trust* me . . . I will tell him not to call anymore. Okay?"

I can tell she's angry. I don't want her to think I don't trust her. Or worse, that I'm the same unstable, insecure boy/man I was years ago.

"I'm sorry, Lisa," I say, stealing a breath. "I trust you more than you know. Please forgive me. I've wanted you back for so long, and now that I have you, I feel like the floor is about to open up and I'm going to drop down into a pit of burning flames."

"Reece," she says in the same soft tone, "you're not playing with matches, I hope. I should have tossed all the packs out now that no one smokes anymore."

I picture the two used matches sitting inside a dirty coffee cup in the sink, the pack of matches still sitting out on the counter.

"No," I say, my eyes drifting to Frankie where she lies fast asleep on the couch.

"Maybe you should go back on your medication. Why not give Dr. Cutler a call? It's been a few months and you know what your doctors said. You need to be in therapy once a week, every week. You've been shirking and you know it. This . . . this phone call. This is what happens when you stop following doctor's orders."

I picture the short, gray-haired, bearded psychiatrist entrusted with my case when I was released from Four Winds in Saratoga a few months after Lisa and I split up. Maybe Lisa's right. Maybe I should call him and go back on the meds.

"Reece," Lisa says. "You still there?"

"Yes, babe. I'm here."

"Listen, I need to go. You sure you're all right? I knew leaving you alone in the house might be a problem. I still think you should call Blood and have him stay with you."

"I'm not an invalid, for God's sakes," I insist. But then I remember her underwear drawer. "But there is one more thing I need to discuss with you."

"Quickly, Reece."

"Your drawer. Your top dresser underwear drawer. I was looking for socks. I saw some things that maybe I shouldn't have seen."

Lisa takes me completely by surprise when she bursts out laughing.

"I'm sorry, Reece. I am truly sorry."

She's laughing so hard she can hardly get her words out.

"What's so funny?"

"It's probably the sedation kicking in. I truly don't mean to laugh in your face. I knew something like this would happen the second I told you *not* to go through my underwear drawer."

"You did? You made it sound like you *wanted* me to go through it."

"I did. I didn't. Or, oh hell, I don't really care either way, honey. It's just that I've forgotten about the things I might have in there. I've been meaning to get rid of that blue toy for a long time. Ever since David and I broke up for good. It's just that I keep forgetting. It's so unimportant to me that it slips my mind. We have a daughter and she's all I think about at home."

"There's photos too, as if my imagination weren't sharp enough."

Her laughter stops. "Oh, you poor soul. I'm soooo soooo sorry you had to see those, Reece. Really, I am. It was entirely insensitive of me to keep them lying around, even if they were hidden. They mean nothing to me."

"I guess you and I . . . way back when . . . we weren't as adventurous."

"Reece, you were drunk way back when. You were blocked and wallowing in self-pity. We didn't have much of a sex life."

"Unlike you and David."

"David is very . . . well, playful."

The word "playful," and the way it sounds coming out of her mouth, is like a swift punch to the stomach.

"I understand."

"I'll get rid of everything when I get home. Don't worry yourself over it all. Remember what I said. Don't let David get to you. You two are very different people, even if you are both writers."

I'm surprised to feel myself smiling, my cheeks taking on a warm red blush. Uncovering the sordid details of Lisa's sex life with her ex is not necessarily something to smile about.

"I'm the better writer," I say.

"That's the spirit. And I'll tell you a little secret too."

"What's that?"

"You're better in bed."

Just then, a commotion coming over the line. I make out a door opening, and the footsteps of people walking into Lisa's room.

"I have to go now, Reece," Lisa says. "The doctor is back and so is Vickie. He's going to put me out now. Bye-bye, bad tear ducts. I will no longer cry for you."

I hear her say something cute and bubbly to the "handsome" doctor. I wonder if he'd be interested in seeing some pictures of his patient dressed in sexy lingerie, minus the panties.

"I love you, Lisa," I say.

But she's already hung up.

Chapter 8

Dad is standing inside the open bedroom door. He's got his arms crossed over his chest, and his hair is parted on the side. He's wearing his serious expression so that the cheeks on his clean-shaven face are slightly caved in. He's younger than me in death, but somehow still older too.

What the hell is wrong with you, Reece?

You sound like a crybaby. And a paranoid one at that. Haven't two stays in the nuthouse taught you anything? Two rounds of electroshock therapy? Did all that lithium go wasted?

You must have some sort of messed-up whore/Madonna complex swimming through that head of yours. So what if Lisa and David talk? What harm can come of it?

You know that if you had the chance, you'd talk to Rachael again. You and Rachael were inseparable for the better part of three years. Only when you were writing and she was in her studio making art were you apart. But now that you've gone back to your ex-wife, Rachael wants no part of you. She's erased you from her life for good, and who the hell can blame her? She hates your guts.

So don't blame Lisa for communicating with David on occasion. Blame yourself for being bothered by it. Sure, Lisa and David used to have fun in bed. So what? You've had your fair share of fun, too, with your book groupies. Remember that threesome at the Toledo Holiday Inn during the book tour for The Damned? *Both women (girls?) were barely eighteen. Then there was the high school English teacher who invited you to speak to her English Comp seniors and who, later on, asked you to "stay after class. You've been a terribly naughty boy, Mr. Johnston."*

You need to get your head out of your ass before Lisa calls the whole thing off, this time forever and ever. This is your dad speaking: grow up, Reece. Face it, Lisa is an adult and she has been living her life over the past eight years, just like you've been living yours.

David Bourenhem was a big part of that life. But now it's over. Just like it's over between you and Rachael. She's gone. He's gone. The sooner you accept that as truth, the sooner you can get on with the job of creating a new life for you, Lisa, and Anna.

You hear me, Reece?

Get a grip, or get used to no Lisa all over again.

Chapter 9

I quickly change into my running clothes and head out the back sliding glass door. Making my way over the wood deck and then through the fence gate, I walk the length of the driveway past my Ford Escape. Turning north on the road, I start a slow, steady jog, trying my best just to breathe in the cool spring air and not think about the events of the morning. I just want to feel human again, with the sun on my face and a good novel in my head.

I take the scenic route through the Albany Rural Cemetery, jogging past century- and two-century-old headstones that have turned gray over time and succumbed to the forces of gravity by leaning at odd angles. Not far from where I'm jogging is the old brick crematorium. It's set down in a valley on the far side of the cemetery. On any given day, if the wind is blowing in the right direction, you can smell the smoke from the incinerator fire that burns the dead.

When I was a kid, my friends and I used to dare one another to run down to the crematorium and sneak inside while the fires were burning. It was a dark, foreboding place that could have been lifted right out of a Stephen King novel. Nothing has changed in the thirty-plus years since I first set foot in this place. It is still dark, gothic, and glowing of death.

Truth be told, I used to visit the crematorium on my own some-times. Mostly during the hours of sad silence that usually accompanied my dad's occasional drinking binges. Binges that almost always ended with his passing out in his easy chair before the television, his whispering my mother's and brothers' names in his drunken sleep, one after the other.

The feeling I got from being close to the crematorium is not easy to describe. It was a combination of fear, curiosity, and a sort of high. The attraction, of course, was not death, but fire. The fact that fire was utilized to entirely consume a human body that only days before had been living, breathing, talking, eating, dreaming, only made the place all the more fascinating.

Once, when I was just piddling around the crematorium on a lonely Saturday afternoon, I saw a hearse pull up outside its front overhead door. Hiding around the corner of the old brick, castle-like structure, I watched one of the overall-wearing workers assist the black-suited mortician with sliding a simple wood casket out of the hearse and setting it onto a gurney. I watched as they wheeled the box in through the open overhead door.

As they worked, I snuck my way around the corner of the building and sprinted to the front of the hearse. From there I had a clear view of what the men were doing to the body inside the casket. I saw the man in overalls open the big iron door on the furnace. The fire inside it was raging. So much so, I swear I felt its heat even from where I was standing out in the front lot. I watched as the casket was slowly rolled into the fire and the iron door closed behind it. I felt an odd sense of satisfaction at watching that body enter into the fire and for a long time, I just stood there, mesmerized.

When the two men turned to walk back out to the hearse, they spotted me.

"Hey, kid," the man in overalls shouted. "Get the hell out of here."

I wanted to shout back, "This *is* hell."

But instead, I ran into the woods and scaled the hill back up into the cemetery. The top of the hill was a good place for watching the smoke that came from the burned bodies pour out from the brick chimney, black at first until it eventually turned snow white. No one bothered you there, because the only people around you were dead. The old cemetery contains many hills, but only one that looks down on the crematorium.

Today, I make sure to run a few of the steeper hills so that by the time I've run a complete lap around the entire cemetery, I've worked up a good sweat. As soon as I exit the cemetery gates, I hook a right and jog along the main road until I arrive back in Lisa's neighborhood. There I reduce my speed to a brisk walk and, with my hands pressed against my hips and my lungs filled with fresh oxygen, I head in the direction of Lisa's ranch house.

The house is barely in view when I spot the strange but all too familiar vehicle parked in the driveway.

Chapter 10

It's nothing special. The vehicle, I mean. One of those cheap 4x4 Honda CR-V hatchbacks that looks barely large enough to fit the driver, much less any passengers or cargo. It's an older model, tan or puke brown, for lack of a better authorly description.

There's a man standing by the driver's-side door.

From where I'm walking along the sleepy suburban road, he looks tall. Taller than me, anyway. Thin, with thick, wavy black hair and dark eyes masked by black horn-rimmed eyeglasses. He's wearing "skinny" cut blue jeans, loafers, and a brown T-shirt that says "HOLLYWOOD" across the front in big black letters. I peg him for maybe forty-three or -four, but going on twenty-six.

The closer I come to the driveway, I can see he's smiling that wide smile I now recall from his Facebook page. He's also holding something in his right hand. Flowers. A small bouquet of red roses wrapped in purple tissue paper. He is David.

The David.

"Can I help you?" I say, forcing the words from the back of my throat.

He smiles. Friendly. Too friendly. His half-squinted brown eyes not looking at me, but into me. Maybe even through me.

"How's Lisa doing?" he asks. "Her procedure?"

I take a step forward. "I'm sorry," I say. "But who exactly am I speaking to?"

He lets loose with a short, faux laugh. "Gosh, where the hell are my manners?" Holding out his free hand. "I'm David. We've met before. A bunch of years ago, in the house you and Lisa shared, before you . . . well . . . you know."

I shake my head. "No, I don't know. And I don't remember meeting you."

"No biggie, bro. We can start all over."

His hand is still there, waiting for mine.

I look at it. It's the hand that touched Lisa in so many ways for so many years. I feel the blood in my veins beginning to simmer. The hand . . . I want to take hold of it and break it. Crush it. Maybe even cut it off and feed it to a pack of wild dogs. Or, better yet, toss it into a fire and watch it burn until there's nothing left but white bone.

But that would be insensitive of me.

Instead of hurting him, I inhale, wipe my sweaty palm on my running shorts, and take the hand in mine. It feels cold, smooth, rubbery, and it sends a charge of ice water up and down my spine. If the hand could talk, it would say, *Never a hard day's labor in my life.* I shake it quickly, then release the cold fish of a limb.

"So how the hell are you, Reece? You've been killing it on the best-seller lists, bro."

"You read my stuff?"

He lights up, wide-eyed. "Dude, *The Damned* is like my favorite novel. Fucking great read. Fire, pyromaniacs, and burning people in caskets . . . What's not to like? I've coined a new term for your particular brand of noir. Do you wanna hear it, bro?"

Is he going to stop calling me "bro"?

"My guess is you're going to tell me anyway."

"Ha, ha. You sound like you know my ass, almost as well as Lisa does." Then, catching himself: "Oh, shit. Sorry, man. Didn't mean that to sound like . . . well, you know."

I nod. I just want him gone. "Okay, what do you call my particular brand of noir?"

"Pyro noir," he says, shaking the flowers so that one of the petals falls off one of the rose stems. I watch the red petal float gently down to the black driveway. "Whaddaya think?"

As much as it bugs me to admit it, he's right. It does have a nice, badass ring.

"Cool," I say.

"I've devoured *The Damned* three times. I never even read Franzen that much, and that dude *rawks*. Your protagonist is so despicable, but at the same time you can't help but pull for him, you know? Even while he's tormenting that family he abducts in their own home, setting out separate pine caskets for each of them, setting them up in the living room. And then later on, when he burns them inside the caskets? And in the end, him getting his due with his own pine casket and a one-way trip to hell thanks to some gasoline and a lit match. Powerful shit. Yet you can't help but like the dude. I don't know how you can write like that. Wish I could."

"It's noir, David," I say. "Or pyro noir, I guess. You're not really supposed to like or hate him. I wrote it from his point of view so that readers might gain some perspective into the essence of a pyromaniacal killer. A coldhearted killer. Mailer's done it. Capote, too, with *In Cold Blood*. Then there's Cain, and even Bukowski."

"The essence of a killer," he says, once more shaking the flowers and once more losing some petals. "Another title for you. You can have it if you want it. No charge, bro."

"Thanks, but Dave Zeltserman already snatched it up for one of his novels." Then, pointing to the flowers, "Those aren't for me, I presume."

He bursts out laughing. "God, what a sense of humor you have. Lisa's lucky to have you back, let me tell you." More laughing. "Well, if you must know, they're for your significant other, bro."

"Oh, that so? Tell me, how did you come to be aware of her surgical procedure today?"

"She Facebooked it."

"I thought she might have mentioned it during one of your telephone conversations or texts or e-mails."

He purses his lips. "You know about those? Hope you don't mind. Lisa and I are still friends. I mean, we were together for nine years. That's like forever."

But he and Lisa got together after we split up eight years ago. He must have his math wrong.

"Forever," I repeat slowly, distastefully, like it's an ugly, bad word.

"Hey, you know, I never did blame you for trying to start that fire at the old house way back when. I realize you were under a lot of strain then. Losing Lisa. Writing the first draft of *The Damned*. I can see where you borrowed from real life with your fiction."

The sweat from my run in the cemetery has now evaporated. But that doesn't mean my blood isn't heating up.

"Thanks, I appreciate it. So you and Lisa are friends?"

"I wouldn't say BFFs. But good friends. Hope it isn't going to be a problem, bro." His face lights up like a Christmas bulb. "Say, how's my little Anna? What a pip that girl is. She's a rock star in the making. You know, I offered to give her guitar lessons."

I bite down on my bottom lip. "Your little Anna?"

"Figure of speech," he says, reaching out with his free hand, patting my shoulder. "You wanna know something, Reece? Lisa has been talking about getting her tear ducts fixed for so long now. She used to talk about it all the time." More shaking of the flowers, more red petals floating down to the asphalt. "I guess she didn't have the money back then, much less the medical insurance to cover it. It's before her parents agreed to give her a monthly allowance since you weren't sending that much her way. You hadn't hit it like you have in recent years. Thank God for e-books, right?" He's back to smiling. "Guess I can't blame Lisa for wanting you back now that you're flush, bro."

While my brain burns with adrenaline, my gut starts speaking to me. Whispering. It tells me David is baiting me. Doing it with a smile and a fistful of flowers for his ex-girlfriend. I have a choice here: I can either take the bait and tell him to fuck off, or I can just pull off the exit onto the higher road by nodding in agreement.

I choose the latter.

"Yup," I say. "It's no wonder . . . *bro*." Holding out my hand. "I'll take those off of you, give them to Lisa."

"Would you? Thanks a bunch. I thought about waiting until she got home, but then I thought she could use a pick-me-up now while she's fresh out of surgery." Handing me the flowers. "You *will* give them to her, right, Reece?" He shoots me a wink of his left eye. The untrustworthy eye.

"Sure," I lie, gripping the life out of the bouquet. "Don't worry."

I walk toward the house.

"Oh, hey, Reece, bro," he calls out.

I stop, turn, exhale. "What is it, David?"

He opens the door to his ride, reaches inside, comes back out with something. It's a book. What's known in the industry as a trade paperback. A novel that isn't as big as a hardcover but isn't as small and squat as an old-fashioned mass-market paperback.

"You mind doing me the honor of signing your latest? I know it's probably weird, but what the hell. I loved it, bro."

Exhaling a second breath, I head back down the driveway, the flowers brushing up against my naked leg. The thorn that scratches against my shin only adds to my annoyance. When I get to him, I take the book in my free hand. It's a copy of *Killer Be Mine*, which came out about a year ago. The novel has been selling steady, but none of my novels do as well as *The Damned* still does, years after its original publication. Judging by the way the book has been dog-eared and soiled, I'd say David has read this one more than once also.

"You got a pen?" I say.

"Do us writers always have ink on hand?" he says, reaching into the console area of his ride and coming back out with a pen. It's a black push-button pen, and there's some special writing on the side. It says, "David Bourenhem, Freelance Writer." Printed below that is a website and a phone number.

I thumb the pen's button and I open up to the dedication page. The dedication is for Lisa, even though we were still broken up at the time and she was still involved with David. It reads, "For Lisa, for what we once had and what we might have again one day." When Rachael read it, she hit the roof. She broke up with me for about a month, but then took me back one last time. The next time she broke up with me several months later, it was for good.

How the hell can I possibly sign this thing?

I write, "For David, thanks for reading."

But what I really want to write is, "For David, How I would love for you to burn a path away from this place."

I hand him back the novel and the pen.

"Oh no," he insists. "I want you to have the pen. You know, if you ever need someone to do research for you or edit your manuscripts, I'm your man." He looks over one shoulder, then the other, like he's making sure we're not being watched. "I'll be frank," he goes on. "I found three typos in *Killer Be Mine* that wouldn't have been there had I gone through it prior to pub date." He puts on a sour face. "Stupid, silly, careless mistakes like that sort of cheapen the novel, wouldn't you say, bro?"

I just look at him, holding back the urge to pummel his skin and bones in the driveway.

"Oh my God," he says. "You'll have to forgive me. I'm rather outspoken on matters of writing and writers. Sometimes I don't know when to stop."

"Don't worry about it."

"Think you'll ever bring back the protagonist—or, should I say, antagonist—of *The Damned* for a sequel?" he asks. "What was his name? Drew Brennen?"

"Be kind of hard when he burned himself to death at the end."

"But you could write a prequel. You know, you could focus on when he was a boy, soon after he lost his family in the fire, and his slow, painful regression into pyromania. It would make a great book."

I hate to admit it, but it's not a bad idea. I wonder if it shows on my face, because he's back to smiling that awful smile that somehow must have attracted Lisa way back when.

"No dice," I say. "Now if you don't mind . . ."

Once again, I start back up the drive.

I can hear him getting back inside the Honda, shutting the door, turning over the little engine. I'm just about to ascend the three concrete steps up to the landing when he hits the horn, startling the living crap out of me.

I turn. Fast.

"Oh, Reece, I almost forgot," he calls out, his head sticking up and out of the driver's-side window.

I have no choice but to go back down to the center of the driveway. That is, if I want to clearly make out what he's saying. "Forgot what?" I say.

His head and shoulders are hanging out the window, his eyes squinting behind the black-rimmed glasses, thick hair mussed up.

"This might sound a little strange," he says. "But if you should happen to come upon any, ummm, let's call them *personal* photos of Lisa, would you mind terribly packing them up and sending them my way? They sort of belong to me."

My blood shoots from simmer to boil. It's all I can do not to sprint back down the driveway and head-butt him like a bull. Once more I'm put in one hell of a precarious position: I can either take the bait or pretend I have no idea what he's talking about.

"Personal pictures of Lisa," I say through grinding teeth. "Sure thing, Davey bro. I'll do my best to see that they're returned."

As much as it hurts, I make sure to smile when I say it.

"Hey, thanks, Reece man. You wanna know something?"

"What is it?"

"You and I are gonna be awesome pals."

His shoulders and head retreat back into the vehicle, and I watch him back out of the driveway. Before pulling away, he gives the horn a couple of honks and tosses me an awesome-pal wave through the passenger-side window.

I watch him disappear from view, hoping that on the way home he head-ons a tractor trailer and bursts into flames.

Chapter 11

Are you really going to take shit from that guy? Dad asks as he follows me back across the driveway and up the concrete stoop to the front door of the house.

    Bad enough he used to have sex with Lisa. He's baiting you, Reece. Tormenting you. He wants you to get angry. Wants you to take a swing. Maybe he even wants you to come after him with fire, just like Drew Brennen did when he went after his enemies in The Damned.

    When that happens, he'll call the police. The police will arrest you. Maybe they'll even toss you back in the hospital.

    You remember the hospital, don't you, Reece?

    You remember those initial, frightening moments? The stripping down, the full-cavity body search, the injection of meds, the burning feel of the medication making its way through your purple veins and capillaries? Then, the never-ending sleep. You remember the sound of the feet outside your door when they came for you with the gurney? The big men dressed all in white who lifted you from your bed and tossed you onto the black plastic mattress before wheeling you to the procedure room?

    You remember all that, don't you, Reece?

Well, take a good look at David Bourenhem, because he'd like nothing more than to see you end up back there. He'd like nothing more than for those electrodes to be strapped to your head, and the switch pulled.

He'd love to see your brain fried, like an egg on a hot skillet. You watch your backside, Son, you hear me? You watch your back.

Chapter 12

I'm not through the door before I toss the flowers down the length of the short corridor. Followed by the stupid black pen with his stupid name on it. Frankie comes running out of the master bedroom, paws at the flowers, and gives the pen a sniff as if she recognizes the scent (which I'm sure she does), then lets loose with a couple of short, sharp barks.

"Let's have it, Frank," I say. "You like David more than me."

She looks at me, licks her chops with her pink tongue. "What are you," she says, "Peter Paranoid?"

"I'm just wondering if you liked David."

"David was an okay guy. He wasn't like you. He was sort of metrosexual-slash-intellectual. You could talk to him about anything. Correction, Lisa could talk to him. You, Reece, not so much."

"She talks to me."

"Not like she talked to David. With David, you could talk things out. No offense, Reecey Pieces, but conversations ain't so easy with you."

"And why is that?"

"'Cause all conversations lead back to you and your own little fiction world."

"In other words, it's all about me."

"Hey, you said it. Now if you don't mind, I'm tired."

With a shake of her head, Frankie trots into the master bedroom and jumps up onto the bed to continue her nap.

Heading into the kitchen, I pick up the phone, punch "Redial," and wait for the ringing.

But this is stupid.

Lisa is the last person on earth I should be calling. No doubt she's laid out cold, her pretty eyes bandaged up. I check the time on the microwave oven mounted over the stove. Ten minutes until eleven. Her surgery was scheduled for ten, and from what she relayed to me last week, the procedure only takes about three minutes per eye. Three minutes and ten thousand dollars for the surgeon. I'm in the wrong business. Me *and* David Bourenhem.

I cut the connection, set the phone down onto the counter. I do it maybe a little harder than I should. It's made of plastic, after all.

"Sorry, Frank," I say, loud enough so that she hears me in the bedroom. But I get nothing more from the dog.

Lisa's house is designed so that only a short, waist-high counter separates the kitchen from the dining room. I glance into the dining room, its polished wood floor occupied with a long, dark wood table. My laptop sits out on the table, along with a yellow legal pad for my notes, and brown, horn-rimmed eyeglasses that house my progressive lenses. Middle age is a bitch. If this were seventy-five years ago, a small Remington portable typewriter like Hemingway wrote on would be placed there, and a pair of round, wire-rim granny eyeglasses, maybe a stack of blank writing paper on one side and a far smaller stack of finished work on the other.

Inside the dining room, I locate my black writing satchel. The satchel has followed me on assignment all over the world, from

China to Africa, back when I made a serious return to both free-lance journalism and a string of novels that followed the comple-tion of *The Damned*. It was an exciting but bittersweet time for me. Exciting because I had my life and my work back, even if I did work seven days a week. Bittersweet because my work and my travels took me far away from Anna, a little girl I hardly even knew.

My life is contained inside this bag. A toothbrush, toothpaste, good-luck charm, maps, first aid kit, passport, checkbook, pens, pencils, and more. Like I said, I don't officially live with Lisa, so I also keep all my travel meds inside a special compartment of the bag, including the medicine for my head.

My anxiety meds.

The medication that keeps the fire from haunting me more than it has to.

I unzip the bag, locate the small, rust-colored, translucent bot-tle, and unscrew the child-protective cap. Pouring out a capsule into my hand, I pop it into my mouth. Returning the meds bottle to the satchel, I proceed to do something I haven't done in years: day drink.

Back inside the kitchen, I open the refrigerator and grab a cold can of beer. Snapping open the aluminum tab, I wash the pill down with a long, satisfying swig.

It takes only a few more swigs to finish off the beer, and in no time, I'm feeling more calm. Calm without having to light fire. Tossing the empty can into the sink, I go back into the dining room and sit down before my laptop. I bring up the novel I'm pres-ently working on. The untitled story of a boy, a teenager, who's lost in the deep woods. No matter how much he tries, he can't find his way back out. Meanwhile, a forest fire is burning. The winds are heavy, and it's getting closer and closer to him, beginning to sur-round him. As the choppers and planes fly overhead, dropping their fire-smothering ordnance onto the distant flames, the boy remains invisible, and unable to call for help. He is doomed . . .

"Fire! Fire!" says the Town Crier; "Down the town," says Goody Brown; "Burn! Burn!" says Goody Stern. "Burn her! Burn him!"

I stare at the screen and try to think things through. Am I angry with David for showing up here unannounced? Showing up here at all? For calling Lisa? Of course I am. But am I angrier at Lisa for allowing it to go on? Angry that she still considers her ex a gentle soul who wouldn't hurt anyone or anything?

One thing is for sure: she still has feelings for him.

That's something I'm supposed to accept. Obviously he still loves her, or he wouldn't have brought her flowers. He wouldn't want her pictures back.

I think some more.

I don't like what I'm thinking, because what if David is right? Maybe Lisa is back with me because of my success, and only my success. Because I can afford her now. Lisa hasn't supported herself in years. Since I left, her parents have been supporting her with a monthly allowance. It's not something she enjoys. She'd much rather be independent from them. Sooner or later, her parents will pull that allowance and it will be me who's supporting her.

Perhaps my problem lies deeper than just photos in a drawer, or phone calls from the ex, or his showing up unannounced with roses. Perhaps Lisa and I do not belong together at all. Maybe there are very good reasons we divorced all those years ago, not the least of which were my struggles as a writer and my near-lifelong obsession with fire.

What did a novelist more famous than me once write? *It's hard to repair a sinking ship once it's sunk.* But there you have it. I place my hands on the keys and type out those very words in big, bold, caps-locked letters. Somehow, just staring at them makes me feel better. It's reassuring to know that someone else has tasted enough of the same complicated, love/hate emotional stew with his ex-partner to have produced those weighty words. Lest we forget, misery loves company.

The doorbell rings, giving me a start.

I slide my chair out and head to the front door. Through the three small, separate windows set into it, I can see that a man waits on the opposite side, a man with a build so large, it fills almost the entire door frame.

Blood.

I open the door, stare up at a man who is head-shaved bald. His narrow face is also shaved smooth, his dark skin rich and youthful looking, even though he'll never see fifty again. He's dressed all in black. Black leather coat, black T-shirt, jeans, and combat boots. In all the years I've known him, I've never seen him dressed any other way. No matter the season.

"Lisa," I say to him in the place of a hello.

He produces just a hint of a grin. An unusual show of emotion for the former Green Haven inmate. "She texted me," he says. "Wants me to check up on you."

"I told her not to."

"Well?"

"Well what, Blood?"

"You gonna be polite and invite me in? Or don't you allow no brothers in the house?"

"You're always invited," I say, waving at him to come in. "But what I don't need is a nursemaid. I'm fine."

He steps in, his presence filling the place with a strange kind of energy. Frankie emerges from the master bedroom, takes one look at Blood, and then, without barking, slowly about-faces and disappears back inside the room. The big man has that kind of spooky effect even on animals.

In my brain, I replay the events of that summer afternoon when I saved his life. I see Blood and me crossing the narrow alley between the wine bar and the Laundromat . . . see Blood walking a few steps ahead of me, his head tossed back while laughing out loud at some silly, now-forgotten joke . . . see the black pickup out the corner of my right eye as it barrels out of the alley . . . see me lunging at Blood, thrusting him out of the alley and down onto the pavement in front of the Laundromat . . . see myself whipping around in time to catch the face of the kid behind the wheel of the pickup as it lifts from the text message he's thumbing, see the eyes widen as he slams on his brakes . . . see myself move to approach the truck and the kid put pedal to the metal and flee the scene.

Those moments persistently occupy the space between us. I'd let them go, but Blood wouldn't think of it.

Blood never lets anything go.

I watch his dark, eagle-like eyes now as they make an inventory of the house. If I were to ask him a month from now what he observed here today, he'd repeat everything in precise detail.

He sniffs something, makes a gesture with his nostrils.

"Am I smelling smoke?"

I'm a little startled by the question. More than startled.

"It's okay to use your words, Mr. Reece," he adds.

"Not at all, Blood," I say, knowing that there are used matches sitting in the sink. I feel my pulse perk up.

"That's good," he says. "'Cause if you was playing with matches, I'd have to slap you upside the head or something." He cracks a hint of a grin again.

"Listen, Blood," I say, "I'm just about to sit down to get some writing done. Tell you what. Let's meet later for a drink and we can go over some stuff I need for you to research. Is that cool?"

He mulls it over. Nods.

"Okay," he says. "Could go for a glass of cab at the wine bar." Then, "Lisa thinks you worried she's seeing David behind your back. You're not worried about that, are you? Because if you are, I can pay David a little visit." Opening up his coat, he reveals the black grip on the 9mm automatic that's holstered to his belt.

I could tell him that David just paid me a visit. But if I tell him that, he will insist on staying. Not because David poses any real danger, but because I might pose a danger to him, if I get mad enough. Either way, Blood has my back. In the end, I decide to play it cool and keep quiet about it.

"I'm not worried about anything, Blood. I promise." I reach out, open the door. "I'll meet up with you later and we can talk about it."

"Up to you," he says.

He steps out the door onto the concrete landing, then turns. "I don't know Lisa like you do, but if you tell me everything is right between you two, that's good enough for me."

"It is," I say.

I'm slowly shutting the door. "Sorry if I'm not feeling social, Blood."

"Go write us a masterpiece, Reece. I'll see you later."

Closing the door behind me, I lock the deadbolt, praying that Blood believed me when I swore nothing was wrong. As I make my way back into the kitchen, I know damn well he doesn't believe a word I said.

Chapter 13

If this were a novel, it would be plot-point time.

By that, I mean the time where I would make my main character take some kind of action to at least make an attempt at reversing his situation. Otherwise, you risk losing the reader. In this case, I need to find a way to put David Bourenhem in his place, without making it look like I'm putting him in his place. In other words, I don't want him to think I feel the least bit threatened by him. I don't have to do something as drastic as send Blood out after him or actually confront him physically. For now, the action I take can be merely symbolic, a prelude to what will come later on when the fire really hits the fan blades.

Here's what I do.

I head back through the kitchen, stepping on flowers as I cross the corridor into the master bedroom. Flicking on the overhead light, I open Lisa's underwear drawer, once more locate the photos. I carry them back out with me into the kitchen. In the cabinet under the sink I find a stack of paper grocery bags that bear the words "Price Chopper Supermarket" on them in red letters. I pull one out, open it up, and dump the photos inside. With that done, I gather up the roses and the purple tissue paper they came wrapped in, and

I toss them in too. As a final (symbolic) fuck-you to Lisa's former lover David Bourenhem, I throw in his black pen.

I find the pack of matches on the counter, stuff them in my jeans pocket. That's when I hear the pitter-patter of four paws trotting back into the kitchen from the bedroom. Frankie. Once again, she looks up at me with her black eyes like I'm crazy.

"I used to be crazy, Frankie," I say. "Now I'm just pissed off." Then, folding the bag closed, "Observe, if you will."

I cross over the dining room and head down the couple of steps into the living room, where I open the sliding door and go out onto the deck. Stored under the barbecue is a bag of charcoal and some lighter fluid. I take hold of the lighter fluid, pull the bulbous metal lid off the grill, and set the bag onto the grate where a thick juicy steak should go. Popping the top on the lighter fluid, I proceed to spray the bag. Then, setting the fluid back down, I pull the pack of matches from my pocket.

"How about a little fire, Scarecrow?" I say, feeling my heart beating fast, the blood speeding through my veins.

I light the match and go to place it onto the bag. But then something stops me. The pen. It has Bourenhem's website address on it. I shake out the match, open the bag and pull the pen back out, store it behind my right earlobe. Then I light another match and toss it onto the bag.

It explodes in a plume of orange fire.

Reaching back down, I once again grab hold of the lighter fluid. Pointing the nozzle at the burning bag, I continue to spray so that the fire never lets up. It only gets hotter and hotter as the paper burns away, revealing the roses and the green stems and the photos. It takes a minute or two, but the petals burn and turn black while the photos, now free of their burned-up manila envelope, blacken and crumple as their moisture evaporates, the fire forever destroying the images of Lisa. Forever destroying the memories.

I don't stop spraying the lighter fluid until everything turns to black ash.

"Fire, fire," I whisper, feeling the last of the fluid empty out of the bottle. "Burn, burn. Burn her. Burn him."

I jump down off the deck, make my way across the back-yard, where I heave the empty can over the fence and into the woods.

"Fuck you, Bourenhem," I say. "She doesn't love you anymore."

Turning back for the house, I know just how wrong I am, but how bloody good it feels to have said it anyway.

Chapter 14

Between the fire I set in the Little's Lake garbage can and the one I sparked out on the barbecue, I smell like a firefighter who's just fought a towering inferno.

Inside the master bath I undress and turn on the shower. While I wait for the water to warm up, I contemplate opening another beer. But I know where that can lead. Christ, it isn't even noon yet.

Minutes later I'm dressed in jeans, boots, and button-down work shirt under my well-worn bush jacket, the pockets of which are stuffed with all sorts of notes, notebooks, pens, pencils, and anything else a writer requires for those unexpected moments when an idea might cross his mind. I've also placed Bourenhem's pen in the left-hand chest pocket. The pocket that sits over my heart.

Back in the dining room, I sit down in front of the laptop, exhale, and set my fingers on the keys. I wait for my brain to kick in. The part of the brain that makes the words appear on a blank page. Words that tell a story. These days, the writer's block that so plagued me when I was married to Lisa seems gone forever. Nowadays I don't get writer's block any more than a lawyer will get lawyer's block or a surgeon, surgeon's block.

But something's not right today.

My body wants to write, but my brain isn't letting me. It's consumed with something else. I can't get David off my mind. Even with the photos burned all to hell, I keep thinking of David and Lisa together. I glance over my left shoulder. Through the picture window I can see the still-smoldering ashes set on top of the grill. What really nags me is my inability to imagine what attracted Lisa to him so strongly that she willingly spent eight years with him. Maybe the evidence of that attraction was to be found in the pictures I just destroyed. Maybe he was able to give her something I never could, and never will.

I pull David's pen from my bush jacket pocket, set it on the table beside the laptop. I switch the screen from Word to the web browser, type in www.DavidBourenhem.com, and anxiously wait for a screen to appear. When it does, I see his face. The thick, wavy, almost feminine black hair, the black-rimmed eyeglasses, the wide smile, the dark, penetrating eyes. The site automatically feeds circus-like accordion and organ-grinder music. The kind of music you might hear coming from the insides of a merry-go-round. Horns blare, drums pound, cymbals crash. The music of a clown.

"Freelance writer David Bourenhem has written for dozens of newspapers, magazines, journals, and more. He's also published short stories in some of the leading reviews and was a top-ten finalist in the William Kennedy Screenplay Prize. He's presently available to assist you and your business with all your public relations writing needs. Don't just be the best you can be. Be better than the best. Contact David today."

I sit back and peer at the page like I'm waiting for something to pop out at me, like a crazy clown head from a jack-in-the-box. There's a link for journalism and another for public relations campaigns. Another for testimonials. The final one reads, "Screenplay Sample."

I click onto the screenplay link. How can I resist?

When the page pops up, I see words on a page in the familiar format. It's the title that glares out at me.

LISA

by

David Bourenhem

There it is again. The dry mouth, the beating heart, the heated adrenaline coursing through the veins and capillaries in my brain. I want to read the sample, but I don't want to read it, either. But, like driving by a car wreck on the highway, you can't help but crane your neck to look.

FADE IN:

Scene 1: Interior. Bedroom. Night.

All around the room, candles are burning. All the lights are turned off, and the firelight flickers off the wall. Sexy music can be heard in the background. Grinding kind of music. The atmosphere is most definitely devilish, bacchanalian even. We see two naked figures occupying a bed. The early middle-aged man, RANDY, is on the bottom facing the ceiling while the thirty-something LISA is on top of him, riding him, her long, lush black hair bobbing and swaying with every thrust of her hips. They are both beautiful people and their skin is soaked with a sheen of sweat. Obviously they have been making love for a long time, as if they cannot possibly get enough of one another. As if they need to devour one another in order to survive.

LISA

Do you love me?

RANDY (between breaths)

I love you . . . with all my heart.

LISA

Then make me cum. Make me cum hard. Do it now.

RANDY

I'm your slave, Lisa. I'll do anything for you. Anything.

LISA

I know you will.

LISA lets loose with a climactic scream as the flames on the candles flicker menacingly.

Scene 2: Interior bedroom. Later.

The couple is lying on their backs, post coitus. They are staring up at the ceiling as the candle flames make their skin glow.

LISA

You meant what you said?

RANDY

Meant what, baby?

LISA

That you would do anything for me?

RANDY (giggling)

What are you, Herod's wife?

LISA, turns over onto her left side to face RANDY. She obviously means business.

LISA

I mean it, Randy. I'm not fucking around.

RANDY (face turning serious)

Okay, I get it. What is it you would like me to do?

She slowly reaches out, starts running her fingers through his chest hair. We see a close-up of the long, stiletto-like fingernails, which are painted fire-engine red.

LISA

Would you be willing to kill for me?

RANDY (swallowing)

What the hell do you mean?

LISA

If I asked you to kill someone for me, would you do it?

RANDY

What a question, Lisa. I guess no one has ever asked me that before.

LISA

I'm asking you now.

RANDY

Who, exactly? Who would you like me to kill?

LISA (putting her mouth to his ear, whispering)

My husband.

RANDY's eyes go wide. He swallows again.

> RANDY
>
> How exactly would I go about killing your husband?

> LISA
>
> With fire.

> RANDY
>
> Jesus, you want to burn him?

> LISA
>
> I want him to suffer.

Once more the candle flames flicker almost violently, while one or more goes out, as if an evil wind has just passed through the room. And it has.

I stop reading there.

I stop reading before my heart spontaneously combusts and burns its way out of my rib cage. Are the Randy and the Lisa in the screenplay the true-life David and Lisa? Naturally, I can only hope that this screenplay is just David's way of having fun, because in my heart of hearts, I could never imagine Lisa even considering something like homicide, much less talking it over in bed with the new boyfriend.

Death by fire.

"Ashes, ashes," I whisper to myself. "We all fall down and we keep on falling."

My eyes still locked on the screenplay, I aim the cursor arrow at the X in the upper right-hand corner and make the words on the page disappear from sight and mind.

Chapter 15

My detective work continues.

Taking a moment to breathe, I then click back to the home page, where I find several links to Bourenhem's personal social networks. I go to Facebook. The face that appears on his profile picture is the same one that I recognize from his website home page. For his cover or banner photo, he's got a picture of his laptop and whatever he's working on. I try to look at the words on the laptop screen, but they are all a blur. Like I said, this isn't the first time I've looked at Lisa's ex's Facebook page. This is just the first time I've looked at it since Lisa and I have been back together. It's the first time that I really care to look at it, if that makes any sense.

My eyes scroll down to his latest post.

"Lisa is getting her eyes operated on today . . . Good Luck Leese!!!"

The post is followed by one of those yellow smiley faces and three big Xs.

XXX

Located directly below the post is a "Like" option. It's only been "Liked" one time. I click on it to see who the "Liker" is, but it's not the least bit necessary, since I know full well who it is. I know it in my gut.

It comes from Lisa.

It gets worse. Because she's also typed "XOX" in the "Write a Comment" area. Makes me feel like there's more than just phone calls going on between them.

My eyes gravitate toward Bourenhem's vital stats.

He describes himself as self-employed at "Fictionalizer, Fibber, Lover." Witty. He went to Siena College and lives in the historic old city of Troy, just across the Hudson River from the Albany skyline. He also lists his relationship status as "It's complicated."

"You're fucking single, pal," I whisper as if he can hear me.

I click on his photos. There's a bunch of pictures of him and Lisa together. Even now that they're supposed to be broken up, I see him arm in arm with my woman. I wonder if I ever looked at the pictures before. If I did, it's only now registering how much they bother me, causing my body to enter into a slow burn.

In the first picture they're drunk and all smiles at some bar, who knows where. In another, David, Lisa, and Anna are standing before a huge pumpkin on a brilliant fall day at a local "pick your own pumpkin" farm. They look like one big happy family.

Yet another picture shows the threesome at some amusement park, Anna riding a carousel, both her hands gripping the thick metal pole that supports the white horse, her face all smiles.

One more photo has David dressed in a tuxedo and Lisa in a minidress and black stockings. They're holding hands at some kind of ritzy function, and judging from the way they're looking into one another's eyes, they appear to be absolutely in love.

The date on the picture is a curious one. It's only a little over two months ago. Maybe one or two days prior to our reuniting on the day my father dropped dead of a heart attack.

I've had enough.

I log off Facebook entirely since I can't bear to look at David and Lisa's lives together anymore. Lives together when they're supposed to be separate. In fact, I come close to tossing the laptop across the room. But that wouldn't be very good for my new novel or my career in general.

What the hell is going on here? How can it be that the two of them attended a black-tie function together just days before we got back together? Did they attend only as friends? Anyone looking at the photograph can tell they are more than just friends. That they are in love. In love *and* lust.

Being back with Lisa for the past two months has been like a dream come true. I have my wife and daughter back at a time in my life when I can enjoy far more professional successes than train wrecks. At a time when writer's block isn't a problem. At a time when my obsession with fire is under control. But suddenly I feel like I'm standing on the edge of a cliff and peering down into a deep pit of fire. And I'm losing my balance.

From where I'm sitting at the dining room table, I spot the keys to my Escape sitting out on the kitchen counter. They beckon me. I go into the kitchen, snatch them up, and leave the house knowing that what I'm about to do is the wrong thing. But then, it's the only thing for me to do.

I'm about to drive to the medical center and demand an explanation from Lisa. Demand nothing less than the naked truth.

Chapter 16

What is it that draws us back to the broken places?

Maybe it's some kind of human perversity and stubbornness. This desire to rein in something that seems, on the surface anyway, to be forever *out* of your control. Of wanting to put things right even if it means going back in time and reentering a life that ended up causing so much pain in the first place.

Love has a lot to do with it, of course. Obsessive love.

I never stopped loving Lisa, even when things were at their worst and I was approaching bankruptcy and a nervous breakdown (the former didn't quite happen, but the latter struck like a firestorm). Throughout the years of our separation, I never had a bad thing to say about her, even while romancing Rachael, whose predilections for hard work, good food, red wine, and sex fit mine perfectly. I suppose that's because I found it impossible to sever the bonds with Lisa entirely, no matter how many times I was required to sign our divorce papers.

It didn't help that we shared the greatest emotional attachment two people can share: our daughter. It certainly didn't help that I could find myself sitting in a park on a beautiful day in another part of the world altogether, like Paris for instance, and upon seeing a young father walking hand in hand with his little girl I would suddenly be reduced to tears.

The divorce didn't really work for us in one important aspect: Lisa and I didn't break off all unnecessary contact. In the modern digital world, you're never totally disconnected from an ex, no matter how hard you try to unplug. Not that we tried. We e-mailed, texted, talked on the phone, and, on more than one occasion, engaged in phone sex. Did it when we were seeing other people. There it is, the admission of the century.

I'll admit something else too: I never once gave up hope that we would one day reunite, no matter how often she'd remind me just how different we'd become as the years of our separation wore on. Love is strange, but obsession is stranger. I'd become consumed with both.

———

I did quite a lot of web research on the topic of getting back together with your ex. It's a touchy subject to say the least. An entire science has been constructed around it and, for the psychoanalysts of the world, it remains both a topic of fascination and a significant boon to the old bottom line.

I talked the matter over with my psychotherapist, and in the end, he issued me a stern warning: "If you go back to a relationship that didn't work out the first time, it will not only fail a second time, it will fail harder and more painfully." What's the old saying? Burn me once, shame on you. Burn me twice, shame on me.

Still, I persisted. Still, I obsessed.

I ignored my shrink, shrugged him off as an academic who had no idea about real life and real love. I consulted with my dad, with Blood, and my agent in New York. Christ, I even looked up at heaven and asked Tommy and Patrick what they would do if they were in my shoes. No one, dead or alive, would tell me what I wanted to hear. Without fail they all said, "Don't go back!" Or, as my agent—a rather hardened, broad-chested man of Sicilian descent—put it: "We have a saying in Italy. Once a toy is broken, you can't fix it. You must toss it into the furnace and find a new one."

Knowing my, let's call it, "complicated" relationship with fire, you'd think he might've chosen another metaphor. Fire burns and destroys. I know that better than anybody. But fire is more than that. Fire can also transform, purify, redeem. Words like his could only make me more determined to become the exception to the rule. To raise the broken toy from the ashes, as it were.

I suspect Lisa felt much the same way.

Case in point: Once, about six months ago, not long before Rachael and I broke up for good, Lisa called out of the blue and asked if I wouldn't mind interrupting my writing schedule to take her to the automotive repair shop so that she could pick up her Land Rover, which was being fixed. The vehicle had been a gift from her parents, who'd elected not to pay the routine maintenance bills on the gas-guzzling foreign 4x4 for the simple reason that Lisa's character might benefit from bearing at least *some* financial responsibility, which is precisely how Lisa put it . . . with a smile.

I picked her up and naturally I asked her where David might be, that I should be elected to do the taxiing honors. She informed me that he was busy with an interview for a local pop culture newspaper. But then, turning away from me, she admitted that they had not been getting along so well as of late. A confession that sent a sudden wave of heated optimism coursing up and down my blue veins. David, she said, for as sweet and gentle as he was, lacked direction and ambition. He could never properly take care of her or Anna.

"He'll never be the writer you are," she said. "He just doesn't have what it takes."

"I thought he was writing a book," I said.

"He did write a book," she said, eyeing me. "Years ago, before we were a couple. Remember? He came to the house to get your opinion on it." Again with this insistent story of hers. "But it was impossible for him to get it published and he hasn't been able to write one since."

I couldn't believe what I was hearing. Years before, our relationship deteriorated over my obsession with my work and, at the time, a dreadful writer's block that just happened to coexist with the precise duration of our marriage. At least, that's the way I remember it, not that I remember a whole lot about that time . . . that horrid, dreadful time when Lisa and I lived in a state of siege while she began rekindling her friendship with a man named David Bourenhem. Now she was telling me that David was able to write a book prior to their getting together, but in all the years they had been a couple, he hadn't written a thing, other than cheesy public relations copy.

Was there a pattern developing here? Was Lisa, as lovely as she was, some sort of anti-muse?

I could only shake my head and smile. I was making too much out of nothing. But as we got onto the highway in what was then my pride and joy, an open-topped Jeep CJ, I told her that I had enough ambition for both David and me combined. She shook her head sadly and looked out the window, no doubt sorely reminded of her bad choices in men.

Then, turning back to me, she turned her frown upside down.

"Rachael doesn't mind you doing me a favor like this?" she said. "From what I'm told, she has a temper."

"The girlfriend and I aren't getting on so well as of late either."

The smile never left her smooth face. "You doing okay?" she said, gently placing her hand on my thigh.

"Sure," I said, feeling the electricity of her touch. "We had what's known in the publishing business as a very good run."

But what I wasn't letting on about was the entire truth of the matter. Rachael loved me very much. Too much, maybe. She wanted to spend her life with me, perhaps even have a child with me. But more than once she'd caught me texting or e-mailing Lisa. More than once she'd heard me utter Lisa's name in my sleep. More than once she'd snagged me staring at Lisa's Facebook page. We were still together, but Rachael had made it very clear she could not, *would not* go on with my still being in love with my ex-wife. I was either going to commit to "us" entirely, or she was going to have no choice but to douse the flame that was "us." As Lisa and I bounced around on a bright, sunny, cool day in my Jeep on the way to the auto repair shop, that flame was officially in the process of being doused.

Later on, as we exited the highway and began driving through a scenic stretch of country road, Lisa asked me what I had seen in Rachael in the first place. My answer might not have been one she liked, but I told her the truth. That Rachael was beautiful, gifted, funny, intelligent, ambitious, and what's more, independent. She was currently taking the New York City art community by storm, and I found something entirely sexy and stimulating in that. Maybe it wasn't exactly what Lisa wanted to hear, considering her role as a full-time mom, but I saw no reason at that point not to reveal the absolute truth. After all, we were divorced.

"So how is she in bed?" she posed after a weighted pause.

I shot her a look, but didn't answer.

She turned away and faced the open road. "That good, huh?"

We fell back into a silence that was neither uncomfortable nor comfortable as we drove further on into the country, flanked by the thick trees that were filled with the rustic golden colors of early autumn. The wind filled the Jeep and made Lisa's long dark brown hair blow back beautifully away from her face. Soon we came upon an old, abandoned farmhouse that was set inside a patch of overgrown second-growth woods. Lisa suddenly perked up and demanded that I slow down and pull into the driveway.

"But your Land Rover?" I said.

"It can wait," she said. "What's wrong? You have something better to do right now, Mr. Best Seller?"

I shook my head, smiled. She knew how much I was enjoying this drive, even if I was trying my best not to let on.

Downshifting, I pulled into the overgrown two-track that led to the farmhouse. Knowing in my gut what Lisa wanted, I pulled in far enough so that we were hidden from the road by the boarded-up two-story house. Without a word, she turned and leaned into me, kissed me. We didn't stop there. We tore one another's clothes off and made love in the backseat of my Jeep as awkwardly and as well as anyone can inside such a cramped space. Lisa finished by taking me into her mouth. She worked me slowly but deliberately, doing things with her mouth and tongue that I had never felt before. She'd learned some new tricks during the years we'd been apart. When I exploded, she didn't back off or away. She kept me in her mouth until there was nothing left of me but an empty, yet happy-in-the-heart, exhaustion. It was the first time we'd made love since we'd split up, and it had come to us unexpectedly and wonderfully.

Twenty minutes later we arrived at the auto repair shop. When Lisa was presented with a bill for twelve hundred dollars that included unanticipated repairs and parts for the Land Rover, she nearly passed out from sticker shock. I jumped at the chance to make good. To pounce on an opportunity to prove to her that I was no longer the broke, unproductive writer I had been when we were married. Despite her protests, I insisted on paying. It took some time, but eventually I got my way.

On the way out of the shop, she took hold of my hand and smiled at me. "Thank you," she said. "That was sweet. I didn't make you come with me as a way of making you pay the bill."

"No," I said. "You made me come with you so you could jump my bones."

"You jerk," she said with a laugh, issuing me a quick little punch to the arm. "Well, okay, but I honestly wasn't planning on jumping your bones."

"You just made sure you wore sexy underwear anyway."

Now I was laughing.

"Hey," she said. "One should always be prepared for those unexpected pleasures in life."

I turned to her, took hold of both her arms. "Lisa, I still love you," I said. "It makes me feel good to pay for things for you, but it's you I really want. I want to try again."

"You want to pay for my stuff? Oh well, Mr. Novelist, I'll just have to remember that."

Ignoring what I'd said about love and starting over, she began walking to her now-repaired sea-green Land Rover, parked just past my Jeep. I couldn't help but notice how beautiful she looked in her torn blue jeans, white Converse sneakers, and long-sleeved, blue horizontal-striped Russian sailor shirt, her long dark brown hair put back in place and draping her tan face. I could only wonder how it was possible I'd ever let her slip through my fingers.

After getting behind the wheel of the Jeep, I called her name.

She looked at me over the Rover's hood.

"That was beautiful back there," I said. "Back at the old house. Really beautiful."

She brought her extended index finger to her luscious lips, as if to say, *Shush. It's our little secret.*

"Will you ever come back to me?" I said as she unlocked the Land Rover door with the electronic key ring, the lock releasing with a bird-like chirp.

She pressed her lips together, made sad eyes. "I do love you too, Reece," she said. "I think I just showed it. But it could be that in the end, we're just too broken. And I am still with David. There's no denying that. But I promise you, I will think about it. Think about it hard."

She climbed into the Rover and drove off, leaving me feeling both sad and elated at the same time. My ex-wife still loved me, but I think as far as she was concerned, common sense stood in the way of our ever reuniting as a couple. I had brought too much trouble into her life so long ago. Too much pressure, anguish, sadness, and, yes, fire.

A short time later, my father dropped dead while tying his work boots in the garage of the house I'd nearly burned down as a boy.

Since I was the father of our daughter, Lisa felt it her duty to come to me, to comfort me, to be by my side through it all. And in my dad's sudden death there emerged a new life for us, like somehow God had struck up a strange bargain with the old man: *"It's either your life, or your boy's love life. So what's it gonna be?"*

Despite the secret hopes and dreams I harbored for years, our coming back together was, in the end, entirely unplanned. But at the same time, it seemed so natural. Now, two months later, as I uncover her still-unbroken connection to David, I'm beginning to think that the shrinks, the websites, and the naysayers might have been right after all. That our coming back together has all been a tragic mistake. That when it comes down to it, ashes are just ashes.

Chapter 17

The Loudonville Medical Center is located on Everett Road, not far from the big house Lisa and I lived in when we were married. A stone and red wood, three-story corner-lot monstrosity for which her father, Alexander, generously put up the one-hundred-thousand-dollar down payment. But even then I couldn't afford to pay the remaining measly monthly mortgage while I was still waking up every morning to the blank page and going to bed with an even blanker one.

When I come to Everett, I take a right and drive along a road that, not too long ago, was surrounded by pristine farm country that supported thick stands of tall pines and oak along its perimeter, trees now long bulldozed in favor of suburban sprawl. Part of that sprawl is a four-story, red brick and glass building that must take up ten or twelve acres of farmland while its surrounding black macadam parking lot spoils at least twice that much land.

I pull into the overcrowded parking lot, slowing my new red Ford Escape so that I won't miss out on an empty space. I'm maybe one quarter of the way in when I discover Victoria's Volvo. And I'm halfway in when I spot a puke-brown Honda 4x4 hatchback.

I punch the brakes so hard the tires squeal and I'm thrust forward.

I sit back and lock eyes on the vehicle like it's the chariot of the devil himself. But then, these Hondas are everywhere these days. They're almost like disposable vehicles. So cheap and small you can practically fold them up and stuff them into your back pocket. Maybe it's not David's at all. Maybe I'm just back to being paranoid. I could cross-reference the license plate, but I never thought to study it earlier when he unexpectedly pulled into Lisa's driveway.

The blaring of a car horn directly behind me nearly sends me through the windshield. Some asshole in a Dodge Ram, his grill practically pressed up against my rear bumper. Redneck.

I throw the Escape back into drive and move forward down the line of cars. When I come to the end, I hook a right and motor my way back up another row in the opposite direction. No spaces are available.

I hit the brakes.

"Jesus," I say aloud. "What the hell am I doing?"

What if my gut serves me right and David has indeed shown up to be by her side?

What good can come out of our being in the same room together?

I can just picture the scene. I would demand an explanation, and that explanation could very well lead to my punching him in the mouth. I've been in my share of bar fights and I'm not altogether unfamiliar with a jail cell. More importantly, what better excuse for Lisa to show me the front door for the second and final time than for me to wallop her ex in the face? The ex she claims is sweet and docile. A man who wouldn't hurt a housefly.

I stomp on the gas.

When I come to the edge of the parking lot, I make a right-hand turn back onto Everett Road. My heart beating inside my throat, I head directly to the Stewart's convenience store on the corner of Everett and Albany-Shaker Road. Parking the Escape, I dig my left hand into my jeans pocket, pull out a twenty-dollar bill. Just enough for a twelve-pack of beer, a pack of smokes, and a Bic lighter. Not exactly the breakfast of champions, but the perfect recipe for a man who is speedily losing his shit.

Chapter 18

I head directly to the back coolers, where I grab a twelve-pack of Budweiser, then hustle to the counter. The college-aged kid standing behind it is wearing an old T-shirt that says "Fuck Bush" on it. He's listening to something on his iPod, nodding his head to the beat.

He looks down at the beer.

"That it?" he says disinterestedly.

My left hand stuffed inside my pocket, I rub the twenty between forefinger and thumb, feel the paper heating up.

"Pack of Marlboro Lights and three mini-packs of Advil," I say, pulling out the money, laying it on the counter. The Bic butane lighter display is positioned beside the register. I choose a red one and set it down onto the counter beside the beer.

"Twenty ain't gonna do it, dude," he says. "Sin taxes will burn a hole in your wallet these days."

I feel a wave of warmth fill my face. Pocketing the twenty-spot, I pull my wallet from my back pocket, open it, slide out the credit card, and set it onto the counter between the lighter and the beer.

Sighing, he runs the barcodes of the cigarettes and the Advils under the scanner, then sets them down onto the twelve-pack and glares at my purchases like he's staring down at a pile of his own charred remains.

"What's wrong with this picture?" he says.

"Just run the card."

"In a rush to get home, are we?"

I wonder what the penalty is for slapping a college-aged kid across the face. Whatever it is, might be worth it.

He runs the card, then hands it back to me along with the receipt, which I sign with a pen stored in a cup that bears a red, white, and blue New York Giants logo on it. "Go Giants!" I return the pen to its rightful home.

"Would you care for a bag to go with your purchases, sir?"

"Don't need one, thanks," I say, stuffing the smokes and the lighter into the left-hand pocket of my bush jacket while I store the Advils in the side pocket. Grabbing the beer by the cardboard "suitcase" handle, I go for the door.

"Sure you don't want a porno magazine to go with that?" the kid chuckles.

But I just stiff-arm the door and make my escape to my Escape.

Chapter 19

Here's what's running through my adrenaline-fueled brain: This whole second-time-around thing is a bust. I was doing just fine on my own before the old man died and Lisa came storming back into my life. I was writing, building my audience, travelling, not thinking about fire, not thinking about Lisa as much as I used to. David Bourenhem was of zero concern to me. I was free.

I'll say it again: I . . . was . . . free.

But now the old paranoia has raised its ugly, scarred head again. The paranoia, the obsessions, the bad habits. The fire. They're all sneaking back into my life. And listen to this: I'm not writing. It's not even noon and I'm sitting in the Escape in the parking lot of a Stewart's convenience store with a twelve-pack of beer at my side and a pack of cigarettes screaming at me to smoke the living shit out of them.

I think it's time I left Lisa again.

I'm thinking the right thing to do is to pack up what little I have in Lisa's house and split-the-scene-Gene while she's still recovering from tear duct surgery at her parents' house. I'll just grab my backpack, shove my laptop into my writing satchel, book a one-way ticket to Rome, and leave this hot, toxic place behind for Lisa and David and the love they still obviously bear for one another.

I pull the lighter from the bush jacket pocket and thumb the trigger, which sparks a tall flame, as if the kid behind the convenience store counter jokingly thumbed the flame control to its highest setting. Not that I'd think of minimizing the flame. Instead I flick the trigger no less than five times, my insides calming down with each and every burst of red-orange flame.

Tearing open the beer's cardboard packing, I pull out a cold one, pop the lid, and take a deep drink, then set the can into the center-console cup holder. I tear off the plastic on the pack of smokes, open the cardboard lid, and pull one out. Firing it up with the Bic, I taste the smoke and feel the heroin-like calmness pour over me with the first glorious drag. I retrieve the beer, steal another mind-numbing drink, and yearn for some peace. But I know in my gut that peace is just a pipe dream with David Bourenhem still in the picture.

I catch my reflection in the rearview mirror.

Jagged veins protrude through the thin skin on my forehead. Both the veins and the fire scars run up deep into my scalp, my ever-receding hairline leaving them exposed like miniature tree roots popping out of a cracked, concrete sidewalk. The three-day facial growth makes me look worn-out. Wired-out would be more accurate. Anxious. The horn-rimmed glasses I sometimes wear might make me appear somewhat smart, but I feel boneheaded stupid for having been lured back into this relationship with Lisa when she still isn't over her life with David.

Or is it more than that?

In my head I begin to rehash Bourenhem's film script:

LISA

Would you be willing to kill for me?

I trigger the lighter and keep triggering it. I take the time to drink another beer. By the time I'm feeling sufficiently calmed, forty-five minutes have passed since I first pulled into this convenience store lot. Tossing the two empty cans onto the floor, I crack open another, set it into the cup holder, and start up the Escape. A new cigarette burning between my lips, I back out of the parking space and drive out of the lot.

Having turned onto Albany-Shaker Road, I head back in the direction of Lisa's house. If I have my way, it will be the last time I ever lay my eyes on the place.

Chapter 20

Dad rides shotgun while I drive. At first he says nothing. He stares down at the center console, picks up the half-full beer can from out of the cup holder, sets it back down. He picks up the pack of smokes, sets them back down. Then, with a disgusted shake of his head, he resumes staring out the windshield. After a beat, he clears his throat and speaks.

Do you remember how you got back to the nuthouse, Reece?

Oh, you must remember how it happened. You finally broke through the writer's block, but that didn't make the loss of Lisa any easier to bear. And when you discovered she was seeing another man . . . another writer, who had just finished his first novel . . . it was all you could do to keep what strings of sanity that remained holding you together from snapping.

They snapped.

You snapped.

You tried to burn them, Reece. You set a fire on their back deck and tried to burn the house down, just like you tried to burn down the little home you and I lived in after Mom and your brothers were gone.

You remember how I found you outside around the back of the single-story bungalow, trying to light the wood siding on fire with some gasoline and a pack of matches? Remember how I dropped to my knees and sobbed into my hands, just like I did on that night back in '77?

That botched attempt on our bungalow earned you your first official hospital visit, and then, what do you do almost three decades later? You go and do it again. This time to the place you shared with Lisa and Anna.

Lisa might have had you arrested, but after I begged her not to, she did you the favor of having you hospitalized. You remember what it was like on that cold, cloudy morning back when they rolled you on a gurney into that white-tiled room? I remember because I drove you there in my truck and watched them wheel you away.

Yeah, Dad, I remember.

I remember my eyes were drawn to the angelic white light that shined down upon me from the ceiling-mounted, stainless steel–shaded lamps. No matter how much it burned my retinas, the light reminded me of heaven, just like it did when I was a boy and kept looking for the faces of Tommy and Patrick in that blazing light. This time around I wasn't looking for my brothers, but my body was still shaking and trembling like a leaf when I felt a gentle hand set itself onto my bare forearm.

"What's this I hear about you setting fires again?" An attractive, brown-eyed, female doctor in her white lab coat. "You should be writing, not playing with matches. But never fear, Mr. Johnston. This time, we'll make sure that we fix you for good. So just try and relax and enjoy the flight."

"Happy to be aboard," I said through chattering teeth.

She knew I'd been here before. Of course she did. She'd read my chart. She'd studied my life. Those records never die, unless they burn.

A long time ago, when I was still just a boy, the doctors thought the best solution for a child obsessed with burning things was to try to erase as much of the past as possible. Or, as the therapists put it, to neutralize the effect the past had on me. Since completely erasing the past was a practical impossibility, they decided upon the next-best thing.

Erasure of my short-term memory.

That took a series of electroconvulsive shock therapy sessions which, in the end, did indeed succeed in erasing my recollections of the fire that killed my brothers and mother. But only for a time. And my obsession with the manner and the means by which they died never went away. Not really. My need for fire only became more controlled, more carefully reined in.

Now, decades later, the electroshock therapy was being applied again. Not only for fire this time, but also for something else. To help me with the loss of Lisa. I was having a bit of trouble with that. Okay, that's putting it lightly. I was having a lot of trouble.

"I'm going to administer the sedative," announced the lab-coated woman. "You might feel a bit of a pinprick."

"I guess that's better than feeling what it's like to set myself on fire," I said with a nervous laugh.

She just stared back at me, then grinned. "Ready?" she said, holding down my arm with one hand and pricking the vein that stuck out of the back of my hand with the other.

The pain shot up my arm, but just as quickly disappeared.

Another man entered the room, a small man of late middle age, also wearing a white lab coat. "I'm your anesthesiologist," he explained. He had a blank, clean-shaven face. "You won't be entirely out for the procedure. But I promise you, as you enter into a seizure state, you will feel nothing. From what I'm told, you already know the drill."

"'Fire! Fire!' says the Town Crier," I recited.

"Excuse me?" said the anesthesiologist.

"Just a favorite nursery rhyme of mine as a child," I said. "My mother taught it to me not long before she died. Before she was burned alive in her bed."

So yeah, Dad, I remember. I remember it all, even if they did try to erase my memory for a while. Or maybe that's not quite right. Maybe in the end, I just remember what I want to remember.

Bringing the cigarette to my lips, I smoke the last of it, then toss the still-smoldering butt out the window.

"Before she was burned alive in her bed," I repeat aloud, the words echoing inside my brain. "Before my mother was burned alive."

I reach out, try to set my hand onto my dad's knee. But all I feel is the empty seat.

Chapter 21

Letting myself in through the front door, I don't take two steps inside before I freeze up. I don't require a third step to make out the destruction. The living room is in a shambles, the couch overturned, the paintings on the wall tossed to the floor, and in one case, the canvas kicked out of its frame. Something's been drawn on the big chalkboard wall in brilliantly colored chalk, but I don't take the time to allow the artwork to register.

Looking over my shoulder, I see that the dining room hasn't fared much better. The china that Lisa stores on floor-to-ceiling shelves has been tossed to the floor and shattered, the jagged white shards covering both the tables and the hardwood flooring. But what shocks me more than the destruction of the china is that my laptop is still sitting out on the table. Whoever did this didn't steal it.

Gun. Go get it.

About-facing, I head back out the open front door and sprint to the Escape. Unlocking the SUV with the electronic key ring, I open the passenger-side door, throw open the glove compartment, and I find my gun. A 9mm Smith & Wesson, like the police carry. It's illegally owned but I don't give a rat's ass right now.

I sprint back to the house, head inside shouting, "If you're in here, motherfucker, I have a gun and I will shoot you dead!"

Heart lodged in my throat, gun gripped in my right hand, I make my way back across the living room, across the dining room, and down into the playroom. No one there. Shooting back up the two steps into the dining room, I head into the kitchen. The entire room has been ransacked. Bowls, plates, pots, pans, and food—everything's tossed about everywhere. I find a big French knife on the floor beside Frankie's spilled water and food bowls.

"Oh fuck. Frankie."

Bending down, I grab the knife, set it on the counter.

"Frankie!" I shout, looking over one shoulder and then the other. "Come out, Frankie."

I step on through the kitchen and into the corridor, make my way toward Anna's room. When I step inside I'm shocked to see that it hasn't been touched. Making ready with the pistol, I inhale and yank open the closet door to my right-hand side.

Just Anna's clothing hanging from the rack.

Closing the closet door, I kneel down, peer under the bed.

All clear.

Back on my feet, I head out into the hall and proceed to the bathroom. Other than the contents of the medicine cabinet having been tossed into the sink, it's relatively untouched. A few steps forward and I find myself in Lisa's home office. It too is untouched, as if the intruder didn't think he'd find anything important in her desk or simply didn't have the time to go through it.

He did have the time to do one thing, however.

A picture of me has been tacked to a bulletin board screwed into the far wall. It's the same photo I've been using for my book jackets. The last couple of books, anyway. The photo was taken by Rachael inside the dining car of the train we rode together from Innsbruck to Venice through the Italian Alps a couple of years back. Nothing funny has been done to the image. No scribbled mustache on my face. No devil horns. It's just been tacked up onto Lisa's bulletin board, maybe to bring attention to my sudden presence in her life.

I stuff the pistol barrel into my jeans, go to the picture, remove the tack. Holding the color image in my hand, I turn it over and see that something has been written on it. It says, "Present day Heretic. Posthumous Bestseller."

I set the photo onto Lisa's untouched desk and then head back down the hall to the living room. To my right, past the overturned couch, is the chalkboard wall—the creative wall Lisa had installed so Anna could write or draw anything she wanted using the colorful chalk sticks set out in a wooden dish atop the piano. It's not Anna's artwork that's presently gracing the wall, though. The drawing is accompanied by some writing. The words fly out at me in their red-chalk lettering: "Hemingway knew enough to blow his brains out after he went crazy. So should you, Heretic."

Below the words is a drawing.

The facial likeness is definitely me, but whoever drew it added a Hemingway-like beard and a roll-neck sweater, just like the famous author photograph printed on the back of my high school edition of *The Old Man and the Sea*. My head isn't all there. In the drawing, I've got the barrels of a shotgun stuffed in my mouth and the cranial cap is in the process of being blown off, spurts of blood shooting out of it like fire.

The intruder is quite the artist.

Turning, I once more cross over the polished-wood living room floor, back into the hall. Walking its length past Anna's room, I enter the master bedroom. The room hasn't been flipped. But something even more disturbing occupies the bed. Set out on the mattress is a set of clothing. A silver chain necklace with a large silver cross pendant is lying on the right-hand pillow where Lisa's head would normally rest. Under that is a short black dress with ruffles at the bottom. A silk see-through blouse has been laid out on top of the dress. Set on top of the blouse is a black lace push-up bra. And set on the skirt are matching black satin panties. The panties are accompanied by a silk garter belt to which a pair of thigh-high stockings are clipped. Laid out over the feet of the stockings are a pair of black patent leather pumps.

It's the same exact outfit Lisa wore to the formal occasion she attended with David just a couple of months ago. Only he would know what she wore that night, both as clothing and underwear. Once more my heart drops into my stomach. My head spins, pulse skyrockets.

My eyes are glued to the bed.

I feel paralyzed. Feet buried in freshly poured concrete. Until I feel something behind me. A live presence. A man, maybe. Gripping the pistol, I pull it from my waistband. I hear something. Breathing. Footsteps. I have the pistol for protection, but it takes all the strength I can work up just to turn around. But somehow, I manage to do it.

I turn. And that's when I see her.

⌣

I let loose with a short scream.

Frankie barks.

We've managed to scare the living crap out of one another. I pocket the gun, then pick her up, cradle her in my arms, tightly.

"Jeez, Frankie, my girl," I say, petting the top of her head and behind her freakishly long ears. "What the heck happened here? Who did this?"

Like I said, sometimes I imagine Frankie talking to me. I imagine what she would say in response to the direct questions I pose to her. It's a way of destroying my loneliness. But she's silent now. Silent and shivering in my arms. Her heart is pounding in her skin-and-bones chest. She's panting. I should be calling the police, but my gut is telling me not to call yet. It's telling me to hold off. Because I know full well who did this. The perp can only be one man.

David Bourenhem.

I saw what looked like his Honda 4x4 parked outside the medical center. He couldn't have possibly been in two places at one time. But then, his puke-brown Honda is not the only one taking up space on the streets of Albany and Troy. Maybe the Honda I saw at the medical center belonged to someone else. Or maybe he flipped the house while I sat in the parking lot of the convenience store smoking cigs and drinking beer, feeling sorry for myself and trying to come up with reasons for leaving Lisa a second time.

Get your shit together, Reece. Lisa needs you now.

It's then that I make the decision not to leave Lisa. Not unless she asks me to leave.

Chapter 22

I head back out to the Escape, replace the pistol in its glove compartment hiding space. I grab what's left of the twelve-pack and carry it with me into the trashed kitchen, where I store it in the refrigerator. With the shards of broken china and glass crunching under my feet, I make my way back into the dining room, brush some of the same shards from my chair, and sit down at my laptop.

The screen saver is changed. It used to sport a black-and-white photo of Hemingway, snapped when he was writing *For Whom the Bell Tolls*. The bear-like writer is seated at a wood desk, the sleeves on his shirt rolled up over bulging biceps as he pounds out the words, key by single key, to his magnificent Spanish Civil War masterpiece.

But now the image of Hemingway is gone. It's been replaced with words.

THE BESTSELLER IS A HERETIC AND LIKE ALL HERETICS HE WILL BURN FOR HIS SINS.

I recognize the line, or most of it, because I wrote it in *The Damned*. It's what my character Drew Brennen says to each of his victims before he burns them alive inside a pine coffin. "You are a heretic and like all heretics, you will burn for your sins." It's a reference to Dante's *Inferno*, Canto 10, Circle 6, in which the heretical souls of those who betray their God, their family, their friends, and supporters are forever burned alive inside a tomb that hasn't been buried but instead, set ablaze.

Back in Dante's day, the worst kind of punishment was to be burned at the stake. Renaissance Florence overflowed with stories of men and women burned at the stake for betraying one thing or another, or for going against church doctrine or that of the state. Crooked politicians often met this fate, as did wayward members of the clergy. So did adulterous husbands and wives.

So did writers.

I don't know what to make out of all this. Lisa has been portraying David all along like he's fucking Gandhi, a gentle man of words and peace who bears no ambition other than to live and let live. A man who wishes no harm on anything or anyone. A man who defies the macho ethic. In literary terms, he is the anti-Hemingway, anti-Mailer, anti–tough guy anything. The gentlest of gentle souls.

Or so claims his ex-lover. "Ex" being a dubious prefix here, folks. Yet, who the hell else could be responsible for the crimes committed in her house during the short time I was gone? Gandhi would never be caught flipping a house.

Holding my breath, I bring up Microsoft Word. I've been working on and off on what will be my sixth novel, which I'm calling *Blood Mountain*. The novel is still there and, scrolling through it, I can see that it seems, on the surface anyway, to be uncorrupted. Like the unmolested desk in Lisa's office, or Anna's untouched bedroom, this doesn't make much sense to me. Why not infect my computer if you're not going to bother to steal it? Or better yet, why not smash it to bits like Lisa's wedding china? Perhaps he didn't have the time. Maybe he heard me pull up in the driveway and had no choice but to run out the back sliding glass doors, and from there into the one-hundred-acre Little's Lake State Park. That's exactly what I'm betting on. He's probably still running.

Minimizing Word, I pull up the web browser, type the name "David Bourenhem" into the search engine. His web page is the first site to come up. I swear I have to hold myself back from punching the screen when the enlarged image of his face appears. Scanning the website's links, I click on "Contact." What comes up is a phone number and his home-office address. As I surmised, it's located in Troy on First Street. I know the area well.

Rachael lives nearby, on Third Street, on the first floor of a renovated brownstone that's more than a century old. I practically lived there myself for three years. The address listed on David's site is 57 First Street, while Rachael's is 38 Third Street. They live only two streets over from one another.

Holy Christ, did I more or less live in the same neighborhood as David Bourenhem for nearly three years and have no idea? Did Lisa spend the night at his house while I was resting my head on Rachael's pillows, just a few yards away?

Standing, I close the laptop lid. I pull the keys to my Escape from the pocket of my bush jacket and exit Lisa's house by way of the front door.

Time for a face-to-face showdown with the ex-lover boy.

Chapter 23

I pull up as close as I can to 57 First Street and immediately spot the tan Honda parked a few yards ahead of me along the side of the road. If I'd just pulled a major B & E on a quiet suburban residence in the heart of North Albany, the last place I'd park my ride is right out on the street. That is, unless I was pulling a head fake, making it look like I'd never left that spot all day.

Turning off the engine, I exit the Escape and immediately turn my attention to the perpendicular cross street that accesses Third Street, where Rachael lives. Maybe it's unlikely that she would park on the cross street, but still I look for her car, a green 1990s-era Toyota hatchback. A utility vehicle that not only got her through the snow when she needed to be teaching a class at the downtown university in midwinter, but that also was large enough to cart her canvases and other more three-dimensional art projects.

She once built a huge dollhouse of wood, inside of which she installed miniature video monitors that played old 8mm flashbacks of her childhood and the father who deserted her family. Then, in a bold statement against men who leave their wives and families behind for other women, she videotaped herself destroying the dollhouse with a chainsaw. The look on her face in the video as she tears into the dollhouse is not altogether different from the expression I must have worn as a child when I tried to light our second house on fire only a couple of years after the fire that destroyed our first house.

The Toyota isn't there, but that doesn't mean she isn't home. But this visit isn't about Rachael. Better that I keep my mind on task, stay focused.

I step out onto the sidewalk and head along the cracked pavement in the direction of number 57. It's only two doors up. With each step I take, my pulse rises, the blood in my veins racing. My brain begins to buzz from the release of adrenaline. It's a pure, primordial animal feeling, but the sound in my ears is like an orchestra stuck on a single note, playing soft at first, but then louder and louder, reaching for a heated crescendo.

I stop when I come to the front steps of a four-story brownstone that hasn't enjoyed the same tender loving care as Rachael's old building. I hop the flight of stone steps up to the front door. It's not only unlocked, it's partially open. Set inside the narrow vestibule wall on the right-hand side are metal mailboxes for all the residents, each with a buzzer that activates an intercom. I scan the names on the mailboxes.

Bourenhem is unit 2C.

Making a fist, I punch the button. A buzzer sounds. I wait.

"Hello," says David—the word long and drawn out, like "Helll . . . lowwww." He sounds almost effeminate when he says it. Like maybe I've just interrupted him in the middle of writing a press release.

"FedEx package for Mr. Bourenhem," I say into the intercom.

"Just leave it, please, Mr. FedEx Man," he exhales.

"Need a signature, boss."

He lets loose with another sigh just to make sure I know how annoyed he is at having his genius moment interrupted.

"I'll come down," he says.

"Tell you what. You sound real busy and the package is heavy. No use both of us breaking our backs. Why don't I just bring it up to you?"

"What a nice FedEx Man you are," he says, his voice brighter, almost singsong.

He hits the buzzer. The inner door unlocks electronically and opens by a few inches.

For better or worse, I'm in.

Chapter 24

I bound up the stairs two at a time. The apartment directly ahead of me at the top of the stairs is B. The black metallic letter B nailed to the six-paneled wood door says so. I glance to my left and see that the apartment that faces the back alley is A. Hooking a quick right, I head for what can only be 2C, the apartment that must face First Street.

The door begins to open just as I arrive at its threshold. My years playing high school football take over and I lower my right shoulder, barrel through the door like a 250-pound fullback crashing through the line of scrimmage. Bourenhem is on the opposite side of the door and he flies back, drops to the wood floor onto his back.

Wide-eyed, he sees me standing over him. He screams.

I slam the door closed, lock the deadbolt. Then, turning to him, I make my approach, slowly. He starts crabbing backward, a tiny trickle of blood now dripping from his lower lip where the wood door caught it.

"My neighbors heard me scream," he says. "They're calling the police."

"Nobody cares," I say, still moving toward him like I'm about to stomp on him. "Go ahead, Bourenhem, scream again. See what I do to that pretty little face. I'm going to kick it so hard your grand-mother's mother is gonna feel it."

He's still staring at me when the back of his head connects with the far, exposed brick wall that separates his apartment from First Street. End of the line.

"You did a real nice job on Lisa's house," I say. "Just so you know, I haven't touched a thing. When the cops go through it with a fine-toothed comb, they'll lift your prints off of everything you touched. Including her fucking underwear, you creep."

"You are out of your mind," he says. "I haven't the foggiest idea what you're going on about."

"I'll give you this, Bourenhem, you have serious artistic skills. Wow, a writer *and* an artist. That image of my skull getting blown off by a shotgun blast is terrific." Standing over him, I press my black combat-booted right foot onto his bare foot and press down hard, make it bend in a way God never intended.

"Oh Christ," he cries. "Stop it."

"Tell me why you broke into Lisa's house this morning and I'll think about not breaking your ankle. Was it to rattle me? Scare me? Intimidate me? Or just plain burn me up?"

"I did not break into Lisa's house," he insists through gritted teeth. "Why would I do something insanely stupid like that?"

"Because you must be insane."

"You're the insane one. Lisa warned me about you a long time ago. You get crazy fucking jealous, she said. You play with fire. You nearly burned your home down when you were a kid and then you tried to torch Lisa's house when she and I first became a couple. You're not like the main character of *The Damned*. You *are* the main character."

I press harder. He winces. For a second or two, I get the distinct feeling he might pass out.

He says, "I went to see Lisa at the medical center right after I left you at her house this morning. If someone broke in, it wasn't me."

In my mind I see the Honda 4x4 parked in the medical center lot. The Honda belonged to him after all.

"That your alibi?" I say. "A visit with Lisa? I wonder if she'll back it up."

"After I dropped the flowers off, I decided, screw it, Reece will probably toss the flowers away. So why not just pay her a visit in person? We're all adults here. Most of us, anyway."

"You're lying and insulting me."

I see him reach into the back pocket of his black skinny jeans. I press harder.

"Stop, please, stop," he whispers, his teeth clenched in pain. "I'm just trying to get at my cell phone."

"Why?"

"Because Lisa will vouch for me."

"Go ahead and call. Fire away, Bourenhem."

"If you get off my fucking foot."

I slide my foot off his ankle.

Immediately he pulls his knee into his chest, grabs his bare foot, rubs the pain out of it. Then, thumbing a single button on his smartphone, he speed-dials my present, and his former, significant other.

Chapter 25

I stare down at him while he awaits an answer that I'm convinced won't come. Lisa just had her infected tear ducts surgically repaired. She will still be under the influence of a waning anesthetic, not to mention the waxing pain from the operation. No way she can answer the phone, much less vouch for this asshole.

I can hear the rings coming through the little iPhone speaker pressed up against his ear.

Then, "Lisa, I'm so sorry to be bothering you right now." I'm shocked she's answered. "But I have a visitor standing inside my apartment. A visitor who knows you as intimately as I do." He shoots me a look from down on the floor with his bug eyes further enlarged by his thick eyeglasses. "It's your husband. Well, correction, ex-husband and current love interest. Seems there's been a break-in at your casa and he wildly assumes that I might, in fact, be the perpetrator. Surprise, surprise." He pauses while she responds. "Okay, I'll put you on speaker."

He thumbs the digital commands that engage the iPhone's speaker system.

"Reece," comes the tinny but groggy voice of Lisa. "What on God's earth is happening? What happened at the house and why are you harassing David, of all people?"

. . . harassing David, of all people . . .

"I'm not harassing him, Lisa," I say. "It's true, a break-in occurred sometime this morning while I was out. I'm not going to get into details, but the method of the break-in indicates to me that the person behind it could only be David. I'm sorry, but that's the way I see it."

"Really? Well, David was kind enough to sit with me for much of the late morning." That hurts, but I let it go. "Have you called the police, Reece? Maybe you should get in touch with Blood, once and for all. Is the dog okay?"

"No. I mean yes. Or, what I mean is, Frankie is fine. But I haven't called the police, nor have I gotten Blood involved. Not yet. I wanted to leave them out of it for now while I spoke with David."

"Maybe you should be talking to the police instead of letting your jealousy get the best of you and lobbing false accusations."

My body feels like it's melting into Bourenhem's dirty wood floor with each groggy word Lisa speaks. Each admonition. Maybe that's why I haven't commanded Blood's presence. Because upon discovering the flipped house, he would have wanted me to call the cops, not take matters into my own hands.

"Tell you what, Lisa," I say, my eyes connecting with Bourenhem's, "my mistake. Go get some rest. I'll take care of the house. I'll call the police."

"Was anything taken?"

"Not that I can see. Some plates were broken, and some paintings were pulled off the wall. But I think I arrived home unexpectedly and Mr. Bourenhem here fled the scene in a panic."

"Damn it, Reece," Lisa says. "He was *with me*. And it's crazy to think he'd do it in any case." She gasps. "Oh God. You haven't hit David, have you?"

I look at him and he looks at me. The little trickle of blood on his lower lip is beginning to dry and cake.

"No, he didn't hit me," David says into the phone while wiping the dried blood away with the back of his free hand. His eyes never leave my own. "He hasn't touched me."

"Good, that's a relief. Just call the police, Reece. We'll talk about all this later when I can keep my eyes open."

The line disconnects. David thumbs "End."

"I'm going to get up," he says. "Please don't try and knock me down again."

"I won't."

I do something I never would have considered just ten minutes earlier: I hold out my hand for him. He looks at it, then grabs it. I yank and help pull him back up onto his feet. For a brief second we both stare at our hands clasped together. Then, realizing what it is we're looking at, we pull our respective hands away.

"No need to show me to the door," I say, turning, walking.

"Reece," he says.

I stop, turn around. "What?"

"I truly mean you no harm. I love Lisa. I spent what seems a lifetime with her and Anna. You just don't walk away from something like that. I want to somehow be a part of her life . . . their lives . . . no matter how small that part might be. Do you understand?"

Over his right shoulder, I take notice of his floor-to-ceiling bookshelves. They're crammed full of paper- and hardback novels. I can't help but notice that there's an entire section of a shelf devoted to my books. All five of them.

He notices me noticing them. He gazes over his shoulder at the books, then turns his attention back at me. "I wasn't lying," he says, his bottom lip no longer bleeding, but swelling up. "I'm a big fan."

A desk made from an old wood door set upon concrete blocks is set beside the bookshelf. The desk supports a laptop computer connected to a printer, with stacks of manuscript pages. Now that I'm able to take a good look, I can see that the place is covered in manuscripts. There are stacks of typewritten paper on the floor, on the dinner table in the kitchen area, on the kitchen counters, and on something else too. What looks to be a genuine pine casket.

"The casket," I say. "Where the hell did you get that?"

"Ordered it special," he says, not without a smile. "It's identical to the ones Drew Brennen burns his victims in in *The Damned*. Pretty fucking cool, huh?"

I don't know whether to be proud of this moment or entirely weirded out.

"How many novels have you written?" I say, my eyes scanning all that paper. "Looks like you're trying to catch up to me."

"*Trying* being the key word here," he says, his eyes suddenly glazing over, like a heroin addict who's just shot himself up. "So far, no one will publish a single word."

"Keep trying. Light enough matches, something's bound to catch fire."

There's a kind of light in his eye that I haven't seen until now. "I'll say it again, bro," he says. "I really am a fan."

"If you're a fan, then why disrespect me by still going after Lisa?"

He cocks his head over his shoulder. "Would an author of your caliber respect me if I laid down like a dead dog, just because I was told to lie down?"

He's got a point.

"Listen," I say. "I'm sorry about today, about pushing you down."

"No harm done." When he smiles, there's blood on his teeth.

I unlock the deadbolt and leave Bourenhem's apartment to the memory of that great big bloodstained smile burning itself into my brain.

Chapter 26

I fire up a smoke as soon as I get back behind the wheel of the Escape. I breathe in the smoke, feel my heart rate speed up and then settle gently, and wonder how I ever managed to quit this lovely disgusting habit in the first place.

I'm back to playing with the lighter, making a new flame every couple of seconds, when, out the corner of my left eye, I see someone coming up the cross street.

It's a woman.

She's of medium height, beautifully constructed, with shoulder-length blonde hair cut in a style not altogether different from Lisa's. She's wearing a green wool overcoat over a short skirt, black tights, and black leather boots. Thick round sunglasses cover her eyes. She's got a wide canvas bag strapped to her shoulder like it's possible she's off to her studio. But her studio is located in the basement of the old brick building she teaches Advanced Oil Painting in, at the university across the river in downtown Albany. My guess is she's on her way for a coffee or a quick drink somewhere on River Street, the historic one-way lane behind First Street that parallels the Hudson River.

Rachael.

I haven't laid eyes on her since we split up.

Instinct takes over and I find myself rolling down the window to call out for her. But then I catch myself. She loved me and I loved her in return, but the pain of being with me when I still had love for another woman was too much for her. She had to make the break and make it as clean and as definite as possible. No communication of any kind.

The last time I heard her voice was over the phone. She said she never wanted to see me or speak with me again. She'd blocked me from all her social media and blocked my phone number on her Verizon account. She told me, in no uncertain terms, that if she spotted me walking in her general vicinity, she would call the police. I'd never given her reason to call the police, but somehow, I sensed a seriousness in her threat. It's because of that seriousness that, in the two months Lisa and I have been back together, I haven't once attempted contact with Rachael. If only David Bourenhem would do the same.

Smoking the cigarette and flicking the lighter, I watch her blonde hair blowing gently in the wind as she turns left at the cross-street corner, walks the two hundred or so feet to the next corner, crosses the empty street, and then disappears from view.

Time to get my head out of my ass, concentrate on the present.

I drop the half-smoked cigarette out the partially open window, return the lighter to my bush jacket pocket, then pull my smartphone out, dial 911. The dispatcher asks me the nature of my emergency. I tell her my girlfriend's home has been broken into. She asks me if I'm inside the home now. If so, she says, I should exit as quickly as possible in order to avoid a violent confrontation with the perp or perps.

I resist the urge to tell her it's too late for that. That I'm not in the house anymore. I'm not even in the same town. But I know then she'll ask why I decided to leave the scene of a crime.

Instead, I recite Lisa's address and she tells me a squad car is being dispatched to the scene forthwith. Thanking her, I hang up, knowing I have only about ten minutes to beat the cops to Lisa's home sweet home.

Chapter 27

It takes me only seven and a half minutes to cross the river and get back to Lisa's house. But it's still not quick enough to beat the Albany Police Department to the place. A blue and white squad car is already parked in the driveway, its front doors open, rooftop flashers all lit up, tinny two-way radio blaring indiscernible words.

Two cops are standing beside their respective open doors. When I pull in behind them, they both turn to get a look at me.

I kill the engine and get out. "Can I help you, officers?"

"You the owner?" says the driver of the squad car. He's clean-shaven and burly.

"I'm not the owner. But I'm the one who called 911."

"Why would you leave the scene?" the second, thinner cop says. "You decide to call 911, then go for coffee?" He cracks a smile.

"No," I say, wishing once again I'd waited to call until I was at least on this side of the Hudson. "I needed to take care of something."

The cops shoot one another a look. I'm not a cop, but the look makes it obvious to me that I am now under suspicion as the perp responsible for the break-in, who therefore called 911 in order to make it look like I *wasn't* the perp. If nothing else, those cop-eyes mean I'm at least under suspicion for being an asshole.

"Have you been inside?" I say.

"Joint's locked up tighter than a snare drum," says Burly Cop. "We did a quick perimeter search. No windows broken, no door locks jimmied. Figured we'd wait until a responsible owner showed up and then check the inside."

My keys in hand, I lead the two cops to the front door and let them inside.

We scour the entire house, Burly Cop taking notes on a spiral notepad as we go. But it doesn't take a rocket scientist to determine that the true perp or perps managed to enter the place without forced entry. Whoever did this had a key, or at least access to one.

There's something that bothers Burly Cop. "Out on the back deck," he says, "someone was using your barbecue to burn garbage. There's ashes all over the place. The fire that produced the ashes can't be more than a few hours old."

In my head, I see myself burning the photos from Lisa's underwear drawer. I feel a similar kind of burn fill my body.

"There's been a rash of garbage can burnings in the park behind the house here," Burly Cop goes on. "He struck again just this morning. Could be the same jerk who's lighting stuff up out there could be responsible for your break-in."

I nod. "Seems logical."

A minute or so passes before a plainclothes detective shows up and starts taking pictures of the place with a small digital camera. He focuses not so much on the destroyed objects—the artwork that's been pulled off the wall, the smashed china, the tossed couch—as on the stuff that, in his words, remains "unmolested."

"Good choice of words," I tell him, but the compliment flies right over his closely cropped head.

Eventually he gets down to asking me who I am and what the nature of my relationship is with the owner of the premises.

I tell him.

He smiles. "Well, that's unusual but cool," he says. Making a 360-degree observational rotation on the balls of his feet inside the living room, he adds, "I've read your novels. *The Damned* is a damned good read. Disturbing, though. A home invader whose MO is to burn his hostages alive in pine caskets. Fuck you come up with shit like that?"

"Fire! Fire!" says the Town Crier . . .

"Tell you what, though," he goes on. "You could use a lesson in proper police procedure. Check out Michael Connelly. Now there's a writer who knows his cop shit."

"Thanks for the advice," I tell him, as though not stung by the Connelly crack.

The detective's a tall, wiry man with a head of thick gray hair cut jarhead short. He wears an old-fashioned gray trench coat and, under it, a spit-and-polish navy blue blazer over a brown shirt and gray tie, the ball knot of which hangs perfectly centered under his muscular neck. He hands me a business card. I glance down at it in my hand. It says, "Detective Nick Miller, Homicide."

"Homicide," I say. "I don't get it."

"No murders yet today," he explains. "But plenty of break-ins. Truth is, Mr. Johnston, we're understaffed, underfunded, and underappreciated, so every now and then I get to play with Criminal Investigations whether I enjoy it or not. And to be perfectly frank, I'm not the least bit crazy about the nature of this break-in."

"I get to ask why?"

"It smells personal." He sniffs in and out, as if he can actually take in the personal nature of the crime.

"Isn't it always personal when someone messes with your private stuff?"

He shakes his head. "No, not really. Inanimate objects are inanimate objects, no matter who owns them. Usually these matters have to do with some junkie looking to hock one of those said

objects so he can score some crack or whatever the drug du jour is."
He pauses as he once more makes one of those complete revolutions, eyeing the living room like an artist sizing up a newly finished
canvas. "Not this one, though. This house was flipped by someone
who's been here before. Been here plenty of times."

I feel the hair on the back of my neck rise up. I stuff my right
hand in my pants pocket, finger the Bic lighter.

He asks me where Lisa is. I tell him and he writes the answer
down in a small notepad. He asks me if I live here, and I tell him
not technically. "But I do stay here a lot."

"You have a key to the place?"

"Of course."

He writes that down.

"Children?"

"One girl. Eight years old."

"Name?"

"Anna."

"Where is she now?"

"With her grandmother."

"You and the missus . . . how long you been seeing one another
again?"

"Two months, give or take a day or three."

"Love interests prior to this one?"

"Why do you need to know that?"

"Suspect elimination," he says. "See? I told you you needed a
lesson on cop procedure. You'd already know why I needed to ask
that question if you were Michael Connelly."

Sad thing about it is, he's probably right. I think over his question
anyway. Naturally, David Bourenhem comes to mind. The bloody lip
I gave him when I kicked his door in. I think of someone else too.

"I was involved with an artist for three years," I say. "Lisa had a relationship with another writer for almost the entire time we were apart."

He asks me their names and I give them to him. I even offer up their respective home addresses.

"Your wife Lisa saw Bourenhem for the entire time you were apart?" he goes on. "Excuse me for asking, but had they been conducting an affair prior to your breakup?"

I feel the electric shock of his question inside my spine. I recall Lisa talking a lot about David during the last year or so of our marriage. Back before Anna was born and then shortly after that, until I left a couple of months later. She used to speak about getting reacquainted with him through Facebook. How magical the digital age could be. She talked incessantly about a new book he was writing back when I couldn't manage a single decent sentence. She claims to have invited him to the house for me to look at his work, which I still have no recollection of. Maybe I just learned how to block him out of my mind.

"No," I say, "I don't think they were cheating on me." But when I say it, I feel that familiar pit form in my chest and I can see them. An evil image flashes into my brain. The two of them in bed, me gawking at them. But the image is fleeting, the endless, cruel working of a fiction writer's imagination.

"Did it hurt?" Miller presses.

"Did what hurt?"

"Your ex-wife going out with another writer? She couldn't have hooked up with a high school teacher? Or a carpenter?"

"It might have hurt Bourenhem more," I say, fingering the lighter in my pocket. "He never got to publish anything, while my career took off after Lisa and I split. He'd probably give his left nut for a book contract."

"He hate you now that you're back with his girl?"

. . . his girl . . .

"He claims to be a fan of mine."

"A fan?" He squints like it helps him compute my answer better. "Strange, isn't it? A wannabe writer goes after your ex like that.

Almost like he wanted to put himself in your shoes. Your bed. Your muse. As if the experience would have some kind of magical effect on him. Make him as successful as you."

"I told you. I wasn't a success until *after* Lisa and I split."

My fingers wrap around the lighter.

He nods. "Still seems odd to me," he says.

"You done with this?"

"Done with what, Mr. Johnston?"

"This line of questioning? Or are these questions Michael Connelly would be better at answering?"

He laughs. "Sorry about all this," Miller says. "I'm just guessing it has to hurt a little, imagining a would-be writer sleeping with your ex and present love interest. Strikes me as strange, is all. It's certainly nothing I've ever encountered in all my years as a cop."

"I'm sure it does seems strange, Miller. But you know us writers. On the outside, we might appear to be a close-knit community, but on the inside we all secretly hate one another's guts and successes."

He stares at me for a minute, like he's sizing me up. And he is. "Tell you what," he says. "For one, I know you've been drinking. I can smell it on your breath."

I wonder if he can also make out the sudden redness in my face from the blood that now fills it.

"And for two," he goes on, "I gotta take a shit, so if you don't mind my using your bathroom, we can take five and get back to some questions of a different nature."

I pull out the cigarettes from my bush jacket.

"Mind if I smoke?" I say.

"Quit for ten years," he says. "But by all means, burn one for me, Mr. J."

Chapter 28

Two cigarettes later, I'm back inside the living room while the two uniformed cops stand shoulder to shoulder in the vestibule by the front door, their protective green evidence booties still covering their black cop shoes. Miller comes back in from the can, waving his right hand in the air.

"I were you, I wouldn't go in there for at least an hour," he says, his cell phone in his hand and a big, satisfied smile on his face. "So where were we?"

"Hatred, jealousy, writers, fucking one another's women."

"Ah yes," he says while pocketing the phone. "Speaking of jealousy and fucking one another's women, I do have another question for you, Mr. Johnston." He gives the edge of his hairline a scratch with the thumbnail on the hand that also holds a ballpoint pen, just like Columbo used to do every Sunday night in the 1970s. "You don't by chance own a handgun, do you?"

In my head I see the unlicensed 9mm sitting in the glove compartment of the Escape. The gun was a gift from a fan. A very illegal gift. But it seemed silly to report it to the police when I could use it to protect myself and my family.

I look Miller in his steely-blue eyes. "No gun," I lie. I feel the blood fill my face when I say it. Feel the warmth.

I sense Miller knows I'm lying through my teeth, since he shoots me one of those ray-gun stares. Fumbling around the pockets of his trench coat, he pulls out a second pad of paper. He reaches into his chest pocket, pulls out a second pen, hands me both.

"Seems silly of me to request this of you," he says, a smirk planted on his face, "but I'm going to have to ask you for a writing sample, Mr. Johnston."

Digging once more into his pocket, he pulls out the dust jacket photograph of me that was tacked to Lisa's corkboard. The one with the writing on the back calling me a "posthumous bestseller." Since taking the photo into custody, he's slid it inside a clear plastic evidence baggy. He stares down at it for a minute before returning it to his pocket.

Then, glancing over his shoulder, he stares up at the chalkboard drawing of my head getting blown off.

He says, "I'm also going to have to ask you to draw something for me too."

"Draw what?"

He cocks his head. "Anything. A face. A bird. A burning casket . . . that gun you claim you don't own . . . I don't care." He shoots me a wink.

I nod, knowing exactly where this is going. "And what would you like me to write?"

"A single sentence will suffice. How about the opening line to your new novel? That should do it."

I peer down at the pen and paper gripped in my hands. "I have a choice in the matter?"

"Sure," he says. "You can refuse and we can all take a ride downtown right now."

"I see."

I move to the dining room table, careful to step over the strewn-about shards of china and glass, and sit in front of my laptop, the words THE BESTSELLER IS A HERETIC AND LIKE ALL HERETICS HE WILL BURN FOR HIS SINS still visible on the screen. Placing pen to paper, I try to think of something to write. Like I said, I haven't been blocked in years, but with a detective standing over me and two burly cops planted by the front door, it's not easy being creative.

I take the easy route, write, "The bestseller is a heretic and like all heretics he will burn for his sins."

I hand it to the dick. He reads it, smiles.

"Reminds me of *The Damned*," he says.

"Very good," I say.

"Don't forget to draw me something," he adds in a patronizing, singsong voice, like he's my sixth-grade homeroom teacher.

I just want to burst up out of my chair and ball my fist in his mouth. But since that would land me behind bars faster than I can say "police brutality," I draw a stick figure, complete with cowboy hat, six-guns, and kerchief wrapped around the neck. I stand up and hand it to him.

He looks at it and giggles. "Nice work," he says, shoving it inside his pocket. "I'd stick to words, I were you."

"Thanks," I say, feeling a wave of relief wash over me. "Now, if you're through here, Detective Miller, would you mind not letting the door slam you in the backside on the way out? I'd really like to check in on my daughter's mother. It's been one of those days."

A cell phone chimes. It's Miller's. He pulls the phone back out of his pocket, glances at what's obviously a text message, then shoots a look across the living room at the cops.

"Slight change of plans, guys," he says.

"Yes, sir," Burly Cop answers.

"Okay, good." Then, his eyes back on me, "You can call Anna's mom from the squad car."

The warm relief in my veins is suddenly replaced by ice-cold water. "Why would I do that?"

"I need you to accompany me downtown in order that you be fingerprinted and photographed."

"Am I under arrest for something, Detective Miller?"

"Let's just say I need a little more information from you, given the present circumstances."

"What circumstances?"

He shows me his phone and the text message, which is too far away for me to read. He helps me out: "Under circumstances I was just made aware of now that Mr. David Bourenhem of Troy, New York, has filed a complaint of assault and battery against you with the Troy Police Department."

Chapter 29

I'm led into a concrete room with no windows and very little venti-
lation to exhaust the heavy smell of ink and disinfectant. Burly Cop
hasn't left my side since we arrived at the downtown South Pearl
Street headquarters of the APD ten minutes ago. There's a pad of
ink set out on a metal table. Beside that is a pad of paper, the top-
most sheet of which contains thick square boxes that will soon be
tattooed with my prints.

I'm a little confused, because although I haven't been officially
arrested, or read my rights, or even handcuffed, I'm still being
printed. My guess is they want to compare the prints they lifted
off Lisa's place to my own. I suppose I could protest, call in a lawyer, scream harassment, but my gut tells me that would just make
matters more complicated. Besides, what the hell do I have to hide?

"Thought you guys were fingerprinting electronically now?" I
say. It's my attempt at showing off at least some knowledge of the
twenty-first-century police department.

"Computer printing devices cost a lot of money," he says,
scratching his nearly bald head. "We're always running in the red.
Or so they tell me."

Burly Cop takes hold of my right hand with his left, tells me to extend my thumb. Then, talking hold of said thumb with the opposing digits on his right hand, he presses the thumb pad onto the ink pad. When the thumb pad is sufficiently blackened with ink, he presses it onto the fingerprint form in the square space provided.

"Don't resist me," he insists.

His grip is tight and for a brief second or two, I feel like he's going to tear my thumb off. When it's done he points to a sink in the corner of the room.

"You can wash up there," he says mechanically. "Careful of the water. It's scalding hot sometimes."

The hot water doesn't seem to bother me. Allowing the steaming water to run onto my hands, I shoot Burly Cop a smile. But he just shakes his head like he's witnessing the actions of a crazy man. If he only knew.

***

Miller, the homicide-slash-criminal-investigations detective, is sitting behind his desk. He's taken his jacket off and hung it on the rack behind him along with his trench coat. His shoulder holster and the automatic it houses are plainly visible. If I were to describe the scene for one of my novels, I'd write, *The gun rested heavily against his left rib cage, close to his broken, but still-beating heart.* That sort of thing.

He's busy reading something when I enter the office. From the looks of it, it's a legal document of some kind.

"Shut the door behind you, please, Mr. Johnston," he says without pulling his eyes away from the document.

I shut it.

"Take a seat."

"You telling or asking?"

"I'm very busy, Mr. Johnston," he says, clearly not in the mood.

There's a single wood chair set in front of his desk. It looks like the kind of chair a prisoner of war might be interrogated in inside a windowless concrete cell that's dripping of damp, blood, and lies. With the only light available in the cramped square office provided by a single desk lamp, I half expect him to turn the light directly onto my face before barking out questions and lobbing accusations.

"Where were you on the morning of October 10?"

But he stops reading and sets the short stack of papers back down on his desk. Then he looks up at me and smiles. "You comfortable, Mr. Johnston? Can I get you anything? Cup of Albany PD burnt coffee or something? Might even be a Dunkin' Donut left over from this morning."

I peer down at my still somewhat ink-stained thumb resting in my lap. "I'd like to get the hell out of here so I can go see my girlfriend," I say. "She had surgery today and her house is ransacked."

"Your ex-wife," he says.

"Yes, you know that already."

"Yes I do." Shaking his head. "Still trying to get that shit to sink in. How does a man get back together with his ex-wife after all that pain? All that suffering? All the fights? All the bad memories?" Then, smirking, "No wonder you drink during the day."

"You learn to look beyond the old pain and begin anew," I say. Then, "Look, is this why you pulled me in here and printed me? To talk about my complicated love life, Detective?"

He smiles again.

"Not at all. My wife died on the operating table a few years ago. I don't even have a girlfriend these days, so I can't help but be curious."

"Sorry to hear about your wife."

He nods. "Thanks." He lifts the document back up off his desk. "Back to your love life. You now have to contend with Lisa's ex-boyfriend who, at present, seems to be a thorn in your side."

I feel him taunting me, trying to make me feel uncomfortable. He's succeeding.

"Listen," I say, "he made an unannounced visit to Lisa's house this morning. He brought her flowers. He's been calling her too, and texting. He's obsessed with her."

"So naturally you assumed he was the one to break in and smash all that good wedding china and to write that nasty note on your computer and to do that crazy drawing on the chalkboard wall. It must have enraged you, knowing he went through Lisa's underwear."

"Detective Miller," I say, my hands now fisted, "are you trying to get a rise out of me?"

"Not really," he says, once more setting down the paper, sitting back in his swivel chair. "I'm trying to get to the bottom of why you would choose to confront him in his own home, and why you let it get physical. You realize he has every right to have you busted on numerous counts, assault with malicious intent being one of them?"

"Whoever said I hit him, much less went to his apartment?"

"He does and I do."

"But he isn't pressing charges, is he?"

"No, but he is requiring you to stay away from him. Now, are we going to stay away from him or do I send this document to the court for a judge to issue the necessary order?"

"Don't know about you, but I would prefer never to see him again."

"I would prefer it that way too."

Silence ensues. It's as heavy and as stale as the air inside the office.

I make like I'm about to get up. "So can I leave now?"

He sits up in his swivel chair, gestures with his right hand for me to remain seated.

"In a minute." He fumbles through the thin stack of paper once more, sliding out two more sheets. "Did you know that we keep meticulous records here at the APD? Even before everything went digital, generations of good cops have managed to maintain a shipshape records department."

"Good for you."

"No. Good for you and Johnny Q. Public. That's your tax dollars hard at work. Or, in your case, royalties."

"I can sleep better now. So why are you telling me this?"

"Because if it weren't for those meticulous records, I might never have known that your ex-wife and current girlfriend, Lisa, also slapped a restraining order on your ass eight years ago."

My heart drops. Before the words come out of his mouth, I know what he's about to say next. And then he says it.

"You really try and get away with burning Lisa's house down with her, Bourenhem, and your daughter inside it?"

"It was *our* house, and the truth of the matter is this: I lit a small fire using a pile of newspaper way out back on the wood deck. It was a way of getting attention. A frustrated scream or tantrum, if you will. Trust me, I should know what I'm talking about. Never at any time was there a danger of the house going up or anyone getting hurt."

Miller clears his throat. "You really believe that?"

"I have to believe it."

"I understand you also tried to light your childhood home on fire. And here I thought *The Damned* and all the fires that dude Drew Brennen starts was just fiction."

"My *second* childhood home, if you want to know the truth. The first one my mother burned down with a cigarette. Killed herself and my brothers. They were all burned alive in their bedrooms. Ever since then . . ." I raise up my hands as if the gesture will complete my sentence better than words ever can.

"Ever since then you've harbored a rather unhealthy obsession with fire."

"You've done your research. My royalties at work."

"Yes, I have, Mr. Johnston. I also know that you were twice hospitalized for your, uh, pyromania. Once as a boy, and again as an adult."

"That's right. Electroshock therapy and all. You should try it sometime. It's like rebooting your brain."

He smirks. "You understand someone, probably you, lit a fire on the grill on Lisa's back deck. Only it wasn't to roast a few weenies. The fire wasn't a means to an end, but an end in itself."

"Excuse me?"

"Whoever lit the fire wanted to play with fire and that's all. By my estimation, he went through an entire bottle of lighter fluid. Probably stood there and poured it into the flame, watching it go sky high. Dangerous shit."

"That so. There a law against lighting a fire in a barbecue?"

"Not really. Unless the man doing it is a pyro who's doing it irresponsibly. But that's not what bothers me about the fire in the cooker. What bothers me is that we've been getting reports of garbage can fires at Little's Lake, which is situated directly in back of Lisa's house. In fact, one of those garbage cans was torched just hours before Lisa's house was broken into and someone started making fires on her back deck."

My throat goes tight. So does my chest. I try to keep a straight face, but it's getting harder and harder.

Miller goes on. "Tell me something, Mr. Johnston. Did you ever threaten your former girlfriend, Rachael, with fire?"

"Listen, Miller," I say, trying not to raise my voice. "I'd never hurt a woman. You got that?"

He raises his hands in mock surrender. "Hey, calm down, Mr. Johnston. And please lower your voice. We're just talking here. You say you'd never hurt a woman, but you not only scared Lisa eight years back, you might very well have killed them all. A triple homicide would look very bad on a writer's dust-jacket biography."

I exhale, loosen up my hands, then once more squeeze them into fists.

"I was going through a bad time. I was drunk and struggling through my first novel after three straight years of writer's block."

"You should have been happy now that you were able to write again."

"You're right, I should have been. But the words weren't coming easy. It was like pulling teeth, tooth by painful tooth. At the same time, I was also struggling with the sadness, the desperation, that can only come from losing the woman you love to another man."

"Fire burns, Mr. Johnston," Miller sighs. "But love kills."

"So what is it you want of me now? An admission that I've made mistakes? Made bad decisions? Been a pyromaniac? What about you, Detective? You ever fuck up now and again?"

He smiles out the corner of his mouth. "Hey, I told you. My wife is dead. I don't have a girlfriend, and no money, or even a house to burn down."

In my head I scream, *I've had enough of this.* I stand.

He stands, comes around his desk.

"I'm not trying to give you a hard time, Mr. Johnston. I like you, and I like your books. It's just that the break-in you reported has personal vendetta written all over it, and I need to turn over a few rocks before I find the right creep living under the right rock. Understand what I'm saying here?"

"Why just print me and me alone? Maybe it would be a smart thing to drag David Bourenhem down here for fingerprinting. My gut feeling is that you won't find the rock, but you will find the creep."

"You leave the police work up to us. Because a crime writer like you knows that before you drag someone in for prints, you must at least possess probable cause, and whoever flipped Lisa's house has a key to her new locksets, which Mr. Bourenhem claims he no longer possesses."

"Apparently your job is to serve, protect, and believe without question the lies of a sick asshole like Bourenhem."

He goes to the door, opens it.

"Joke all you want, Mr. Johnston. But just keep in mind, I don't like this situation one bit. I've dealt with people like you in the past who possess two personalities. The first, as they perceive themselves when looking in the mirror. And the other, as the world perceives them when they are doing things like lighting houses on fire, or beating people up, or who knows, maybe even murdering them. They tend to possess selective memory and they can be very dangerous both to themselves and to others."

"You're going to give psychoanalysis a bad name, Detective Miller."

"Just doing my job." Now working up a smile, "You're free to go."

He doesn't have to tell me twice. I head for the door.

"Oh, and Mr. Johnston," he says, as I step on through the open door and into the larger booking room.

Stopping, I give him a look over my shoulder.

"Please don't leave town for a while," he adds. "You know, until this thing at Lisa's house gets straightened out. Okay?" He points to Burly Cop, who's standing at the far end of the room, apparently waiting for me.

I nod.

"The officer will be happy to give you a lift back home."

"Let me ask you something, Miller," I say. "If I were truly a suspect in the ransacking of Lisa's home, wouldn't it have made more sense for me to have just burned the place to the ground? You ask me, just making the place a wreck doesn't fit my MO."

He shrugs narrow but solid shoulders.

"Maybe you altered your MO to throw us off. That's how I'd write it if I were a novelist. Unfortunate for me that I'm just a stupid upstate cop."

For a few long seconds we just stare into one another's eyes. Until I turn my back on the detective, knowing that I fit the bill as the number one suspect in the ransacking of Lisa's house, regardless of my love of fire.

I leave without saying good-bye.

Chapter 30

As soon as Burly Cop drops me off at Lisa's house, I head inside and pop a cold beer. I drink it down right on the spot, with the refrigerator door wide open. Tossing the can into the sink from across the kitchen floor, I grab a second beer and close the door.

Now, standing at a counter still covered in scattered knives, forks, Scotch tape dispensers, pens, pencils, rubber bands, and everything else that the now-turned-over junk drawer contained, I pull out my cell phone and stare at the display.

No calls.

I wonder how Lisa is doing. If she's resting at her parents' house by now. I wonder if she's awake and if the anesthesia has worn off. If it has, in fact, worn off, then why hasn't she attempted to call me? Maybe she's talking to David. Maybe she has been made aware of the restraining order that he's applied for.

I pull the red Bic lighter from my jeans pocket, thumb a new flame. Too many things running through my head right now, including one very bad memory, resurrected by both David Bourenhem and Detective Miller. The memory is more than eight years old now, but it still haunts me as if it occurred just minutes ago.

———————

After weeks of discussing what was quickly becoming our inevitable legal separation, I finally rented a U-Haul and moved all of my stuff into a small apartment in the city. I recall the date I moved out: Monday, September 11—like that other godawful September 11, weather sunny, dry, and pleasant. I remember the day vividly because it was the Monday after NoirExpo, a popular mystery writers' conference that was taking place in New York City and for which I had worked up the courage to attend. I recall some other things vividly too: from the moment I moved out, I proceeded to drink myself to sleep every night for weeks. Maybe I was feeling sorry for myself, but at the time, I felt that if anyone had a right to feel sorry for himself, it was me.

I had no publisher, no income, and now I'd lost my wife and daughter. About the only thing I had going for myself was *The Damned*, which I was making steady progress on.

Mine was a tale of two emotions. I was miserable over losing Lisa, but excited about writing again. But I would have given it all up to get Lisa back. I still loved her more than anything in the world. I not only obsessed about my love for her, I obsessed over her loss, and about something else too: the fact that she had found another man.

I recall leaving the house. Recall the van backing up to the garage, recall loading my things into the van and driving away, tears falling down my cheeks. But now, since having spoken with Miller and since having finally met Bourenhem in the flesh, my mind is beginning to fill with images that just don't make any sense. In my head I see a closed door. I see myself walking toward it. I see myself opening the door. The door opens—but there's nothing. The flare-up of images . . . memories? . . . ends there.

Why did I choose to leave Lisa on that one particular day? Why not leave weeks before or months after? Why did I decide to leave on September 11, 2006? All I truly recall is this: As one month of separation began to turn into two, I decided to do something about it. I took a few days to get my act together. I showered up, shaved, and put on some clean clothes. I bought a big bouquet of red roses (Lisa's favorite) and went straight from the flower shop to the front door of our big house in the suburbs. With her Land Rover parked in the driveway, I knew she had to be home. But when she came to the door, she frowned, told me I might have called first. I nodded, because after all, she was right. But I also told her she would never have agreed to having a quick drink with me if I called first.

"You're right, I wouldn't have," she said, standing in the open doorway, her long hair blowing back behind her ears in the breeze.

I handed her the flowers.

"So what will it be, then?" I said. "Are you up for a quick drink? *Real* quick, I promise."

"Why? What purpose will it serve? Our separation papers haven't even been signed yet."

"Let's just talk. Please, Leese."

Sensing I wasn't about to give up, she finally agreed to the plan. She also said she needed someone to watch Anna. But as luck would have it, the next-door neighbors didn't mind at all. We got inside my Jeep and headed downtown to a Mexican joint that we used to frequent back when we were dating and my future as a novelist looked as bright as a flame.

"You had to choose this place, didn't you," Lisa said.

I smiled as I parked the Jeep in the lot across the street. Lisa looked ravishing with her long dark hair, long black skirt, and sandals. She had a real glamour about her, and I felt like the saddest son of a bitch in the world for having allowed her to slip through my fingers like so much melted candle wax. Looking at her as she got out of the Jeep, I felt like I was seeing her for the first time. Like she was new to me again, and I wanted nothing more than to get to know her, and to be with her always.

I got us a table outside on a slate patio that was lit up under brightly colored strings of lights that had been strung around a metal, vine-covered arbor. We sipped our margaritas for a while in silence. After a time I took hold of Lisa's hand. I could tell the gesture made her uncomfortable, but I held it anyway. She had that look on her face. The ten-mile glare in the eyes that told me she was hiding something.

"I want to come home, baby," I said. "I need you and I'm sorry. For everything." My eyes teared up.

"Reece," she said, "you're not giving the separation a chance. We need to be apart for a while. You need to work some things out for yourself. Your life, your career. You're no good to us as a couple, to Anna as a father, to anyone, if you're no good for yourself. You need to find some peace and stop tormenting yourself." She smiled then, sadly. A smile that quickly morphed into a scowl. "From what I understand, you have a book going. It's what you've always wanted, isn't it? To have your own book completed and published. Well, let's hope it gets published and you can become a huge success and leave us alone."

She yanked her hand away from mine, angrily, and suggested I take a field trip somewhere. Europe maybe. Mexico. Anywhere. She just wanted me to get out of town like she never wanted me to see her or Anna again.

"Go back to writing freelance journalism," she insisted. "Write some travel stories to make money. Or, I'll give you the money. Just go. Take your book and your talent and be free."

"You'll give me your parents' money, you mean," I said.

"Does it really matter where it comes from?"

I supposed it didn't, and I knew that arguing the point would be futile.

I took hold of her hand again, squeezed it hard. "Please, baby. You're my muse."

For a second time she pulled her hand away. Only this time, she burst out laughing while she did it. "Don't give me that muse crap, Reece Johnston," she said. "You were writing fiction before you met me, but as soon as we got married and settled down, you couldn't write a goddamned word if someone put a gun to your head. You call that a muse? More like a literary cock-blocker."

I couldn't help but think about the word count I'd miraculously managed to put in on *The Damned* even in the short time we'd been separated. It also told me that as much as it hurt to admit it, Lisa was telling the truth. But that didn't mean I was going to give up on her. I loved her too much for that. I wanted her too much, physically, emotionally. I needed her.

"The writer's block was all my own fault," I argued. "Too much pressure to make money. To pay for the house. To pay for you and Anna."

"You're speaking the truth," she said, staring into her drink. "The pressure was too much for us all. You just need to make it happen on your own, Reece . . . without the pressure of *us*."

"You can say it, Lisa," I said. "It's not a dirty word."

"Say what?" she said.

"Family," I said. "Without the pressure of our *family*."

She sat up, finished her drink, looked at her watch. "Damn. I've really got to go." She stood.

"What's the rush?" I said, dropping a ten-spot onto the table. My last ten-spot. Then, through a short chuckle, I said, "You got a date or something?"

She turned to me. "Something," she said, and started walking.

My gut had served me dead right. She was seeing someone tonight, and I knew precisely who that someone was.

"It's the writer, isn't it?" I said. "The one you met on Facebook."

"Really, Reece. After all that's happened, you have to ask that question?"

Standing under the lights on the patio of the Mexican restaurant, I felt my blood turn to hot oil as Lisa turned her back on me and walked out.

Back in the Jeep with her, I fired up the engine, backed out of the space, and positioned the vehicle so that it was facing the empty, wide-open lot. I was feeling completely out of balance, as if the entire world had shifted on its axis. My mind was spinning and I felt almost faint. I was feeling angry and alone and desperate. It was the way I felt as a boy as I watched our house burn to the ground, taking my brothers and my mother along with it.

"Who is this man, the writer?" I said as I shifted the Jeep's transmission into neutral.

She exhaled, profoundly. "You know exactly who he is. You know what he's written. You better than anyone know what he's capable of as a writer. So just please take me home."

I tried to recall the writer, but I couldn't. I couldn't picture what he looked or sounded like. All I recalled was her talking about him. Talking about him incessantly.

"Tell me his name," I said. "I want to hear you say it."

"I'm not telling you another goddamned thing at this point. You'll have to figure it out for yourself. Now can you please, please, please take me home? I knew this was a bad idea."

I wasn't conscious of it at first, but my booted foot was leaning heavily on the gas as we sat there. The eight-cylinder engine was beginning to rev louder and louder.

"I see," I said. "So where are you meeting the writer?"

"It's none of your business." Then, shooting me a glare, "Now can we please go once and for all?"

By now, my foot had almost completely depressed the pedal to the floor. The engine noise was deafening.

"Reece," Lisa shouted. "What are you doing?"

I threw the tranny into drive. The tires spun, until they caught on the gravel and the Jeep began to race across the parking lot, picking up speed as we barreled toward the exterior brick wall of the building across the lot.

"Reece, you're going to kill us!" Lisa screamed.

I'm not sure if at that moment in time I wanted to kill us both, or truly intended to kill us, but it took all the power and strength I could work up to slam on the brakes. We came to a screeching, fishtailing stop only about a half-dozen feet from the wall.

"You surprise me, Reece," she said after catching her breath and through bitter, angry tears. "I thought your method was fire. I'm calling David to pick me up." Opening her door, she jumped out and ran away into the darkness.

That night, after many drinks, I drove back to the big house and parked the Jeep along the curb. I killed the engine and the headlights and I watched them through the plate-glass window. They were seated on the couch in the living room. The same couch where Lisa and I made love many times before. The couch where I was convinced we'd conceived Anna.

When finally they both stood up, I made out a tall, thin man with glasses and black hair. He was wearing jeans and a button-down with the tails hanging out. I tried to recall him from previous visits and I simply could not. Lisa was still wearing the same dress she'd been wearing when we had our drink at the Mexican restaurant earlier. Even from out in the Jeep, I could see how much fun they were having with one another. Laughing, dancing to music.

When she leaned into him and kissed him, I felt like my heart would melt and spill out onto my feet. I began to cry. I wanted to get out of the Jeep, run up to the front door, kick it open, toss in a Molotov cocktail. But what good would it do?

Starting the Jeep back up, I pulled away from the curb and drove on.

I wasn't halfway down the block before I decided to burn the house down.

———

The details are still a little fuzzy, but I remember driving to the Lowe's and buying a red, plastic five-gallon gasoline can. I also bought a new Bic lighter, or it's possible I already had one on me. On my drive back to the house, I stopped at a gas station, where I filled up the can and bought a newspaper. Five minutes later, I was back in my old neighborhood. Parking far enough down the road so that no one would notice my presence, I grabbed the gasoline can, the newspaper, and the lighter, and I exited the Jeep.

I made my way around to the back of the house where it was dark. There was a wood deck attached to the back of the house, which was accessed by a door off the kitchen. The deck supported a Weber grill we'd gotten as a wedding present from one of Lisa's friends. Crumpling up some of the newspaper into fist-sized wads, I gathered them into a small pyramid on the deck floor and then soaked them in gasoline.

Then I thumbed the business end of the lighter and produced a high flame.

I brought the flame within inches of the gas-soaked paper. I touched the top most piece of paper with the flame, watched it ignite. But the breeze blew the flame out as soon as it started.

I might not recall everything that occurred that night or, for that matter, during the days and weeks leading up to it. But I do remember this: something stopped me from bringing the flame to the paper a second time, not the least of which was knowing our infant daughter was inside, asleep in her crib. I just stood there staring at the crumpled-up heap of newspaper, the flame from the lighter burning so hot in my hand a big water blister began to form. Once again, I began to cry. I knew Lisa was inside the house and I knew what she was doing on the couch in the living room. I knew that he was inside her and that she was loving it, needing it, wanting it. Dropping the lighter onto the deck away from the newspaper, I turned and made my way back to the Jeep.

The next morning I was awakened by the telephone. It was Lisa. She was screaming at me, angrily asking me if I had been at the house the night before. Was that my lighter? My can of gasoline? Had I made the little mound of newspaper balls and soaked them in the gasoline? Had I intended to burn the house down with our daughter inside it? You just don't forget a telephone conversation like that. A conversation filled with so much anger, accusations, and hatred.

"No," I said. "I intended to burn the house down with your new boyfriend inside you."

"I'm calling the fucking police," she said before hanging up.

I can tell you this: she never did press formal charges, but true to her word, she did call the police. Later that next day I was served a restraining order stating I could not come within five hundred feet of Lisa or our daughter without express permission or else face immediate arrest by the APD.

They tell me that exactly one week later my father let himself into my studio, pulled me out of bed, and dragged me to the Four Winds Psychiatric Center in Saratoga Springs, where I was diagnosed with a nervous breakdown.

Chapter 31

I stuff the lighter back into my pocket, feel its flame-baked metal head through the thin fabric against the skin on my thigh. The door to the cabinet over the coffeemaker is open, the entirety of its contents spilled out onto the counter and floor. I gaze down at the counter, search for my pills. But I don't find them. My heart begins to pound. I feel the heart muscle beating against my ribs. Suddenly, my head needs my pills like my lungs need air. Like fire needs oxygen.

I drop to my knees, run my hands over the utensils, spice bottles, chipped coffee cups, and too many drinking glasses to count, until finally I locate them. I pop the top on the small caramel-colored, translucent bottle, shake two pills into the palm of my hand, and dry swallow them while down on my knees. Returning the lid to the bottle, I stand and replace it on the cabinet shelf.

It looks lonely sitting there by itself.

I begin to smell something. It's a familiar odor. It's a smell that brings me back to when I was a kid and hanging around the crematorium. I see something reflecting against the dining room wall over my shoulder. The reflection is moving in waves or movement.

I turn quick and, looking through the picture window that provides a view out onto the backyard, I see something I should not see.

I see fire.

Chapter 32

Bolting through the dining room, I jump down both steps and throw open the sliding glass door. Something has been set aflame out on the back lawn. Something maybe five and half feet in length and two feet wide. It lights up the dark of the late fall afternoon. I jump down off the deck onto the lawn and try to get a look at it. But the heat is too intense and it prevents me from getting too close.

I do my best to get close anyway.

I'm not ten feet away from the burning object when I see that it's human. That the smell of burning flesh wasn't a figment of my imagination.

"Oh my sweet Jesus," I say aloud as my knees grow weak and my head spins out of control.

Dad stands off to the side.

For Christ's sake, do something, Reece.

Attached to the back of the house is a garden hose that's attached to an exterior spigot. I sprint to the spigot and crank it all the way on, pick up the flowing hose, and, pressing my thumb against the hose opening, create a pressured spray which I use to douse the burning body.

It takes me maybe two minutes of constant spraying to stop the fire entirely.

Dropping the hose, I see the dead, now badly burned body lying on its back, face up, steaming in the waning orange/red sun of the late afternoon.

"My God," I say with a dry mouth, as if talking to my dad. "Is this what poor Mom looked like when she burned up in her bed?"

All the clothing has been burned away. Everything but the shoes, which are short leather boots. Ladies' boots. The body belongs to a woman. Some of the hair on her head has been spared. Golden brown, curly hair. Her face is too badly burned for me to make out any features, so it's impossible for me to recognize her. But she's wearing a silver necklace that supports a medallion. The medallion consists of a single word or, as it turns out, a name.

Gingerly, I touch the medallion, bringing it closer so I can read it.

It says, OLGA.

Chapter 33

Dropping the medallion back onto her burnt chest, I try to picture Olga.

She is Lisa's neighborhood friend. A recent divorcée and Russian expatriate, she lives—lived—up the road, alone, in an identical ranch. I've met the attractive, soft-spoken woman only once or twice in the two months Lisa and I have been back together.

"What the hell's happened here?" I say to my dad. "Who could have done this to Olga?"

Maybe you should call the police, Son. Call them now.

But I can't call the police. Miller not only suspects me of ransacking Lisa's house, he knows that I went after Bourenhem. Knows I've been lighting fires on the deck and more than likely torched those garbage cans at Little's Lake. He wants nothing more than to bust me for real.

I think hard.

Did the neighbors hear or spot anyone in the backyard either just before or immediately after I got home from the police station? If Olga were being burned alive, wouldn't she have put up a struggle? Would the neighbors see the flames or smell the smoke? At least, that's the way I wrote it in *The Damned*. When the paperboy shows up at Drew Brennen's house, the pyromaniac lures the teenager inside, then out the back door into the yard, where he swiftly hits the boy over the head with a framing hammer. From there he douses the unconscious boy in gasoline and sets him on fire.

While he watches the boy's clothing and flesh burn away, Brennen feels something incredible happening inside his body. The feeling is euphoria, peace, calmness, serenity. It's the feeling most people get from making love to someone they can't live without.

As for the neighbors, sure, they saw the flames, and they might have even heard the sounds of a brief struggle. But the neighbors didn't want trouble. They knew enough to close their blinds, turn a blind eye to the strange sights and sounds coming from Brennen's house.

I recall the screen-saver note on my computer and the casket inside Bourenhem's apartment. Both were lifted right out of *The Damned*.

"*Bourenhem,*" I whisper through clenched teeth. "You did this, you son of a bitch. You sick son of a bitch. I will get you for this."

Staring down at the charred body, I try to figure out my next move. I steal another glance at Dad, see him standing beside me— stocky, gray-haired—peering down with me at the mutilated body.

Reece, whoever did this is an animal . . .

Dad knows what he's talking about. As a father who's already lost two sons to fire, he must be thinking of his last remaining son, and the threat these smoking remains pose to him.

This is a horrible, terrible thing, Reece. But you also have to look at it for what it is: someone is after you, and they are willing to do anything to see that you are buried alive. Your only choice is to get rid of the evidence, and get rid of it fast . . .

With my dad's advice ringing in my ear, I consider the cell phone stored inside my right-hand pocket. If I call Miller, he will answer right away. But I don't call him. And I don't call Blood, because why get him involved in this nightmare? And I sure as hell don't call Lisa, because she will be horrified and sick.

Instead I choose to listen to my dad.

I must bury her, and I must do it alone.

Chapter 34

Frankie is standing under the dining room table when I come back in through the sliding glass doors. She stares at me with those dark marble eyes, her body shivering, like she knows someone has just been murdered out on the back lawn. Turning, she issues a growl and trots off through the kitchen, back into the master bedroom.

It's not my fault, Frankie.

From the linen closet in the hall, I grab an old blanket Lisa keeps around for Anna's occasional sleepover guests. I know it's inevitable that she will miss it, but I have no other choice. Right now, I just want to get rid of the body as soon as I can.

In the garage I find the pair of Carhartt overalls I wear on frigid fall and winter days for ice fishing or bird hunting. Lisa has allowed me to store them here, but she doesn't want the old, badly stained overalls in the house, so they're hanging by a sixpenny nail that's been pounded into the wall. Unzipping the legs, I slip into them, zip the legs back up, then zip up the front all the way to my chin. Turning to the metal shelf pushed up against the wall opposite the car, I locate a pair of leather gardening gloves and a flashlight. There's also a shovel leaning up against the shelf. I grab hold of that too. With the blanket tucked under my arm, I carry everything out with me to the backyard.

Standing over the charred body, I try to figure out the best place to perform a burial. It's possible I could bury the body on the opposite side of the wooden security fence, but then maybe the better place to bury her is inside the fence. The fewer eyes there are to see the freshly dug-up dirt, the better. But what if the police make a surprise visit to the house? What if they inspect the backyard? What if the neighbors decide to get nosy?

"Where would you bury her, Dad?" I say out loud.

As if answering my question, it suddenly dawns on me that burying the body anywhere near the house just might be one of the most terrible ideas I've come up with in a while. But there is always the river. If I dump Olga in the river, chances are she will never be discovered.

Dropping the shovel, I go back into the house, retrieve the keys to the Escape, then shut off all the lights. Back outside, I roll the body up in the blanket and heft it over my shoulder, praying that the body remains intact while I carry it to the vehicle.

It does.

Cursing the dome light's glow, I store the body in the cargo bay of the SUV as quickly as I can and close the hatch. Back inside the garage, I locate two cinder blocks that were left behind when Lisa bought the house. I find some rope and some duct tape too. Storing everything in the Escape beside the body, I start the SUV and drive in the direction of the Hudson River.

I'm on my way to destroy the body of evidence for a crime I did not commit.

Chapter 35

The river just north of the city is flanked on both sides by deep woods. There's a bicycle path that traverses a major portion of Albany riverbank, but on a dark, late afternoon in October, the path is abandoned. Driving the Escape up over the curb, I maneuver a two-tracked maintenance road that runs perpendicular to the bicycle path. Crossing over the path, I drive into the tall grass until I come to the edge of the steep bank, then kill the engine.

Opening the back hatch, I grab hold of the body and drag it with me down to the edge of a section of riverbank wall that's constructed of huge black boulders rising up vertically some four or five feet above the surface of the fast-moving, deep water—a mile-or-so-long section of river that's been dredged in order to accommodate the big cargo ships that dock at the Port of Albany only a few hundred yards downriver. Jogging back up to the truck, I grab the two cinder blocks and set them down beside the body. Making one last trip to the Escape, I snatch up the rope and the duct tape.

Unwrapping the body, I tie one section of rope around the wrists and another around the ankles. Running and tying off the opposite length around both cinder blocks, I cut away the excess rope with my pocketknife and then proceed to wrap as much of the body as possible with duct tape in order that the limbs and head don't show up on either bank as they decompose and separate from the body. By the time I'm done, Olga looks like a gray mummy.

Dad steps up beside me.

Be careful you don't fall in with her when you push her over the side . . .

Dad's got a point.

Taking hold of her duct-taped feet, I shift her body so that it rests parallel with the very edge of the riverbank wall. Then, setting both blocks flat onto her stomach and making sure none of the excess rope is wrapped around my feet or ankles, I brace myself and heave her body unceremoniously into the river. The body and blocks make a splash, but then disappear entirely from sight.

"How'd I do, Dad?" I whisper, feeling a cold sadness wash over me.

But my dead father has nothing to offer.

Chapter 36

On the way home I pull into a Mobil gas station, drive around the back of the main gray block building. Parking beside an overfilled blue Dumpster, I pull off the soiled Carhartts and stuff them, along with the gloves, as far down into the trash as I can. Closing the black Dumpster lid, I get back into the Escape and drive on.

Parked once more in Lisa's driveway, I try to make sense of this whole thing. How did Bourenhem manage to sneak into the yard and burn Olga? He must have come back to Lisa's while Miller was interrogating me. That's when he must have spotted Olga. Maybe she forgot that Lisa was having her eyes operated on and came by to see if she wanted to take a walk. I have no idea. All I know is she must have come here and Bourenhem must have used her sudden presence as an opportunity.

Or maybe something else happened.

Maybe she caught him doing something. Something bad, like once again breaking into the house. She might have threatened to call the police. Whatever happened, he killed her. Burned her alive, mimicking almost perfectly one of the pivotal murder scenes from *The Damned*.

Olga died on Lisa's property from a fire that quite possibly was fueled by gasoline stored inside her garage. I know in my bones that there will be no evidence of forced entry into Lisa's house and that it will be my prints plastered all over everything. That evidence will only point toward me as the culprit.

But simply getting rid of Olga's body isn't enough.

Now there's the matter of cleaning up the lawn. Eventually she's going to be missed, and one of the people the police will interview is Lisa. I get out of the Escape and make my way into the backyard. I pick up the shovel, scrape away as much of the charred lawn as I can, examining the area with the flashlight. Collecting the burnt grass and dirt in the shovel, I toss it over the fence. Then, covering up the exposed area with fallen oak leaves, I spread them out to look as if they haven't been touched by human hands. By the time I'm done, you would never know that a grown woman was burned to death there.

Back in the kitchen, I open another beer and drink half of it down, setting the can on the counter near the sink. I pull out the lighter and go to trigger a flame, but the lighter falls to the floor. Sinking slowly and carefully onto my right knee on the glass-strewn floor, I feel a sharp pain and shoot upright again.

Looking down, I see the small, round spot of thick blood on my Levi's. When I press my hand against the knee, I feel the sting. I must have cut my knee on a piece of shattered glass. Unbuckling my belt and unbuttoning my jeans, I pull them down below my knees, careful not to upset whatever is stabbing me.

It's worse than I thought.

A jagged piece of crystal-clear drinking glass has impaled itself into the side of my knee. It's gone clean through my jeans and into the skin and flesh. Oftentimes, pain doesn't really kick in full force until you see the wound. Just bringing my fingertips to the piece of jagged glass ignites my nervous system and makes me see stars. Blood trickles down my skin and a painful burn shoots up and down my leg.

I don't have much choice in the matter.

Reaching around behind me, I grab my beer off the counter and down what's left of it. Then, inhaling and exhaling another breath, I clamp the piece of exposed glass between thumb and index finger and yank it out of my knee.

I nearly black out.

As the glass comes free, glazed with my richly red blood, my legs grow wobbly. I grab the counter to hold myself up and take a moment for the sting to go away. I know I have to clean the wound. Tossing the triangular, inch-by-half-inch shard of glass into the sink, I pull up my jeans just enough to allow walking without stumbling and head into Lisa's bedroom and the bathroom at the back of it.

I need Band-Aids. Lots of them.

By the looks of it in the bright bathroom light, the wound would more than likely require four or five stitches. But no way in hell I'm going to the hospital. Not when doctors and nurses can start lobbing questions at me about how I managed to cut myself. They'll smell the alcohol on my breath and the smoke in my hair and they'll ask me if I have a history of violence or if I've ever been diagnosed with a psychotic ailment. Even if I lie and tell them no, they'll do a computer search on me and discover that not only have I been diagnosed, but that I've been nailed with not one but two violence-related restraining orders, the most recent of which was issued today.

No bandages inside the medicine cabinet. No alcohol.

I close it and open the doors to the cabinet under the sink. The space contains several rolls of toilet paper stacked one on top of the other, a toilet brush, and bingo, a white bottle of rubbing alcohol. I pull it out and rest it on the sink. I also spot a much nicer first aid kit, which means I'm in business.

I pull out the kit and gaze upon the big red cross printed in the box's center. Opening it, I find a roll of thick medical tape, a few packages of gauze bandaging, and some cotton balls. I proceed to soak the cotton balls in the alcohol and then, gritting my teeth, press them to my leg wound. The burn is electric and sends another wave of stars flying past my eyeballs. Tearing open the gauze bandage package with my teeth, I apply the clean bandage, securing it with four separate strips of surgical tape.

When it's all done, the wound doesn't feel nearly as painful, but, judging by the crimson-red stain expanding on the gauze, it's going to be a while before the bleeding stops.

Pulling up my pants, I go to set the alcohol and first aid kit back into the bottom cabinet, setting them down beside the stack of toilet paper. That's when something stored behind the rolls of paper drops. It's a little white CVS pharmacy bag.

When I open the bag, I find a bright purple box with a glossy finish to it and white lettering. The front of the box contains a familiar white graphic of a Trojan warrior. Above that can be found a gold-rimmed frame that bears the words "Trojan Pleasures. America's No. 1 brand of condom. Trusted for over 90 years." This particular model is said to be extended for "longer lasting pleasure."

Longer lasting fucking pleasure.

I stare at the box, not quite believing what it is I'm holding in my hands. Lisa and I don't use birth control. My vasectomy officially took me out of the gene-spreading pool three years ago, when Rachael and I started dating and spontaneity usually took the place of safe sex.

So why the hidden box of condoms?

Maybe it's left over from months ago, from when Lisa was still sleeping with David. That's got to be the answer. Reaching down into the plastic bag, I find the sales receipt and pull it out. The slip is dated one month ago, almost to the day. Lisa and I have been back together for two. My stomach grows as hard as a rock. I open the package and see that out of the twelve, four are missing.

For a brief, heated second, I feel the urge to stuff the box into my jacket and drive it out to Lisa at her parents' house. I'll bust in through the back door off the kitchen, march upstairs, and even if she's still asleep from the sedatives, I'll wake her, shove the box in her face, and demand an explanation.

But it would be the wrong thing to do.

I've never had a reason not to trust Lisa, so why should I be jumping to conclusions now? If she has a box of condoms hidden in the master bathroom sink cabinet behind a stack of toilet paper, there must be a good explanation for them.

Yeah, you go with that, Reece.

It's not my dad who's whispering into my ear this time, but instead, my big brother Tommy. I can just see him rolling his big brown eyes while he stuffs his thick hands into the pockets of his worn Levi's.

Dropping the condom box back inside the plastic bag, I tuck them back behind the toilet paper where I found them, close the cabinet door, and leave the bathroom.

A man with a wounded knee, a brain on the verge of meltdown, and a heart full of distrust.

Chapter 37

Distraction.

I need distraction real bad. Something to take my mind off the madness of the day and the anger that's building up inside me like the hot lava inside an active volcano. I discover that distraction when I see her standing in the middle of the bedroom floor looking up at me with sadder-than-sad eyes.

Frankie.

"Oh dear God, Frankie," I say aloud. "I haven't fed you at all today and the house is still a train wreck." Leaning down, I pick her up, check all four of her paws for any cuts she might have suffered on the broken glass and china. She seems okay, and to prove it, she starts licking my face like I'm the second coming of Jesus. At least she isn't growling anymore, now that Olga's burned body is resting at the bottom of the river.

"Can we eat now, Reecey Pieces?" she asks. "And my bladder is about to burst."

"Yes, ma'am, Frankie. Been one hell of a horrible day."

"Have another beer. It'll make you feel better."

"After I get you fed."

First I set her outside the sliding glass doors, where I watch her relieve herself only a few feet away from where Olga was burned to death. When she's done, she can't help but trot on over to the now leaf-covered burned-out patch of grass and start sniffing. Heading back outside, I take her into my arms and carry her back inside and into the kitchen, setting her down on an empty space of counter. I order her to sit and she obeys. While she's still, I locate both her water and food dishes. I clean them both and fill them with water and dry food, then set them before her on the counter. While she eats, I go about the business of cleaning up the kitchen. It takes a while, but I manage to get it done, even with a wounded knee.

With Frankie safely back inside her crate, I head into the dining room and sweep up all the broken china and toss it away in the trash in the garage. Then I set to work straightening out the bedroom, returning Lisa's clothing and underwear to the chest of drawers. All that's left to do is erase the chalkboard, which I do, only too happy to do away with the drawing of my brains being blown out.

When I go to set the wooden chalk bowl back on top of Anna's upright piano, I see the earring. It's caught between the loose pages of a piano lesson book that's leaning upright on the piano's music holder. I take the earring in my hand and stare at it. From what I can see, it's homemade and constructed of small pieces of jade strung on thin wire.

Is this Lisa's earring?

Possibly, although I can't recall her making her own jewelry. But that doesn't mean it wasn't a gift from someone. Still, the long earring doesn't seem like her style. But then-what the hell do I know?

Is it Anna's?

Certainly not. Anna hasn't had her ears pierced yet. Mom's orders.

Maybe one of Lisa's mom friends. I'll never know, and right now, with my adrenaline-filled head on fire, I can't really care all that much. Stuffing the earring in my pants pocket, I decide the time has come to pay a visit to my girlfriend/ex-wife, even if she hasn't called me yet to give me the "all clear."

Back in the kitchen, I make one last check on Frankie in her crate.

"Gotta go out, Frank," I say.

"My love to the girls," she says.

Grabbing the car keys, I head out the front door. In my over-heated head, I'm already building a list of the twenty questions I plan on shotgunning at Lisa.

Point-blank.

Chapter 38

Here's the deal with Lisa's father, Alexander Reynolds: While Victoria treats me with a degree of civility, he is downright hostile to me. I've been in his presence only once since Lisa's and my reunion and, even then, it was only for a few minutes . . . the time it took to sing "Happy Birthday" to Anna and for her to blow out eight candles plus one to grow on, and for her to silently make a wish. When Lisa told her not to speak a word until she finished making the wish and took a bite of cake, Anna peered up at me with big, brown, loving eyes. Eyes that didn't go unnoticed by the entire family. Eyes that said, *I'm glad Daddy's back and my wish is for him never to go away again.* At least, that's what I wanted to believe at the time. But Lisa's dad wasn't having any of it. He ran his hands through what's left of the salt-and-pepper hair on his head and walked out of his daughter and granddaughter's house, letting the screen door slam behind him.

There's supposed to be two sides to every story, right?

Not according to Alexander. He warned her a long time ago about me. Back when we first got together. "He's a writer, Lisa," he said. "An artist. He's broke and always will be broke, and he'll suck off of you like a leech if you allow it."

But even after we were married and she told him I was in the process of writing the great American novel and that my agent promised to sell it to a big New York publisher for a million dollars, he responded, "You just wait. Even if your new husband does manage to sell his book, he'll find a way to lose it all and then you'll be on the hook all over again."

The old man's hard words festered inside Lisa's head, because what she couldn't reveal to him was that I wasn't writing at all. I was suffering from a seemingly incurable bout of writer's block, the symptoms of which included heavy drinking and self-imposed isolation. I would never write that first novel, at least while we were married, which made Alex's words prophetic to say the least. Lisa was indeed on the hook for me, and it was something that began to tear us apart even before David entered back into her life.

I pull into the long, private driveway and take it slow along its entire quarter-mile length until I come to a big, brick French Colonial home. Technically speaking, the estate is located in the city, in the ritziest suburb of North Albany, but Lisa's father laid out the cash to buy up a ton of acreage so that the mansion is three-sided by thick second-growth woods. The backyard contains a giant lawn, groomed gardens, and a kidney-shaped swimming pool with attached hot tub. A black fence surrounds the entire back lawn and immediately beyond that, the woods.

The fence is made up of iron, spear-like rails. It's the kind of fence an intruder can easily impale himself on, which I suppose is entirely the point. Not too long ago, a deer trying to jump the fence did indeed impale itself on one of the spikes, right through the belly. He hung there for hours writhing in pain until Victoria discovered him. The police came, shot the deer in the head, took the carcass away in a black rubber body bag, and later cremated the animal in the city pound. To this day no one knows what the deer was running away from, but a second deer was also discovered that very same night, impaled on an identical fence located not a half-mile away.

Instead of making my way to the front door, I let myself in through the back gate, which I knew would still be unlocked at this time of night, and follow a path of neatly laid brick pavers all the way to the back door off the kitchen. Through the big picture window looking out onto the gardens of the big back property, I can see them both sitting at the round kitchen table.

Victoria and Alexander Reynolds.

She's got a ceramic mug of something set in front of her. Tea, probably, since, other than the occasional bottle of wine, the house is mostly dry. He's sitting with his legs crossed in his business suit minus the jacket, reading a newspaper.

Sucking up a calming breath of the cool evening air, I step up onto the concrete landing and thumb the bell. My heart beats inside my throat. One of the major reasons Lisa and I have worked so well these past two months is that I've managed to avoid her parents like the plague. But Lisa is still very close to them. She relies upon them for support, both financial and otherwise. Anna loves them. Even I must admit how good they are to her. It's as if they don't recognize an ounce of me in my daughter.

Out the corner of my eye, I see Victoria getting up from the table. I see her not through the picture window, but through the glass on the door. She says something to Alex that I can't make out. But judging by the look on her face, it's something like "Be nice." She spots me through the glass, frowns, and begins unlatching the deadbolt. Don't let the unlocked back gate fool you. The Reynoldses are freaks for security.

She opens the door and issues me this up-and-down gaze with wider-than-wide eyes, like I've just stepped out of a meat grinder. But then, she just as quickly assumes a faux smile, saying, "You should call first." Her tone is one I recognize entirely. Agitated and nervous.

"Thought I'd surprise you," I say. "Sorry I didn't have time to pick up some beer or donuts maybe, but as you can see from my less than kempt appearance, it's been a hell of a long day."

"That's okay," comes a deep voice from behind the newspaper. "We don't drink on weeknights and you won't be staying long."

"Alex," Victoria barks, shooting her husband a look that could singe.

It never ceases to amaze me how, with her long dark brown hair and deep-set brown eyes, she resembles the Lisa of the future.

"Come in, Reece," she says. "It's getting cold out."

I step inside, close the door behind me. The heat is always on high, since Victoria finds it impossible to get warm inside the drafty old house once the summer is over. Must cost them a fortune in utility bills. But then, Alex, having combined a sizeable payout from the profits of his own law firm with some prime real estate in Manhattan, is worth not a fortune, but a fortune and a half.

"Hello, Alex," I say to the man still hiding behind the newspaper.

"Alexander," Victoria says, "don't be rude. Reece is trying to say hello. Don't forget, he's Anna's father and our daughter's partner again."

The paper comes down hard, revealing a man with closely cropped and retreating salt-and-pepper hair. His face is long and clean-shaven, his cheeks and nose slightly flushed from hypertension and late middle age. If you look him in the face, you can't help but notice that his ears are slightly too big for his head. But pity the poor fool who would dare point that out to him.

"Partner, eh? Is that what you are now, Reece?" he says through a crooked grin. "At least she isn't with that other lazy fruitcake anymore. He called himself a writer too."

"You tortured that poor boy, Alex. It's a wonder he stayed with Lisa for as long as he did."

"Not my fault his lack of ambition didn't earn him much more than minimum wage. Sound familiar, Reece?"

"I'm all about the ambition, Alex, and I make quite a bit more than minimum wage these days, thank you very much."

"That so? Okay, you're not lazy, thank God, but I will say this: I thought when Lisa kicked your ass out the door it was for good. You still lighting shit on fire?"

"Alex, please," Victoria once more jumps in. "I thought you promised to be civil."

He shoots her a glance. "I am being civil. He tried to burn Lisa's house down with our granddaughter still inside it. Reece should feel lucky I'm not knocking his teeth down his throat right now. Isn't that right, Reece?" His grin widens, his ears twitch. "By the way, you look like hell and back."

I feel the slow burn from the fire he's lighting under me. He's provoking me and he knows that I know it. But then, the man is not all wrong. I did try to burn a fire on the deck of the home Lisa and I shared together. And if it wasn't for him and Victoria and their sizeable funds, Anna would have had to endure day care while I was off trying to build my career.

"Well, Alex," I say, "people change. I was a bit sick back then."

"Sick and broke and drunk and violent. A man with a history of violence. Need I go on?"

"Please do," I say.

"But you'll have to forgive me, Reece," he says. "Credit where credit is due: you have managed to sell a few books. Unlike that other jerk she was with. What's his name, again?"

"His name is David," Victoria says, "and he was very sweet. He was very good to Anna when Reece . . ." Her statement trails off, like she doesn't want to finish it.

"When I wasn't around," I say for her.

"You were out lighting fires," Alex interjects. It's his idea of a joke.

"Listen, Alex," I say, "I'll admit I haven't been the best father in the world, and that I wasn't the best husband in the world either. Like I said, I had some issues I needed to work out. But now I'm healthy, wealthy, and calm. Lisa's taken me back. Why not get used to it?"

"Wanna talk about it outside, writer man?"

"Alexander," Victoria barks one more time. "Stop making the same mistakes you made with David."

"Hey," he says, "the fruitcake would never have given me a fight. At least Reece has some tough guy in him. Be a fair fight at least." He laughs.

"How fair?" I say. "I'm younger than you, Alex. Okay, you're bigger than me, I will give you that. But I'm not sure that knocking my teeth down my throat is still something you're capable of, no matter how much you try and peacock those old feathers of yours."

"Never underestimate years of experience, Reecey boy," he says, picking his paper back up, pretending to casually read it. "But just remember, I have my good eye on your ass. If you harm even a single hair on either Lisa's or Anna's head, I will come down on you like the devil himself. Understood, Fire Starter?"

My blood is hot, but I listen to my gut and keep my mouth shut. Like I said, he's not all wrong.

Victoria gets up from her chair. "Reece," she says, "why don't you go up and say hello to the girls now. Then maybe think about making it an early night. Lisa needs her sleep, and I sense just by looking at you that you could use some serious rest too."

"Thanks for thinking of me."

I'm gladly heading out of the kitchen into the dining room on my way to the wraparound *Gone with the Wind* staircase off the vestibule when she stops me.

"Reece," she says, slightly under her breath as she steps out of the kitchen to come closer to me. "Are you sure you're okay? You really don't look so good, and it worries me."

She's looking at my wounded leg. The blood spot has grown to the size of a beer coaster. And my jeans are torn at the knee. I probably need another shower and I've got ink stains on my finger pads from the fingerprinting at the APD. I might say something about the break-in at Lisa's, but I'm guessing that if she and Alex don't already know about it, then Lisa doesn't want them to know. Can't say I blame her.

"Oh, that," I say, looking down at my bad leg. "I tripped and fell outside the house getting the mail."

"You been drinking, son?" Alex calls from the kitchen.

His ears are not only large, they still work pretty damn well at his advanced age. That's when it dawns on me that I have been drinking since the late morning. I can't help but wonder if they've smelled it on my breath along with the cigarette smoke.

Of course they have, Reece, whispers my dad. *You can't get anything past these people. They're living, breathing, walking radar stations, and they've finely tuned them to detect threats to their daughter and granddaughter, like you and David Bourenhem, from a million miles away.*

"No, Alex, I haven't been drinking," I lie. "But I could sure as hell use one right about now."

"You might have that leg looked at by a doctor," Victoria says. "Maybe the emergency room. I'll bet the mortgage you need stitches."

"I've cleaned and bandaged the wound," I say. "I was working in the yard raking leaves, burning the piles. I got a little dirty in the process."

"If you say so," she says.

I just want to get the hell away from them. Turning back toward the vestibule, I make for the stairs.

"Don't you bleed on anything," Alex barks. He can't resist a final jab. "The cleaning lady just shined the crap out of the joint."

"Wouldn't dream of it, Alex," I say. "'Sides, you know what they say."

"No, what do they say?"

"You can't shine shit."

Chapter 39

Upstairs, I find Lisa lying on her back in her old high school–era queen-sized bed, the wall-mounted plasma her parents had installed for the occasional sleepovers with Anna tuned into the Bravo channel. I recognize the program that's currently broadcasting. It's *Housewives of Beverly Hills* or *New York City* or *New Jersey* or one of those quote–reality shows–unquote that's full of cosmetic-surgery-fixed tits-and-ass and plenty of staged catfights between sex kittens. Lisa is keeping perfectly still while both her eyes are covered with white ice packs.

"Howdy, stranger," Lisa says, trying to work up a smile through some obvious facial discomfort. "Thought that was you talking to the 'rents. So how you getting along with the out-laws anyway?" Her voice is a bit groggy, but not as bad as I thought it would be. Must be the sedative wears off quickly.

"Peachy," I say. "They make me feel like Charles Manson on a bad acid trip. Your old man asked me if I'm still playing with matches. They're obviously still convinced I'm the old Reece." Wiping the sweat from my forehead with the back of my hand. "Didn't occur to you to call me, tell me you were okay?"

"I've been sleeping, honey. My bad. You sound stressed. Is it because of the house? Because of David? You all right?"

Oh, just a little beat after cleaning up a murder on your back lawn.
Looking around the room.

"Where's Anna?"

"Bathroom," she says. "Wish I could see you."

"Count your blessings. After today's shit storms, I'm not exactly a pretty sight."

Raising both her hands, Lisa shifts the ice packs down so her eyes are uncovered. They're glazed and swollen. I'm not sure how she can watch the television, much less keep them open.

"Can you see anything?" I say, sitting gently on the edge of the bed, taking her hand. "Does it hurt much?"

"I can't really see," she says, raising up the clicker, turning off the bickering housewives. "I can hear, though. And it doesn't hurt so much as my eyes feel irritated. Like I keep burning them with soap." She makes a couple of exaggerated sniffs. "Someone's been to the bar," she adds. "And is that cigarette smoke I smell?"

"No bars," I say. "But I needed a couple of pops. Bought a twelve-pack and, ummm, a pack of Marlboro Lights."

"Wow, just like old times," she exhales. "David comes to visit me at the medical center and you turn to the bottle and the cancer sticks."

"At least I'm owning it. That's the first step."

"I'm sorry about David. But he really means no harm and you had no right to do what you did to him at his apartment."

I feel her hand in mine. I fall just short of filling her in on his having filed for a restraining order. But then, maybe he's already told her.

"I'm really sorry, Leese. It's just that your house . . . the break-in . . . It seemed like he was responsible." In my head I'm seeing Olga on fire. But no way am I letting Lisa in on that right now, if ever.

"Impossible."

"From where I'm standing, I see a man who still loves the shit out of you, is still obsessing over your ass. *You* broke up with *him* because of *me*, remember? That little fact might not be sitting too well. He might be thinking of revenge."

"He'll get over me," she says. "The real issue is my poor house. I can't believe I'm taking all this lying on my back. If I wasn't so drugged up on oxy and anesthesia, I'd be screaming. But somehow, lying here right now, feeling like crap, I can't even think about it. I assume you've called the cops, and you're absolutely sure nothing was taken?"

"Nothing. Does Anna know?"

"No, and that's the way it stays. My parents too. Now, as briefly as possible, tell me what happened."

Releasing Lisa's hand, I get up and go back around to the foot of the bed. I proceed to relay the high points of the break-in, one after the other. I tell her about the clothes laid out on the bed, about the chalkboard drawing, about the "posthumous bestseller" photograph tacked to her office bulletin board, about the "heretic" screen saver comment on my laptop that was lifted right out of *The Damned*, and finally about her office and Anna's bedroom being left totally untouched. Then I quickly tell her about Detective Miller. About his insisting it was a personal job by somebody who might have a key to the new locks, and about his insisting on taking my prints and making me provide both writing and drawing samples.

She opens and closes her swelled eyes.

"Something is definitely not right," she says. "This is all very disturbing. If my parents knew about it, guess who they'd blame?"

"From the sounds of it, your folks like David almost as much as me."

"Yeah, another struggling writer. They were about ready to commit me to a mental hospital when they first learned about David . . . No offense, Reece."

"None taken. What makes you so sure David isn't capable of doing bad things to you and your house just to make a point?"

"What point? Whoever laid my clothes out like that is most certainly not David. That's just way too creepy for him."

"Maybe you just want to believe that, Leese."

"Possibly. But I know him as well as any woman can know a man. And I refuse to believe he'd do such a thing."

It pains me to hear her say how well she knows David. I'm reminded of the condoms hidden under the sink. I inhale a breath and release it.

"Lisa," I say, "I don't know how to say this, so I'm just going to say it. I found a package of condoms in the cabinet under the sink. The purchase date on the package receipt is for one month ago." Pausing for another breath, in and out. "Four are missing."

At first she says nothing. Then, despite her pain, she begins to giggle. "Oh my God, Reece, you have had a bad day, haven't you?"

"Word."

"Those were for us," she says.

"I'm snipped, remember?"

"Yes, but I got paranoid when I started hearing that a lot of vasectomies don't take, so I bought them. But then I got over my paranoia."

"Excuse me, but I don't recall using any."

Her giggle turns into a laugh. "That's because I gave four of them to Olga down the street. You can check with her if you like . . . if you don't trust me, Reece."

So that's why Olga came to the house. To get more condoms.

"I trust you, hon. No need to investigate."

I hear the toilet flush and my daughter singing what I recognize as a Selena Gomez song, which I pray doesn't get stuck inside my head.

"Quickly," I say, "before Anna comes back in."

"Quickly what, Reece?"

"Do you have any idea who might have broken into your place? Like I said, Detective Miller called it a personal job. Not a random act. Nothing stolen, no sign of forcible entry. He's going to want to talk to you when you feel better in a day or two."

"When I do, I'll tell him the same thing I've been telling you. I don't know anyone specific who would do something like that. But I do have an idea who might."

I hear the bathroom door open, and after a couple of quick seconds, Anna comes rushing in, jumping on the bed.

"Anna, please!" Lisa barks.

"Oops, sorry, Momsies," Anna says. She makes an exaggerated frown and shoots me a roll of her big brown eyes like she thinks Mommy is being dramatic. "How's it going, Reecey Pieces?"

She's holding one of those glossy teenybopper magazines with smooth, peach-fuzzed boy-band faces on the cover. Settling in beside her mother, she opens the magazine and continues where she left off in the bathroom.

"What's your idea, Lisa?" I ask, deciding to carry on the conversation even with Anna present, hoping she won't pick up on the subject of our talk.

"You're a popular author, Reece—"

"Not that popular, Reecey Pieces," Anna interjects. "You're just an Amazon best seller."

"Ha-ha, squirt." I pinch and tickle her toes. "Amazon is where it's at these days."

"Daddy!" she screams before busting out in laughter. Just looking at her smooth, round face taking on one of her sly, tight smiles makes my heart ache. But then, that's a good thing. It means the love I have for her is so big, my heart is too small to hold it all.

"Okay, so I'm sort of a popular author," I say. "On Amazon."

"That's more like it," Anna says. Then, peeking out from behind her magazine. "What happened to your knee, Reecey? It's all torn up."

I gaze down at the ever-growing spot of blood on the ripped jeans.

"Oh, that's nothing, honey. I cut it on a piece of glass."

"Keep drinking beers, Reece," Lisa chimes in. "One day you're gonna cut your wrists by accident."

"Wow, thanks for that commentary, Helen Keller."

She opens her eyes and, gently bringing her hands to her face, shifts the ice packs back into place over them.

"Back to the subject at hand, Reece," she says. "What I'm saying is this: You're always getting strange women making advances at you on Facebook. And what's worse, you encourage them because it strokes your ego. You've shown me some of their e-mails because that's an ego-stroker too. Remember that one who wanted to kill herself if you wouldn't marry her? She said she was going to find your house in Albany if it was the last thing she ever did."

"Really?" Anna says, laying the magazine in her lap. "That's like total whack."

"That woman lives all the way out in Boston," I say. "I don't think she'd make the drive here just to flip your house. Besides, no one knows where you live. Plus, I never talk about you or Anna on Facebook. What's private stays private."

"What's 'flip your house' mean?" Anna asks.

"Nothing that concerns you, angel," Lisa answers. "Daddy and I are having an adult conversation."

"About houses that do flips?" Anna says. "Cool."

"People, especially women, have a way of finding things out," Lisa continues. "I'm putting my money on one of your stalker fans. Maybe even the Boston chick. You should talk to Miller about them, and then you need to shut them out of your social network."

"Stalker fans?" Anna says. "J Beebs gets stalkers all the time. But he's like really famous, Reecey. Not fake famous like you."

"Thanks, Anna," I say. "You have a way of keeping my life in perspective."

But Lisa has a point. I often get women, and sometimes men, who chime in on my social media or even send my agent notes declaring their love and undying devotion to me. There was a time when I thought I might enjoy the attention, and for a while I did. Or, as Lisa put it, their attention stroked my ego. But now it only creeps me out and, on occasion, makes me concerned for my safety and the safety of my family.

"It's settled, Leese," I say. "I will shut out the bad Facebook friends."

"Are you staying at the house tonight?" Lisa poses. "Maybe it's better if you stay at your studio. You don't sound very good. I'm thinking you need a good night's sleep."

"You can stay here with us, Reecey P," Anna says. "It will be fun. We can pop some corn and drink Kool-Aid. A slumber party in Mommy's old bedroom."

"I'm not sure Grandma and Grandpa would like that," I laugh.

"Oh yeah," Anna says. "They hate you. They think you're like a bum or something. And what did Grandpa Alex say? You have a history of violins. Wow, you're a writer *and* a music man, Reecey P."

"That's violence, honey, and you know it," Lisa says. "And as much as they love you, that's where your grandparents are wrong. They're just concerned for their daughter and granddaughter, is all." She draws in a breath. "Daddy just went through a very bad period a long time ago, but he got some help and now he's doing just fine. Everyone deserves a second chance in life."

"Yes, they do hate me," I mouth to Anna with a smile.

She smiles back, wide-eyed, nodding.

"Reece," comes the sound of Victoria's voice from the bottom of the stairs. "Maybe it's time Lisa got some rest."

"Speak of the she-devil," I say.

I come around the bed, lean down, and kiss Lisa on her lips. It gives my heart a start every time I kiss her. No matter how small or delicate the embrace, each kiss is an event in itself to be relished and cherished. Then I go around the other side and give Anna a huge kiss on her cheek.

"Gross, Reecey Pieces," she giggles.

"I love you guys," I say. Then, speaking directly to Anna, "You ever gonna refer to me as Dad?"

"Love you too . . . Dad-man," she says and grins. "That better?"

"Much," I say, feeling a wave of warmth travel up and down my body.

"I don't want you to worry about us, Reece," Lisa insists. "Stay at your studio tonight. You'll sleep better. In the meantime, close down your Facebook account. You, me, all of us will be glad you did."

I'd love to believe Lisa. That maybe the house was broken into by one of my stalker fans. But my gut tells me it's not the truth. Whoever broke into the house and whoever killed Olga has a key to the place. That can only be one person. One thing is for certain: tomorrow, I'm having the locks changed again.

"Consider it done," I say. "It'll give me something to do tonight other than worrying about you two."

"We managed for a lot of years without you, Reece," Lisa says. "Anybody or anything decides to break into this impenetrable castle, my dad will slap them with his ears."

"Reece!" Victoria shouts out again.

"Coming, Warden," I shout back.

"Nice, Reece," Lisa says. "Way to make friends."

My laughter that follows is entirely faked. Because as I turn and make for the stairs, I feel a burning sensation inside my gut. It tells me that the break-in at Lisa's house and the murder that followed are just the start of something much worse.

Something none of us will escape.

Chapter 40

Making my way past Alex, who is still conveniently reading his newspaper, I leave by way of the back door. I don't so much as open my mouth to issue even a faint good-bye and neither does he. But I'm sure I hear him issue a grunt as I open the door and walk out.

The night seems to have grown darker since I first arrived at the Reynoldses' mansion, and wall-mounted lamps now light my way along the narrow footpath leading to the top of the driveway. I'm caught by surprise when I come to the gate because it's been left wide open. I'm sure I closed it when I got to the house a half hour or so ago. I wouldn't think of leaving it open and giving Alex and Vickie a chance to come down on me for my carelessness.

Like I've already said, Alex is a security nut. He insists on locking all doors and windows even when he's home. He also switches on the security system, which he claims is connected directly with the local police department.

I stare at the open gate as if it wants to tell me something.

Turning, I look out over the dark back property beyond the perimeter fence. Nothing seems to be stirring in the thick woods. Not even a church mouse. But something doesn't feel right. My writer's gut is speaking to me. My overactive imagination, maybe.

My need to create plot and story around nothing at all. My paranoia, perhaps. But as I stand there at the open gate, I feel ice-cold water travel through my veins, and the short hairs on the back of my neck rise up at attention. For a brief instant, I consider turning back for the house and insisting on staying the night. But I know my presence would be looked upon with contempt, if not open hostility.

Lisa wants me to spend the night at my studio all the way in downtown Albany. But it's simply too far away from my family. If I stay at her house, I can at least take some solace in knowing that we're no more than one mile apart. So what if the place was the scene of a break-in this morning and a murder by fire this afternoon? Tonight is gearing up to be a sleepless night, anyway.

Back behind the wheel of the Escape, I start the engine. But before I turn around and pull out of the drive, I open the glove box, reach behind the owner's manual, and take hold of the pistol. I thumb the magazine release and inspect the nine-round load. All rounds present and accounted for. Slapping the mag back home, I rack one into the chamber and thumb on the safety, then I set the pistol barrel into one of the empty center-console cup holders. Easy access. Shifting the vehicle into drive, I pull out of the driveway.

In my mind I see the ransacked house, the drawing of my brains being blown out on the chalkboard, and a note calling me a heretic on my laptop. I see the woman burning to death in Lisa's backyard and I see the face of David Bourenhem as he looked up at me from the floor of his apartment just a few feet away from a pine coffin, countless unsold manuscripts, and multiple dog-eared copies of my novels.

I'll say it again. It's going to be one hell of a long and sleepless night.

BOOK II

Chapter 41

Parking midway up Lisa's driveway, I kill the engine and cut the lights. Blackness. I never got around to turning the exterior lights back on before I left for the Reynoldses' house.

Taking hold of the pistol, I exit the Escape, stuffing the key ring into the pocket of my bush jacket, and make my way up the drive and then up the three concrete landing steps to the front door. I slide the pistol barrel into my pant waistband, open the screen door, and unlock the deadbolt. I'm a little surprised because all it usually takes for Frankie to start barking like crazy is the initial sound of the key entering the lock.

Opening the door, I pull the piece back out and thumb the safety off.

"Frankie?" I say into the darkness.

I know I should turn on a light. But I'm not liking this. I sense something. A presence. Like whoever burned Olga is still lurking inside the place. I feel eyes staring at me. Into me. It's the same sensation I got outside the open gate at Lisa's parents' house. Someone or something hidden in the dark shadows, staring me down, waiting.

Maybe I should about-face, head back outside, run. But what about Frankie? I need to know that Frankie is okay. I take another step forward along the corridor, past Lisa's office and the bathroom.

"Frankie?" I repeat.

I get nothing in response. No barks, no howls, no sobbing. That's not like the Frankie I know.

The gun gripped tightly, I move on down the corridor until I come to the kitchen. That's when I decide that I can't continue making a check on the house in the dark. Feeling along the wall, I find the light switch. I flick it up and, at the same time, raise the pistol fast, aiming it at the head of the man I'm sure will be standing in the middle of the kitchen floor.

A man named David Bourenhem.

But Bourenhem isn't there.

No one is there.

"Fuck," I say aloud. "I'm fuck, fuck, fucking losing my mind, and I can't find my goddamned dog."

Heading out of the kitchen, I cross over the dining room and step down into the playroom, my eyes focusing in on Frankie's crate. The door's been opened. My chest grows tight, and I feel my heart beating in the back of my throat.

"Frankie," I repeat. "Frankie, how did you get out?"

I go to the sliding glass doors, turn on the exterior lights, and look at the spot where Olga was burned to death. The spot is covered in leaves and looks perfectly undisturbed, like absolutely nothing happened there. Turning, I once more eye Frankie's crate. Is it possible I never put her in there in the first place? Am I losing my mind? Holy crap, have I really been drinking too much? Was it smart to combine booze and prescription anxiety meds? Did I simply imagine Olga's body being burned alive? Had I passed out and dreamt that I was inside my own novel? Acting out a chapter of *The Damned*?

I look down at the palms of my hands. Once more I make out the black ink stains on my fingers.

Maybe I only thought I secured Frankie in her crate before I left the house, but one thing is for sure: Olga most definitely died on the back lawn. I'm just having trouble believing it.

Moving back through the dining room and the kitchen, I head out into the hall, check Anna's room and Lisa's office, including the closets. All clear. I do the same in Lisa's bedroom and bathroom. When I discover that they are also empty, I find myself back in the kitchen staring at the basement door.

You gotta go down there, Son. You know what resides way down there.

"Yeah, Dad. I know what's down there."

Shifting the pistol to my left hand, I wipe the cold sweat that now coats my palm onto my pant leg. Then I switch the pistol back to my shooting hand. Opening the door, I flip on the basement lights and start down the stairs.

"Frankie?" I say again, my voice louder but higher pitched. The voice that comes from a man with a dry mouth.

No response.

At the bottom of the stairs, I look to the right into a concrete-floored area that houses some free weights and a weight bench that Lisa has allowed me to set up here. It's empty. I look to my left onto a carpeted space that serves as Anna's playroom. Other than the dozens of scattered toys, dolls, clothing, and discarded wrappers from candy bars she's snuck down into the basement, the space is also empty. Shifting myself to the left, I walk the short, carpeted area on my way to the last Sheetrock-partitioned room in the basement.

The laundry room.

Holding the pistol at the ready, I throw the hollow wood door open.

The laundry room is vacant.

No intruders.

My heart beating inside my throat, I feel like I've been injected with a sedative as a wave of exhaustion washes over me. I press my back against the Sheetrock wall and slide down onto my backside, my knees tucked into my chest. Other than the sting in my injured knee, I feel nothing.

My eyes lock on the white washer and dryer stationed at the opposite end of the room. A red plastic laundry basket that's filled with dirty clothes is set atop the dryer. My eyes shift to the metal shelving pushed up against the painted cinder-block wall to the right of the dryer. The shelves house the banker's boxes in which I've been given the go-ahead to store the drafts of all my manuscripts.

I focus on the box positioned on the left-hand side of the top shelf. It's the box that contains all the work-in-progress drafts of *The Damned*. I shift the pistol into my left hand and shove my right hand into my pocket, fetching my lighter. I thumb a new flame and take a breath, my eyes still locked on that first box. I'm not sure why, but my eyes fill with tears, my chest grows tight. It's like I'm not looking at a box filled with words on pages, but at the caskets of my mother and brothers. I feel their presence like I felt the searing heat that took their lives on that early damp morning back in 1977.

Two words are written on the side of the box in thick black Sharpie.

THE DAMNED

"I don't want to look at you right now," I say, but it's not my voice speaking. I'm not consciously making the words that are coming out of my mouth. Still I speak them. *"I can't bear the sight of you, of what you've done. You're the heretic. You betrayed us all. And you know what happens to heretics, Reecey Pieces. They burn. They burn up along with all the damned."*

I shake my head, force my eyes away from the box. All I want to do now is head back upstairs, grab another beer from the fridge, and slowly drink it at the dining room table. And when that's drained I'll drink another, and another.

It's exactly what I would do too, if not for the heavy pounding on the floor directly above my head.

Chapter 42

I bound back up onto my two feet, shove the lighter back into my pocket. My breath comes and goes in rapid-fire spurts. So rapid I feel like I'm barely a short hair away from passing out. That is, if I don't get some kind of a grip. Get it fast. I try to control the heavy breathing by closing my mouth while inhaling and exhaling slowly and deeply through my nose.

"Frankie!" I call out yet again. Louder this time. More forceful. But I'm not sure I'm calling for the dog so much as letting my presence be known to whoever the hell is roaming the place upstairs.

Exiting the laundry room, I cross over the playroom and begin climbing the stairs back up to the kitchen. The door is open, so when I get to the top I make my way into the kitchen swinging the 9mm from left to right. Whatever came down hard on the floor sounded like it came from directly overhead. That means the noise originated in the full bathroom situated between Anna's bedroom and Lisa's office.

I go into the hallway, shuffle past Anna's room until I come to the bathroom. I step inside. To my right are the sink and the toilet, and a black plastic shelf with folded towels stored on it. Directly ahead of me is the slider window, which is presently locked. To my left is the combination bathtub/shower. It's concealed by a white plastic shower curtain.

As I take hold of the curtain, I feel my heart lodge itself inside my throat. It's like a stone. My stomach has cramped up tight, and my temples are pounding like timpani.

I swipe the shower curtain open.

It's then I come face-to-face with the source of the noise.

Chapter 43

He's sitting in the far corner of the bathtub, his knees pressed up against his chest. He's got Frankie in his arms.

"How the hell did you get in?" I say, forcing the words from my mouth, the pistol barrel pointed at his face. "Or maybe you never left after murdering that poor woman out in the backyard."

David stares up at me through slits that look like they've been cut into black-and-blue eyes that are nearly swollen shut. His wrists are duct-taped together, as are his ankles. His light blue button-down shirt is torn where the chest pocket should be. Some of the buttons have popped off.

"You brought me here, you bastard," he says, his lips so swollen and bleeding that he's slurring his words. "And what's this about murder? Another fiction, Reece?"

I feel the weight of the pistol in my hand. I'm wondering how he could have grabbed hold of Frankie with his wrists bound like that. But then it dawns on me that maybe Frankie came to him, jumped into his waiting arms.

"Why would I bring you here?"

"Are you that fucked up? You came to my home again. You put that fucking gun to my head. You shoved it in my mouth. You made me walk out to your SUV. When you pushed me inside you started beating the living shit out of me. When you were through and I was barely conscious, you drove me here, dragged me into the house, made me sit in the bathtub so that I don't bleed on anything. Those were your words."

"Bleed on anything."

"Yes, bleed. Sound familiar, Reece? It's what you do to those teenagers in *The Damned*. Drew Brennen drives to the college students' apartment in downtown Albany. He makes them drop to their knees while he shoves a pistol barrel into their mouths, one at a time. Then he leads them out to his car and beats them, ties them up, drags them into his own home, makes them sit in the bathtub so that they don't fucking bleed on anything."

I try to remember *The Damned*. He's right. Chapter fifteen. Or is it sixteen? The college student chapters. Brennen steals them away, beats them, burns them. While he's lighting them on fire, he chants a nursery rhyme aloud over the sound of their pleas and cries.

"Fire! Fire!" says the Town Crier. "Burn! Burn!" says Goody Stern. "Burn her! Burn him!"

"Don't you remember, Reece?" he says, gently petting Frankie with the edges of his bound hands. "You've just gotten through collecting the gasoline that's left over from that poor innocent Russian woman you hit over the head and burned on the back lawn. You have just enough to burn Lisa's house to the ground along with me inside it. You're going to finish the job you tried and failed at once before."

"What gasoline?" I say. "Show me."

"Take a look out in the hall, Reece. It's all there. What's left of it. How the hell can you not remember?"

I take a step back, and while keeping the gun poised on him, peer out into the hall. Sitting on the vestibule floor by the door, two fire engine–red five-gallon gasoline cans. The heavy-duty plastic ones you can easily purchase from Lowe's or Home Depot. I have no idea how they got there. Why they're there. The only explanation is that David put them there. But then, how the hell did he manage to tape his wrists and ankles together? Who beat him up like that?

I step back inside the bathroom.

"Let go of Frankie," I demand.

"Frankie is my dog, Reece," he insists while stroking her back. "Frankie is my baby. Lisa's and my baby. We rescued her together."

"Dude's got a point, Reece," Frankie says. "He's speaking gospel. Lisa and he picked me up at the shelter just minutes before I was gonna take that lethal-injection ride to doggy heaven."

Then comes the sound of sirens.

"Finally," David says, a string of bloody drool falling from his lips onto his torn shirt.

"Finally what, you son of bitch?" I say. I'm shouting, my pulse pounding. "Finally what?"

I aim the cocked pistol at his head.

"The police," he says. "Shooting me is a waste of time. Once the cops find out about the shake-and-bake you did on Olga, you will get the death sentence and then you will be the damned, and you will burn for all eternity. And then I'll once more have Lisa all to myself."

"The police. How do they know?"

He somehow manages to work up a smile under all that battered flesh. He struggles to shift his bound hands into his lap beneath Frankie and produces his iPhone, the answer to my question.

"Reece, bro, you are such a good writer. I want to be you. I want to write like you. I want to fuck Lisa like you do. But you are careless when it comes to the psycho killer business. You never thought to check me for my smartphone before kidnapping and beating me. You need to pay better attention."

The sirens grow louder. The police rounding the corner onto the street. In my head I see the silver-haired head of Detective Nick

Miller, and I see his blue-uniformed sidekick cops. I see their service weapons drawn and aimed for my face. I need to do something. I can stay right here, try to explain myself to an APD that already suspects me of crimes. Or I can do something else entirely.

I can flee the premises.

"You're not going to cremate me alive, are you, Reece?" David asks, tears falling from his swelled eyes. "But that's how it happens in *The Damned*."

I find myself backing out of the bathroom, my eyes never leaving him, the sirens growing louder and louder, until a spray of red, white, and blue police cruiser flashers spills in through the living room picture window. I look away then and make out not one but several cars pulling up into the driveway and onto the lawn. I hear doors opening, men yelling, shotguns being cocked, locked, and loaded.

I look one way and then the other, then fix my gaze once more upon David and Frankie.

Whaddaya gonna do, Reece?

"The only thing I can do, Dad," I whisper.

I run.

Chapter 44

I sprint through the kitchen and dining room, then down into the family room. Yanking the sliding door open, I don't bother with pulling back the screen door. I'm so anxious to get the hell out, get away from the police, I barrel right through it.

Out on the deck, I hear the heavy, thick-soled boot steps of the police as they sprint up Lisa's driveway. In a few seconds they'll be running alongside the house and entering into the fenced-in backyard by way of its unlocked gate.

I don't wait for them.

I jump off the deck, run over the spot where Olga burned to death, and make my way through the darkness to the fence. I know that if I can somehow make it over the fence, I will have a good chance of disappearing into the wooded lot beyond it. From there I can make my way across the adjoining hundred-acre state park under the cover of night. In theory.

When I come to the fence, though, I realize there is no practical way of climbing over it. I certainly can't jump it. But the fence hasn't been painted in years. It's practically rotted out from neglect. Raising up my boot heel, I kick. An entire two-by-two section of wood slat disintegrates before my eyes. I kick again and again, until a hole appears that is large enough for me to crawl through.

Dropping down onto my knees, I snake my way through the opening just as the police enter the backyard through the fence gate. One of them screams, "Stop! Stop now!"

Down on all fours, I crab my way through the thick brush, briars scratching at my face and exposed hands, catching on my bush jacket. Coming from behind me, the screaming intensifies.

"Go around," someone shouts. "He's going for the park."

I feel for my 9mm, where I tucked it into my pants. It's no longer there. I feel all around my waist, reach into both bottom pockets on my jacket. It's not there either. Christ, I must have dropped the piece when I was crawling through the hole in the fence. That unlicensed pistol will be enough to convict me of illegal possession of a firearm once the cops locate it. And they *will* locate it.

There's a gravel road on the opposite side of this brush. If I can get to it before the cops do, I can make my way into the park and find a place to hide.

I burst through the bush on my hands and knees. Looking left I see a pair of headlights poking holes through the darkness. It's an APD blue and white cruiser, speeding down the road in my direction. I bound up and, turning to my right, make an all-out sprint for the end of the dirt road.

"Down on your stomach," bellows a bullhorned voice from the cruiser. "Down on your stomach, arms spread!"

The end of the road is no more than a hundred feet in front of me. It's hidden in the darkness, but it's there all right. I've climbed the fence dozens of times before as a shortcut to the lake.

I hear a pop, and then something whizzing past my head. It's like a bee flying by my left ear. It's a bullet. Motherfuckers are shooting at me. I'm wondering if that single round constitutes a warning or if they're actually trying to drop me.

I pick up my speed. If that's even possible.

Fifty feet to go until I come to the chain-link fence that separates the suburb from the park.

Another pop. Another bullet. The round ricochets off the hard gravel road only inches before me, sending up sparks. I can almost feel the heat from the engine on my backside as I lunge for the chain-link fence, grabbing onto it with all fours. I'm like a desperate spider monkey climbing a tree as the cop cruiser speeds toward the fence as if the driver intends to smash through it.

The cruiser is coming to a gravel-skidding stop as I reach the top of the fence and, swinging my injured leg around, drop down onto the other side and throw myself into brush as thick, if not thicker, than the stuff behind Lisa's fence. Three more pops come from the direction of the cruiser. The leaves and branches above my head explode from the rounds, but I keep on churning in a crouch through the woods and the darkness, deep into the parkland in the direction of the lake.

I take it double-time through the woods, the branches of the trees slapping me in the chest and face, stinging so badly my eyes begin to water. I feel the little cuts opening up on exposed skin and I feel the wound in my right knee throb like I've reopened it. In the near distance I can make out the lake and its calm, flat surface reflecting the light of the full moon.

Seconds later I bust out of the woods and come upon the picnic area where I started the fire in the garbage can this morning. To my right is a swamp that's filled with snapping turtles, frogs, and snakes. To my left is the small beach. But it's not empty. From this distance I'm able to make out the round white light that can only come from a police-issued Maglite. The cops are already combing the place for me.

Choices: I can try and make the one-mile swim across the lake to the other side and, from there, disappear into the city. Or, I can try and make it through the swamp, which is bordered on its opposite side by yet another gravel road. If I can make it to that road, I can find a dark place to hide out long enough for the cops to disperse and start looking somewhere else. Then I'll make my way out of the park and maybe, if I'm lucky, make the one-mile trek back to Lisa's parents' house, where David is sure to show up sooner or later. That is, if Alex lets me in to begin with. That's a chance I'll just have to take.

I need time.

Time to heal and time to figure a way out of this mess. Time to figure out why David Bourenhem would go to such lengths to set me up to take a fall I don't deserve.

The little round speck of light moves and shifts rapidly in the hand of the cop who's holding the Maglite. In a darkness lit on occasion by a moonlight that shines through breaks in the clouds, I take one last glance at the lake and I come to the realization that swimming its length with a wounded leg is an impossibility.

No choice but to head into the swamp.

Chapter 45

I move as quickly as possible along the narrow strip of sandy beach to the edge of the swamp and I don't hesitate for a second. I step into it and sink immediately past the tops of my boots in the muck. My progress is slowed almost to a crawl as I battle the suction created by the layer of swamp water over the muddy silt. I fully expect to leave my boot behind every time I yank my foot out.

My gashed knee stinging with every step, it takes me almost a full minute to move only ten feet from the shore. At this rate it will take me a full ten minutes to get to the opposite side. Ten minutes I do not have.

I shoot a glance over my shoulder. I see that what only a couple of minutes ago was a speck of round halogen flashlight has now become a large never-still circle. Soon the light will shine on me in the swamp and it will be all over.

I turn away from the light and keep on moving, trying my best to pick up my pace in the foul-smelling bog. For a brief moment, it seems like I'm speeding up, like I just might make it to the other side without being spotted. That's when I see the reflection of the flotilla of heavy, ovular shells cruising toward me on the water's surface.

Snapping turtles.

Turtles are supposed to be gentle creatures. Docile, slow-moving, noble prehistoric animals that can live for a hundred or more years and that feed only on aquatic life. But here's the dangerous truth about the snapping turtles that live in this in-city park: at least one or two people per year lose a toe or a finger when making the mistake of swimming in the lake. Signs are posted all along the swampy area warning swimmers of the dangers of both snakes and snapping turtles, the latter of which can achieve a weight of more than one hundred pounds from a protective shell that can measure two feet by three feet. Their jaws are like powerful vise-grip clamps outfitted with razor-sharp teeth. Just for good measure, their feet are equipped with claws that can open up the flesh on a human being with the ease of a steak knife slicing through semimelted butter. Snapping turtles might be slow on land, but in the water they are speedy swimmers, and they are coming after me now.

I stop where I am. If I make like a tree, maybe they'll leave me alone. What I wouldn't give right now for my gun.

The turtles come closer.

I force myself to go as rigid as possible while they close in on me. By the time they are within inches of my waist, the pounding of my heart in my head is competing with the noise of the insects swarming me. Mosquitos sting my neck and face. What feels like a spider is climbing up my right forearm. Still, I have no choice but to remain perfectly still and composed. I want to scream and thrash and barrel my way out of the swamp, police or no police, but I can't.

The first turtle comes within a half-inch of me.

In the dull moon glow, I focus on its hairless head while imagining a dinosaur-like jaw opening wide, exposing sharp, jagged teeth. I'm sure it's about to take a bite out of my stomach and then proceed to disembowel me with a single well-placed swipe of its claws.

But it does something else instead.

It proceeds to swim on by me. I can only assume he must be the alpha turtle, because as he moves past me, so too do the others, following him in perfect formation. When the final one is at a safe-enough distance behind me, I allow myself a breath and then resume my fight for the far shore.

I'm thinking I might just make it when the bright white beam of a Maglite flashes on the swamp's surface to my right and begins sliding my way.

Chapter 46

No choice but to drop.

Crouching down, I submerse myself entirely in the approximately four feet of swamp water, hold my breath. As I go down, I feel the cold, soupy water envelop my head. The water is murky and the night dark, but with the moonlight breaking through the clouds once more, I can make out the faint silhouettes of ferns, reeds, and other vegetation floating and dancing before me. On occasion I can catch a glimpse of the round white Maglite that scans the water's surface.

My oxygen-starved lungs begin to tighten, fill with pain. My need for air becomes desperate. I have no alternative but to wait for the light to pass by me before I position my mouth up over the water's surface so that I can suck in much-needed oxygen.

I do it.

I manage a quick, watery breath before dropping back under. Keeping an eye on the ever-searching flashlight, I wonder how long it's going to take for the cops to figure out that searching the swamp is a dead end for them and that they should move on to another area of the park.

That's when I see the snake swimming toward me, the moonlight illuminating its smooth, scaly skin like the memory of a vivid nightmare.

Chapter 47

Some of the snakes that live in the lakes of upstate New York are a version of the same rattlesnakes that can be found out West and south of the border. They are just as deadly. A long time ago, someone who migrated from the Wild West had the bright idea of getting rid of his pet rattlers by tossing them in a lake way up in the Adirondack Mountains. Since then, the snakes have multiplied and spread throughout the state like wildfire.

The snake swimming toward me must be a half-dozen feet long, its girth maybe four or five inches. Most definitely a rattlesnake. It's not always visible in the dark, silt-colored water, nor is the rattle in its tail audible, but I can feel it when it swims past, running the entire length of its long, sleek body over the skin on my exposed neck. The feel of the snake sends an electric charge throughout my body. It freezes me, makes me catatonic. Paralyzes me down in the swamp with no air to breathe.

But then, just like that, the snake is gone. But not gone for good. It's swimming somewhere behind me. I have no idea if it's coming back or not. No idea if the next thing I feel will be two sets of fangs burying themselves in my neck.

The cop aims his Maglite directly ahead of my position. My lungs are about to burst. I can't hold my breath for one second longer.

The battery-powered light skirts away.

I lift my face up and out of the water, suck in the damp air, then drop back down into a crouch. I try and hobble my way across the slimy bottom. It's nearly impossible to move with almost no breath in my lungs and my boots stuck in the mud and my right knee sending electric pulses of pain up and down the length of my leg. I inch my way forward despite the difficulty.

Again I'm making some tortured headway when the snake returns, wrapping itself around my neck like a fucking boa constrictor. Instinct takes over and I grab its head with my left hand while trying to pull its coiled body off my neck with my right. The snake is squeezing me, choking me. The more forcefully I pull on it, the more strength it gains, squeezing me even harder. Its head in my hand is thrusting at me, aching to bury its fangs into the flesh of my neck. I'm swallowing rancid swamp water, fighting and drowning at the same time.

With eyes wide open, I see the small round beam of Maglite cutting through the silty haze, moving rapidly along the swamp surface toward me. The commotion I'm making in the shallow water is giving me away. I can't stay down in the water for much longer, the snake choking me. If I do, I'll drown.

I lurch up out of the water, shout, "Don't shoot. Please don't shoot."

I'm still wrestling with the snake, barely managing to keep it from biting me.

The Maglites hit me. Out the corner of my eye, I see the cops come to the edge of the swamp, clearly not sure what to do.

"Don't just stand there," comes a voice I recognize as Detective Miller's. "Help the poor bastard before we have to rush him to the hospital for a snakebite."

A few more seconds pass before I hear the sound of someone sloshing through the swamp in my direction. It takes him only a minute to get to me, but it feels like an hour. It's the same tall, burly cop who seems attached to Miller at the hip.

"Hang on," he says while pulling a pocketknife from his utility belt, opening the blade.

He proceeds to press the sharp edge of the blade onto the snake's neck, out a ways from where I've grabbed hold of it, before cutting off the head in one swift, downward slice. The effect of the beheading is immediate. All strength bleeds out of the snake and its long body releases from my neck, drops down into the water, making a small splash.

"Dinner for the snapping turtles," Burly Cop says. Then, pocketing his blade, he pulls out his automatic. "Oh, and this time you really are under arrest, Mr. Johnston."

Chapter 48

Here's what goes down after that: I'm once again transported to the Albany Police Department South Pearl Street headquarters inside Burly Cop's blue and white cruiser. Detective Miller rides shotgun. He remains silent for the entire five-minute ride, as if to engage me in conversation, no matter how unimportant and trivial, would be a breach of protocol.

Once accompanied inside the century-old stone building, I'm processed for the second time in a single day in the general booking room. I'm relieved of my personals, including shoes and belt, and then escorted by Burly Cop not to a basement jail cell, but to an interview room on the first floor, not far down the facility's main corridor. Since they already have my prints on record from this afternoon's unpleasantness, they need not print me a second time.

Throughout the entire legal procedure, a grisly slideshow rolls in my head, the image of the battered David Bourenhem replaced by the torched body of Olga, to be replaced in turn by a bloody and bruised Bourenhem. Rinse and repeat. I know I could demand a lawyer, but then, I haven't yet been informed of the charge or charges.

The interview room is four-sided by cinder-block walls painted hospital white. There are no windows, but a long two-way mirror has been installed on the wall opposite a steel door containing a thick wire-reinforced glass pane. The institutional, black-and-white clock on the wall reads 7:07 p.m.

The day was long but the night has only begun.

I've been seated at a metal table containing a metal ring that's welded to its underside and to which the chain on my handcuffs has been attached by means of a second, shorter chain and padlock. I've been waiting here alone for someone or something for about twenty minutes, but it feels like an eternity in my filthy, swamp-soaked jeans, boots, and bush jacket. On the bright side, my knee no longer throbs so long as I keep it still.

The wait has not been without its entertainment.

For nearly ten out of the twenty minutes, I've been listening to Miller arguing with someone. Arguing and shouting. I can't always make out what's being said with the heavy metal door closed, but I do make out the words "service weapon" and "illegally discharged," and "not following fucking standard operating procedure," and my favorite, "Johnston is a public figure. A popular author. I can have your badge for that shit and I *will* have your badge if he decides to sue our asses for unlawful use of excessive force."

No wonder Miller has conveniently avoided the subject of my calling a lawyer.

Finally the door opens.

In walks Miller and, of course, his burly, clean-shaven sidekick.

"Unlock him," Miller says, slapping a manila file down on the desk, sitting down hard in the metal chair directly across the table from me.

Burly Cop comes around, pulls a key ring from his belt. He unlocks the small chain and then the cuffs, making my wrists feel a whole lot better. He stuffs the cuffs back into his utility belt while hanging on to the chain and padlock in his beefy hand.

"You want I should stay in here with you, Detective?" he says while turning back to Miller.

Miller glances at his watch, shakes his head. "It's late," he says. "Go get a coffee."

"Can't argue with that," says Burly Cop. He opens the metal door and leaves, slamming it closed behind him, giving Miller a start.

"That boy doesn't know his own strength," he says, clearly nervous and agitated.

"Likes his free weights," I say. "Me too."

"He's got youth on his side."

Miller might not be young anymore, but even at this late hour in the working day he's still looking put together in his pressed white button-down oxford, perfectly tied necktie, and neatly groomed gray-and-white hair. Not a hint of five o'clock shadow has risen on his narrow, if not concave face. But then, I'm not sure it's physically possible for him to grow a beard in the first place.

"We done small-talking?" I say.

"What is it you'd like to talk about, Reece?" he says, cracking just a hint of a smile.

"For one, you've had my cuffs removed and for two, I haven't been given my complimentary one phone call. That mean I'm not under arrest anymore?"

"You're pretty smart," he says, the grin growing into a smile. "You should write books for a living."

"Very funny. But my knee hurts and probably needs stitches and if I don't get out of these clothes soon, I'm going to need some serious antibiotic ointment for multiple skin infections. Who knows what the hell was crawling around that swamp besides man-eating snakes and turtles."

He stares into me, exhales.

"A profound exhale?" I pose. "Or significant sigh?"

"Your boy Bourenhem has dropped all charges against you," he says. "He's even withdrawn the restraining order application." He pauses for a minute, looking not at me but into me. "Tell me, Mr. Johnston. Why the hell would he do something like that?"

"If you're looking for a logical answer from me, you're not going to get one."

"Why's that?"

"I didn't beat him up."

"Didn't say you did. But you did flee."

"Look, Detective Miller, I'm the one who brought you and the entire APD into this mess in the first place. If I were a criminal intent on doing serious crimes, why would I want the police hanging around all the time? I ran because I didn't know what the hell else to do. All I know is I woke this morning, said good-bye to my girlfriend—"

"Ex-wife."

"Okay, ex-wife, but current significant other. All I know is I woke up, said good-bye to her and my daughter at the front door, and from there on out my life has been turned upside down and almost terminated on several occasions, most recently by your very own APD."

His eyes go wide, but then quickly return to their half-closed, half-open cynical state. The same look Clint Eastwood took years perfecting in Hollywood.

"They weren't shooting to kill, Reece," Miller explains with a gentle shake of his head. "They were firing warning shots at a fleeing suspect. It's SOP."

He's lying and he knows that I know he's lying. Which could be the real reason behind him not maintaining the order of arrest even if Bourenhem has rescinded his charges against me. I'm a thriller writer and I've done my research. Not only am I suspected of ransacking Lisa's home, but I was fingered as a possible perp in Bourenhem's assault at his apartment in Troy. Then I fled the cops, dropping my unlicensed 9mm in the process. And then there's the woman who was burned to death in Lisa's backyard. Does Miller know about that, and he's just not saying anything about it? Is he looking for me to slip, mistakenly say or do something indicating that I might get some kind of perverse kick out of reenacting some of the death-by-fire scenes I wrote in *The Damned*? The truth of the matter is that I should be looking down the barrel of three or four major felonies, all of which would carry significant prison time. And yet, I'm about to be set loose, and I suspect that's got something to do with the APD's loose cannons. Pun intended.

"One of those bullets flew so close past my left ear it nearly singed it," I point out. "Might have to explain it all to the most expensive ambulance-chasing shyster lawyer I can find in Albany."

Miller's face goes taut, his cheeks caving in. Whoever shot at me truly screwed up.

"I plan on having a talk with my support staff regarding what might be perceived as their use of excessive force," he says.

But judging by the chewing-out he gave an as-of-yet-unnamed officer outside the door, he's indeed fearing a major lawsuit from a not-so-anonymous author. I've decided to call him out on it, just to let him know I'm perfectly aware of my rights *and* my little bit of leverage in the matter.

"That the reason for all the shouting out in the corridor?" I ask.

Miller just looks at me like a poker player whose bluff has been called and busted. At this point I'm quite certain I'm not even going to need a lawyer.

"You've had a rough day," he says, changing his tone entirely. Bad cop to good cop. "One trip down here is enough for a lifetime and you've had two."

"Yes, rough day. I agree. And do you know what the common denominator for this rather rapid change of circumstances in my life just happens to be?"

"David Bourenhem," he says.

"Bingo."

He leans back in his chair, exhales once more. "So what exactly would you like me to do about it? About him?"

"You don't think it's weird the guy just shows up at my house today, out of the blue?"

"Your house?"

"Okay, Lisa's house."

"Just trying to maintain some accuracy to the proceedings, Reece. You know, for the record." He cocks his head in the direction of the two-way mirror.

"He shows up at Lisa's house with flowers, long after they're broken up. In the meantime, he's been calling and e-mailing her obsessively. I see his ride parked outside the medical center where her eyes are being operated on. But that doesn't mean he didn't make a pit stop at the house while I was out. Because when I come home, Lisa's place is trashed, complete with threatening messages and drawings. Even Lisa's underwear is laid out on the bed. I'm convinced it's Bourenhem who's responsible, so I confront him at his apartment about it. He gets scared, files a restraining order. Later on, he shows back up inside the house, in the bathtub, all beat to hell. He blames my ass, and I'm forced to flee you and your bullets by trudging through a goddamned swamp. Through some miracle I'm not killed, and Bourenhem gets what he's after: I'm locked up, fingered for beating the crap out of him and a laundry list of other charges he's lined me up for. But then what's he do? He drops all charges against me.

"Now, why would he do that? I'll agree, he's a little erratic. A little tough to figure, though it helps to keep in mind that he's fucking batshit crazy. But there's one constant in his demented thinking, all the way through: he's setting me up for something even more fucked up than he's set me up for already. Don't you see that?"

The detective shrugs. "Maybe," he says. "But that's awfully complicated. My experience, it's better to build off of what's clear and simple, if there's anything at hand. Like, say, what we found when we searched your vehicle. We found some duct tape, plus traces of blood, which we're having tested. We found some gasoline cans inside the house, and something strange outside on the back lawn."

My heart stops. I guess I haven't been thinking about the burning body any more than I've been thinking about dumping the body in the river.

"Don't know what you're talking about." I swallow.

"Someone torched something there recently. Something big."

"I've been burning piles of leaves there," I say. "It's fall and Lisa has a lot of trees all around the property. I know it's illegal, but . . ."

"Just so you know, I've ordered a forensic team to scour the place." Another smile. "Hope you don't mind."

"Why would I mind? We're all on the same page here."

"You of all people should know better than burning a leaf pile on the back lawn."

"Hey, how else can I get my fix?"

He cocks his head. "For a minute there, I thought you might be trying to act out some scenes from *The Damned*, like when Brennen burns those college students alive in the bathtub."

I swallow something cold, bitter, and dry. "That's why they call it fiction, Detective."

"One thing that isn't fiction, Mr. Johnston, is something we stumbled upon down by the backyard fence." He reaches down into his blazer and pulls out my unlicensed automatic. "And wouldn't you know it? It's not only unlicensed, its serial number has been scraped off."

I lift up both hands in surrender.

"You got me on the gun. But I have no idea how duct tape or blood got in my Escape."

He stands, returns the pistol to his blazer. "Just another puzzle piece in a day of mismatched puzzle pieces," he says.

"Isn't that the truth," I say.

"The truth?" he says, looking me in the eye. "What the hell is that?"

We sit in silence for maybe a minute. It feels like forever.

"Listen, Reece," Miller finally goes on, "I'm going to level with you." He tosses a look at the two-way mirror, crosses his arms. "But I need to do it off the record."

"I'm listening."

"I don't like what's happening in your life, either. Today has been bizarre to say the least."

"What was your first clue, Detective?"

"For one thing, someone really did beat the crap out of Bourenhem."

"You sure he didn't manage it himself?"

"Not a chance. Those bruises on his face didn't come from his own hands. The black eyes aren't a good makeup job." He pauses, looking down not at my face but at my hands. "But look at your fingers."

I look at them.

"I'm not seeing any sign of a struggle there. No cuts, bruises, or scrapes on the knuckles. No broken digits."

I nod. "What if I used thick black leather gloves like OJ?"

"At the very least you'd still show signs of bruising, Reece. You ever been in a bar brawl?"

"All the scrapes I've gotten into in the past always ended up in a wrestling match with no one winning or losing."

"Exactly," he says. "It's hard to accurately punch someone in the face unless you ask them to stand perfectly still."

He picks up the manila file from off the table.

"You got another place to stay tonight?" he says. "Technically speaking, Lisa's home is no longer a crime scene. But I would consider it a personal favor if you stayed away from it."

"Problem with that," I say, "is I want to be close to my girls tonight, but my studio is located way inside the city."

"Okay," he says. "Use your own discretion."

"What about Bourenhem?"

"With everything that's happened today and all the police that have gotten involved, I'm hoping he stays quiet for the night. In the meantime, we'll keep an eye on him."

"And I suppose you'll be keeping an eye on me too?"

"You know, it's within your rights to file a grievance against him," he says. "By the looks of it, he did let himself into Lisa's house and your vehicle uninvited. At this point I'm guessing he somehow acquired a key for the former and for the latter, well, maybe you forgot to lock it."

I nod. His comment about Bourenhem still having a key to the place doesn't sit right with me. Lisa has told me on more than one occasion that David returned his keys when they broke up. Then she had the locks changed.

"It's possible I left the front door open after I'd discovered that the house had been ransacked. I wasn't thinking straight when I left to go confront Bourenhem about it. But later, just prior to visiting Lisa at her folks' house, I'm sure I locked it. Later on, when I got back, the place was pitch dark and locked up."

"Just make sure everything is locked from now on. And as soon as you get a minute, have the locks changed again."

"I'm on it," I say. Then, "So, am I still a suspect in the breaking and entering of my own significant other's home?"

I wonder if I'm also a suspect in the backyard fire and he's just not letting on about it. Of course, they would have to have a body in their possession as evidence. Or at least, some kind of proof that a living, breathing human being was burned alive there and not killed somewhere else, then transported to the backyard and set ablaze.

Miller purses his lips.

"I wish I could say you're entirely out of the woods," he says as the sound of a cell phone chiming comes from his suit jacket. He pulls the phone out, looks at the digital readout. "But not yet," he goes on. "I do, however, need you to continue to stick around town for a while until I give you the green light."

He answers the call.

"Miller," he says into the phone. Then, "You're sure? Burned or drowned? Which is it? Okay. I'll be right there."

He ends the call.

A hot pit settles itself inside my stomach.

"Listen, Reece," he says, returning the cell phone to his jacket pocket. "Our little meeting has to come to an end. A woman was just fished out of the Hudson by a late-season striped bass fisherman."

"A woman?" I say.

"Yes, a woman. My people tell me she was burned severely, then tossed into the Hudson." He looks at me, grins. "Sounds like something your man in *The Damned* would do."

I stand and wonder if he sees the blood draining from my face. Maybe I should just level with him, tell him the truth. That I found her burning on the back lawn. But my gut tells me not to say a word. That Miller wouldn't hesitate to pin Olga's death on me, no matter what problems Bourenhem has been giving me today. After all, I wrote *The Damned* and I am already acting suspiciously in Miller's eyes. And how the hell would I explain my having dumped the body in the river? My not having called the police in the first place?

He opens the door, steps on out of the interview room. Burly Cop is there to greet him.

"My associate here will return all of your personals before seeing you back home for the second time today, Mr. Johnston," Miller says, once more taking on a formal tone. "Don't worry about all this. It will all work itself out. Try and get some sleep."

"Thanks, I will," I say.

But it's a lie only the devil could like.

Chapter 49

It's while Burly Cop drives me home that I'm reminded of Miller's question about how Bourenhem was able to get into the house if the locks had been changed and he no longer had a key. Like I indicated to the detective, it's possible I left the front door unlocked when I drove to the medical center. For certain I might have left it unlocked later on, when I went to confront David at his apartment. I also might have done the same when I went to visit Lisa at her parents' house. I wasn't acting in my right mind on any of those occasions.

But now I'm not so sure about anything. Not so sure I can trust my own story. What if I did lock the house every time I left it and Bourenhem was still able to get in without having to bust a window or jimmy a door lock? No sign of forcible entry was one of the issues that made Miller focus on me as one of the possible perps in the first place. That means one of two things. Either Bourenhem is in the possession of a new house key that Lisa entrusted him with. Or, he somehow came up with one on his own.

As the ever-silent Burly Cop takes a left into Lisa's neighborhood, I feel my pulse pick up.

Why would Lisa give David a key after having the locks changed? That doesn't make an ounce of sense to me. And even if there is a good and logical explanation for that, how do I explain him getting into my Escape and setting the vehicle up to look like I not only bound him up with duct tape but beat the snot out of him? He'd have to have access to a vehicle key. A seeming impossibility.

But then it hits me just as Burly Cop pulls into the driveway.

I picture the events of early this morning. Lisa trying to get Anna out the door. Lisa's mother pounding on the horn of her Volvo out in the driveway. Lisa rummaging through her pockets for her stuff. For her ring of keys that she claimed she did not need. A ring that not only contains the keys to her Volkswagen, her house, and her parents' house, but also to my Escape. As I open the door to the cruiser and get out, I picture Lisa leaving the keys on the bench rail in the vestibule.

I get out and watch Burly Cop back out of the driveway and exit the neighborhood. I don't walk casually to the front door. I run. Unlocking the door, I hit the light switch on the wall to my right and immediately focus my eyes on the bench rail directly before me. A chill fills my empty belly.

The keys are gone.

I look to the side of the bench on the floor. The keys are not there. I look on the bench itself. Even after raising up the cushion I can plainly see that Lisa's key ring is nowhere to be found.

I stand there and try to think things through. Maybe Lisa did take the key ring with her after all. But then, I know different. I know she left them behind on the rail. It explains how Bourenhem was able to get into my vehicle and how he placed duct tape inside there along with some bloodstains. But then, how did he manage to get into the house this morning prior to having the key ring in his possession?

There's only one answer to that question.

Lisa must have given him a key. There's no other way around it, and now we're all paying the price for her moment of weakness.

My stomach grows tight.

Now that Bourenhem has the keys to Lisa's entire life, what else is he about to do with them? How else is he going to exact his revenge and, in the process, further set me up as a psycho killer?

I'm not about to wait around to find out.

Pulling my cell phone from my coat pocket, I dial Detective Miller.

Chapter 50

"I catch you sleeping?" I say when it takes him four rings to pick up.

"I gotta answer that question? What the hell else are desks for?"

"Must be the journalist in me."

"Thought you lied for a living, Reece."

"Started out as a journalist. But your double entendre has not gone unnoticed."

"Must take some skill to fabricate shit convincingly enough to make serious cash at it."

"Okay, I get it. You don't trust me. But I have something of concern I need to report."

"New developments since we last talked a half hour ago, Mr. Johnston? Things happen fast in this town. But make it quick. I've got forensics barking up my ass about that woman we fished out of the Hudson."

"Bourenhem not only has a key to Lisa's place, which explains how he got in this morning, but he also stole Lisa's key ring."

"How do you know?"

"It's missing. It's not where she placed it when she left for the medical center earlier today."

"Sure you didn't grab it and put it somewhere else?"

"I'm sure or I wouldn't be calling you and waking you up from your office nap."

"He has a key. How'd he get one of those if you made Lisa change the locks?"

"She must have given him one."

"Ouch. What keys she have on the key ring?"

I tell him.

"Might explain how he got into your vehicle, that is, if you locked it in the first place."

"I'm sure I locked the doors on the Escape. I always lock them. It's instinctual."

"You say the keys to Lisa's parents' house are on there too?"

"Yes."

Once more I picture the gate that was left open in the backyard of the Reynoldses' estate.

"You might want to give them a call. Meanwhile, I'll have somebody make a drive-by ASAP."

I give him the address.

"Ritzy part of town," he says.

"Ritzy people."

"We'll also make a flyby to Bourenhem's apartment, if that will ease your mind."

"I'd appreciate it." Then, after a pause, "You find out what happened to that woman in the river?"

He clears his throat. "Not yet. Her body is pretty messed up. Could be anybody at this point. Why do you care?"

"The fiction writer in me. Thought you said her body was burned. You gonna blame me for that too?"

Man, you should just tell him, Reece, Dad says. Maybe you should just tell him the truth. Bourenhem lit her up. But then, on the other hand, what if there ends up being no evidence to prove that Bourenhem killed her? What if all the evidence, physical and circumstantial, ends up pointing to you? Christ, you were the one who dumped her in the river. You were the one who cleaned up the murder site and white-washed the evidence. You're the one who's been lighting fires in Little's Lake Park and out on Lisa's deck. You're the one who's been withholding the truth from the police . . . On second thought, Son, mum's the word.

"I promise," Miller says, "soon as I know something, you'll know something. You can write a novel about it."

I go to hang up. But then I hear him take a breath as if he's about to say something else.

"Reece, do me a favor, will you?"

"What is it?"

"Leave the police work up to us. You're in enough hot water as it is."

"I'll try and restrain myself."

"Make sure that you do."

"I'm no cop. I write fiction for a living," I say. "You can trust me."

I kill the connection.

Chapter 51

While standing inside the vestibule, I dial Lisa's cell phone. Like I anticipated, she doesn't answer. I end the call and dial the Reynoldses' house phone. Also as expected, they don't pick up. Instead a machine comes on. I don't bother with leaving a message. I just hang up. Alex and Victoria usually hit the sheets early and it's already after eight o'clock. They will be in bed by now. At the very least, Alex will be dozing off while Vickie will be up watching TV in bed, fighting the onslaught of sleep. The phone ringer will have been turned low since Alex is such a light sleeper.

Hanging up, I check on Frankie, who is sleeping on the end of Lisa's bed. Then I make sure her bowls are filled with food and water. Heading into the bathroom off the bedroom, I wash my hands and face. I'd change my clothing too if I thought I had the time. But I don't. I need to run an important errand before it's too late.

I need to see a man about gun.

Chapter 52

Blood lives in a depraved and crime-infested part of downtown Albany that once upon a time was considered the city's most exclusive residential district. Arbor Hill is filled with old brownstones and townhouses that in the mid-nineteenth century were home to the state capital's wealthiest landowners, lumber barons, steel mill operators, and even politicians like an upstart presidential hopeful named Teddy Roosevelt.

But in the decades that followed, the lumber barons and steel mill operators all moved away in search of cheap labor, leaving the buildings vacant and ripe for the renting by one absentee landlord after the other. As the 1970s and '80s rolled in, and along with them, Section 8 federal government–assisted housing, Arbor Hill became better known for its heroin dens and crack houses than its long-fled multimillionaires. When my mother would have no choice but to drive us boys through the neighborhood in order to get to downtown Albany, we'd lock the doors and close the windows, even in the heat of summer. We also learned to keep our heads down should the ear-piercing discharge of a gun ring out in the near distance.

Blood's crib is located on Sherman Street, on the far western edge of Arbor Hill where it meets up with Central Avenue, Albany's main east-west artery. While Sherman is still set inside the gangland borders, all you have to do is cross the avenue less than one block away and you suddenly find yourself standing in the safe zone. I knew I would find Blood standing on the corner of Sherman, since the former Green Haven inmate turned self-appointed "Sentinel of Sherman Street" is always guarding over the area at night. Even though the self-written code of honesty, righteousness, and honor Blood lives by might not always strictly adhere to the law as written by mortal man, the cops are only too glad to have him take rough justice into his own meaty and scarred hands on his turf. The fact that I once pushed him out of the way of an oncoming vehicle is something Blood did not and will not take lightly for the rest of his days. He will always feel indebted to me and therefore, he will always act as my protector. If I want him to, that is.

The drug trade still exists on Sherman Street. But with Blood overseeing it, you will not find crack, heroin, or anything else that young students might decide to inject into their white-bread veins because they think it's the cool thing to do or their parents refused to buy them a new iPhone. Only recreational drugs can be found here. Pot, baby-powder-diluted cocaine, oxycodone, and occasionally, some X. That's as far as it goes. None of the heavy junk you can find down on Clinton. Those are the Sherman Street rules, and you can either abide by them or face Blood's wrath.

Blood is also a top-notch fixer, which means he can also get you things, be it an unlicensed pistol or a hot car (VIN number scraped clean off) or a fake passport. He's even been known to provide undercover and bodyguard services for private detectives in the area, among them a gumshoe friend of mine who goes by the unlikely name of Dick Moonlight. Having earned himself a master's in English literature during his decade in the joint, Blood makes the perfect research resource for my crime novels. He's a tough, imposing, rock-solid individual who doesn't come cheap, and don't even think of asking him to go against his principles. He will tell you to your face that he is living proof of the possibility of prison rehabilitation, and he bears the knife and gunshot wounds to prove it.

Like I was counting on, I find him standing on the corner of Sherman and Lark Streets. Wearing the same black leather coat, black jeans, and shiny black boots that he was wearing when he stopped by unannounced this morning, he looks like a phantom or a superhero, which is not exactly stretching the truth.

I pull over, come to a stop at the corner, and watch his big, solid linebacker frame emerging from out of the darkness until it's blanketed in an inverted arc of sodium lamplight. I hit the switch that rolls down the Escape's passenger-side window. Leaning down, Blood sets his forearms on the door so that I'm level with his tight-skinned, hairless ebony face.

"You shouldn't be driving 'round here after sundown, Mr. Reece," he says, his unblinking obsidian eyes staring into mine. "You must need some research material real quick, or staying at Lisa's house all by your lonesome has you good and spooked."

"Need your help with something, Blood."

"Must need it pretty bad you take a shot on coming out here at night. You can always call or text me, you know. How many times I gotta tell you that?"

"Too late for that. Besides, you'll try and talk me out of whatever it is I want."

"You probably right about that."

I tell him why I'm here, giving him a quick, bulleted rundown of the day's events, including the burning of Olga in my backyard. In typical Blood fashion, he takes a moment to digest it all without giving away a hint of emotion, either through words or facial expression. Then, without asking me, he opens the car door and gets in.

"I know Miller as well as a Sherman Street resident can know a top APD cop," he says. "He a decent man. But he still a cop. And cops go by the law, and the law ain't always right. You catch my truth?"

I nod.

"You right goin' with your gut and not telling Miller about the burned body. If Bourenhem burned her there, he did it for a reason. To set you up, make you look like the pyromaniac killer. You already wrote that shit in *The Damned*. Cops latch on to that fact, they never let it go. He never would dream you got the balls to clean up the backyard and dump her in the river. Only thing you fucked up with is not weighing her down enough. You should have called me in. She still be at the bottom."

"You're right, Blood. I should have called you."

I recall this morning, when Lisa suggested I call him to stay with me at the house. I also recall his just showing up and offering to hang out with me. I can't help but wonder if any of this would have happened today if I had agreed to his babysitting me instead of listening to my pride.

"You a decent man too, Mr. Reece. Wired a little tight for my tastes, but a good man. I like your books and I'm gonna help get you out of this calamity."

"You read my books, Blood?"

"Gots to read them. You put my name in the acknowledgments. Blood, spelled out in black-on-white letters."

"I thought you only read highbrow European postmodernists like André Gide or Max Frisch."

"Sometimes I slum and read crime thrillers by Reece Johnston. *The Damned* is classic noir lit. You should be proud, Mr. Reece."

"Classic pyro noir, I'm told," I say, recalling Bourenhem's earlier description. But hearing this kind of compliment coming from a man like Blood stands the fine hairs on the back of my neck right up at attention. I also feel warm blood filling my cheeks. I must be as red as a stoplight.

"What do we do now?" I say, making the shift back to the subject at hand.

"You need cash," he says.

Never dawned on me to bring money. Real money. Not the measly two twenties I have stuffed in my pocket. Can't exactly pay for an unlicensed firearm with a credit or debit card. It's precisely what I convey to Blood.

"What's your bank of choice?" he asks.

I tell him.

"Got one of those on Lark Street," he says. "Computer lets you withdraw as much as five hundred. You need more than that, I spot you the rest. You can owe me."

"Thanks, Blood," I say, shifting the Escape transmission into drive.

"Don't be thanking me," he says. "You shouldn't expect a thank-you in life just for doing the right thing. That's something the politicians will never understand. Priests too."

"Priests?"

"Let's just drop the subject. The good Lord be out of my humble jurisdiction."

I drive on to where the money is.

Chapter 53

The Key Bank is located on the corner of Lark and Central. I pull up to the corner and, while Blood waits behind, get out and pull five hundred dollars from the ATM. When I get back behind the wheel, I hand the bundle of cash to him without bothering to count it first.

"Where to?" I say.

He directs me to make a U-turn, then head back to Sherman Street. As soon as the avenue is clear, I spin the Escape around and hook a right onto Lark. When I come to Sherman I turn left.

"Keep driving until I tell you to stop," he orders. "We going to a section of Sherman Street that don't belong to me."

He tells me to stop as soon as we come to an area of the city that's ceilinged off by a big piece of inner-city highway thoughtlessly erected back in the late 1960s. The buildings surrounding us on all sides are old, and mostly made of wood that's covered with asphalt shingles that were designed to resemble bricks but instead scream despair. If you didn't know any better, you'd say the entire section is abandoned. It's actually plenty lively . . . and deadly. It's far enough from South Sherman Street not to fall under Blood's self-appointed jurisdiction and hidden away enough for the Albany cops to turn a blind eye to the nasty business transacted in its crack houses and brothels. The police spend only enough time here to clean up after the more-than-occasional drive-by shooting or to assist in carrying a body bag out from one of the houses to an awaiting EMS van.

"Pull over there," Blood says, pointing to a four-story house to my left, the windows of which are boarded off with sheets of plywood so weathered they've turned gray.

"Wait here," he says. "Anybody come up on you, you tell them who you with right away. They leave you alone after that."

"Now I feel better," I say, hoping the opportunity doesn't present itself.

Keeping the engine running, I watch the big sculpture of a man walk up to the house, knock on the plain steel gray door. When it opens a few seconds later, a man emerges from behind it. He's shorter than Blood, but bare-chested. Like Blood, his musculature is ripped and shredded. He eyes me from across the short expanse of dead no-man's-land with a combination of curiosity and anger, and then Blood follows him inside, shuts the door behind them.

I wait, careful to keep one eye on the rearview and the other alternating between the side-view mirrors and directly ahead through the windshield. After about a minute, I pull out my cell to see if Lisa has called. But she hasn't.

How are you? I text her. *I love you.*

I anxiously wait for a reply that I know in my gut is not coming. When the steel door opens again, I pocket the phone and focus instead on Blood's return to the car. The shirtless man, who seems not to mind the cool October air in the least, shoots me one last burning glance before closing the door. I hope I never have to lay eyes on him again.

As he walks, Blood keeps both hands hidden in the pockets of his black leather coat. Without so much as glancing in my direction, he comes around the back of the Escape and gets in.

"Drive," he says.

I slowly pull away from the curb.

Blood tells you to do something, you do it.

———⌣———

Less than a minute later he tells me to pull up alongside a mammoth concrete pillar that supports a short section of the elevated roadway. Reaching into his side pocket, he comes back out with a black-plated snub-nose revolver that has black electrical tape wrapped around the grip. It looks like a relic from a bygone gangster era.

He flicks open the cylinder with a quick snap of his wrist, then raises the six empty chambers up to eye level. Satisfied that they are clean and debris-free, he then pulls six fresh rounds from out of his opposite pocket and proceeds to load the piece. When he's done he gives the cylinder a spin and wrist-flicks it back home.

One unlicensed snub-nose revolver, officially locked and loaded. He hands it to me by its taped grip.

"That's a .38," he says. "Cost you the entire five hundred, even. It'll blow a man's respiratory system clean out his back at a range of ten feet. Preferably a creepy white man like your Mr. David Bourenhem."

I feel myself go light-headed at the thought of shooting a man, much less Bourenhem. I shoot plenty of men and women in my novels, but the sight of real blood is a different story altogether.

"Let's hope it doesn't come to that," I say. "Let's hope this is all a great big misunderstanding."

"Man drawing a great big picture on the living room wall of your head getting blown away like Hemingway? Man leaving a note about heretics burning to death lifted right out of *The Damned*? Man burning your neighbor on the back lawn? That what you call one great big misunderstanding, Mr. Reece?"

I look down at the gun resting in the palm of my hand, feel its solid, heavy metal construction.

"Guess I wouldn't have dropped five hundred bills for this if I thought it was all a big misunderstanding."

"You sure Lisa okay? Anna?"

"They should be okay at her parents' house. And besides, Bourenhem's problem is me. Not them."

"His problem is with you, then he gets to you through them, no matter how much he still in love with Lisa. He took her keys. He might hurt them to get even with you. He psycho enough, that is."

My stomach goes so tight at the notion of Bourenhem or anyone else hurting my family, a wave of nausea runs through me. Makes me feel like I might get sick inside the Escape.

"Miller has promised to watch out for them. He's promised me some drive-bys at the Reynoldses' estate and at Bourenhem's apartment building."

"Miller suspect you of lying about Bourenhem," Blood points out. "He suspect you might be the guilty one in all this. That you the real crazy psycho one. He might be telling you what you want to hear when he promise you he watching Bourenhem. Truth is, the man he really keeping an eye on could be you."

More nausea followed by a searing liquid that shoots from my stomach into my mouth. I force the hot bile back down and shake my head, once more feeling the weight of the pistol in my hand.

"You want me to help you out with anything," Blood adds, "you just say the word."

"Thanks, Blood, but you've done enough. I'm going to take you home."

Pulling forward, I turn the car around and head back to South Sherman Street.

Chapter 54

I drop Blood off at the same corner where I found him half an hour before. I steal a moment to watch him disappear into the night.

My new five-hundred-dollar revolver rests in my lap. As I drive back through the war zone that is Arbor Hill, I'm not sure what it is I'm feeling inside. More secure, maybe. More empowered. A part of me wants to hook a sharp right, head east, cross the river into Troy, and once more confront Bourenhem in his apartment. Maybe, with the .38 aimed directly at his face, he might get the message loud and crystal clear: stop fucking with me and my family or else face the consequences.

But I can't do that.

Pointing a gun at him will only land me in jail for a third time in a single day. Three strikes and you're out.

So then, what do I do now? First things first. Make a flyby past the Reynoldses' place. Sure, Miller promised he'd watch out for them. Sure, he warned me about taking matters into my own hands. But can I really trust the Albany cops when I know how little they trust me?

Up ahead, a small bonfire is burning on the street corner. A gang of red bandana–wearing young black men surround the fire. Bloods. Some of them are talking on their cell phones. They wear baggy hoodies and blue jeans that aren't buckled around narrow waists but instead around their thighs, so that their underwear is entirely exposed, as if shouting a very loud "Fuck you!" to the viewing public. Over their bandanas are extra-wide-brimmed Yankees baseball caps with the gold tag still stuck to the bottom of the brim.

As I pull up to the red light next to them on the corner of Clinton and Henry Johnson Boulevard, the entire gang turns to gaze upon me. Their glares say it all. I'm just another piece of meat to them. I am the enemy. My sudden death by gunshot would be considered their entertainment for the evening.

From behind the wheel, I can see that they're burning some wooden chairs and a couple of empty pallets right on the sidewalk. The stone stairs that lead up to the entrance on the brownstone behind them are occupied with young women, not a single one of whom appears to be over eighteen. There are a couple of toddlers running around in diapers. It's nine o'clock on a chilly October night. A school night. The women are drinking some kind of alcohol from bottles covered in brown paper sacks. A single cigarette is being passed around. Something tells me there's more between the cigarette paper than just tobacco.

Back in the late nineteenth century, men dressed in tuxedos and women in gowns would be arriving home from a night on the town in their horse and buggy, the gaslights on Clinton illuminating the peaceful neighborhood street in a yellow glow. Now, a scrap fire burns while the present-day occupants of this neighborhood get high and plot out crimes. One of the Bloods tosses some wood scraps onto the fire, causing bright sparks to fly up into the night.

As the light turns green, one of the gangbangers lifts up his shirt, exposes the grip on a 9mm automatic. I'm guessing the cock between his legs isn't big enough. He issues me a menacing smile full of gold crowns. I reach down into my lap, raise the .38, aim it directly at the smile that glistens in the firelight. The smile dissolves as he lowers his shirt, once more concealing his weapon.

A sudden honk from the horn on the car directly behind the Escape startles me. The driver is also white and because he's white, he's in a hurry to exit this neighborhood. This lowest level of the inferno. Can't say I blame him one bit.

I hit the gas and pull on through the traffic light, on my way out of the war zone.

Chapter 55

Once inside North Albany I drive the largely wooded road that will lead me back to the Reynoldses' estate. It's just a few minutes past nine o'clock. By now, everyone must be fast asleep, but just making certain that their situation is secure will help me calm down.

I hook a left onto Alexander and Victoria's sleepy suburban road and slowly make the drive past their mansion. The exterior lights are on as usual. The downstairs looks closed up for the night, as does the upstairs. All looks normal, considering this is a family that likes to pack it in on the early side.

But then I catch a flicker that I initially take for firelight coming from the far right-hand, second-floor master bedroom. My stomach tightens and my pulse picks up before I realize that the flickering light is coming from a television. Victoria, allowing cable TV to lull her to sleep. Again, situation normal.

I pull the cell phone from the pocket on my bush jacket, check to see if Lisa has called and if I somehow didn't hear it. Nothing. For a brief instant, I consider texting her. But it will only go ignored. Lisa is sleeping, healing, our daughter curled up beside her. Tapping the gas, I pull ahead, my eyes looking out for a place to turn the SUV around.

A wave of adrenaline shoots up and down my backbone when the Escape interior fills with bright, flashing red, white, and blue light.

I pull over, throw the Escape in park.

The cop cruiser pulls right up on my tail. So close I not only make out the face of Burly Cop sitting behind the wheel, but I can make out his five o'clock shadow in the rearview reflection. Does the man ever take any time off? Maybe he's a cyborg.

Miller is being good to his word. As promised, he's ordered Burly Cop to make a flyby to the Reynoldses' place in order to keep an eye out for suspicious activity. Activity like, say, his number one suspect lurking around outside.

A number one suspect with a .38-caliber snub-nose revolver set on his lap.

I place my right hand on top of it as the cop opens the door to the cruiser and steps on out. Remaining as still as possible, I slide the revolver to the edge of the seat, allow it to drop to the floor. Then I use the boot heel on my right foot to start pushing it back under the seat and, hopefully, out of view.

But there's an obstruction between the foot well and the carpeted area directly beneath the seat. The obstruction rises up maybe three or four inches, and it houses the mechanical device that raises and lowers the seat. No way I'm pushing the gun under the seat unless I do it by hand. But that would mean bending over. A move Burly Cop could potentially interpret as threatening.

A knuckle tap on the driver's-side window.

Slowly, I set the sole of my right boot on top of the snubby and silently pray that Burly Cop hasn't yet taken notice of it. I thumb the switch that makes the window go down.

"Was I speeding, Officer?" I say, trying for humor.

"I thought Miller told you to stay away from here, Johnston," he says. "The safety and well-being of the family inside there is a police matter."

"The safety and well-being of the people in that home, which includes my daughter, rests with me first." For a split second I think about adding "you big, dumb asshole" to the end of my statement, but quickly discount the idea.

He nods like I have a point, but that doesn't mean he has to like it.

Both my hands grip the wheel the way I was taught in driver's education all those years ago should I happen to get pulled over by a great big officer of the law.

"Go home," he says. "Try and get some rest. In the morning, Detective Miller will have a few more questions for you."

"Gee, thanks."

He places both meaty hands on the door frame and sticks his head inside. He comes so close to me I can smell his cheap cologne. Aqua Velva. He looks right and left, up and down. As his eyes continue to peer down at my feet, I feel a nauseating wave of coldness fill my veins.

"What's that under your foot?" he asks.

The ice cold in my veins turns immediately hot. My brain begins to buzz, mouth goes dry. I'm about to be arrested right out in front of my out-laws' house. If he busts me for being in the possession of yet another unlicensed, unregistered weapon, I won't have a chance in hell of convincing Miller that I'm not the lying, psychopathic, paranoid pyromaniac that he already thinks I am. He might even assume that I'm on a quest to kill my ex-wife's former lover out of pure raw jealousy.

Something erupts on Burly Cop's chest.

His radio. A tinny but insistent dispatcher voice bursts forth. "We have a positive ID on Caucasian female pulled from Hudson River two hours ago. Detective Miller requests your immediate presence back at precinct."

I feel my stomach drop.

Burly Cop raises his right hand, thumbs the chest-mounted mic.

"Car one niner en route," he says into the mic. Then, looking back at me, "Things heating up, Johnston. I haven't passed my detective's test yet, but something tells me that badly burned stiff and you have something very much in common. And to think, all you been burning on that back lawn is leaf piles. That is, when you're not busy lighting garbage cans on fire."

He smiles like he's on to something. And he is.

"Roger that, Officer Burly," I say under my breath.

"Excuse me?" he says, his eyes going slanty, lips tight.

"Nothing."

"The thing is, Mr. Johnston, nothing always turns out to be something in the end, now doesn't it?"

Turning, he jogs back to his cruiser. When he gets back in, he's not even finished with closing his door before he peels out, making an abrupt three-point turn in the road. The sleepy suburban neighborhood erupts in a second explosion of bright rooftop flashers and a piercing siren.

I don't breathe until Burly Cop is completely out of sight.

Chapter 56

As I've said, Alex is a light sleeper. He will have noticed the flashing cop cruiser lights by now as they shine against his bedroom walls. He will have heard the sound of the cruiser's siren in his dreams. There's a real good chance he will get out of bed, throw on some pants, and head down to the street to investigate. Which means I don't waste any time making my own three-point turn and getting out of the neighborhood as fast as the speed limit will allow.

I head back in the direction of downtown Albany and my studio apartment, knowing full well that I have just dodged a speeding bullet. The pistol still sits on the floor of the Escape. Every now and then my boot heel comes into contact with it. What did John Lennon sing? "Happiness is a warm gun"?

Driving down toward the east end of the downtown, not far from where I dumped Olga's body in the river, I turn onto Broadway and make my way to the old brick building that houses my studio. I pull up to the curb and throw the transmission into park. But I don't kill the engine. I feel the revolver barrel resting against my boot heel and in my head I see the narrow face of David Bourenhem, see his black eyes hidden behind his thick black-framed eyeglasses and his painfully wide smile. I see my books on his bookshelf and the many unsold manuscripts set on the floor of his Troy apartment. I can't help but see him laying out Lisa's underwear, can't help seeing him drawing my head-blasted image on the chalkboard wall, can't help seeing him sitting in the bathtub accusing me of beating and binding him. Worst of all, I can't help but see Olga's body burning in the backyard.

Reaching into my bush jacket pocket, I pull out the Bic lighter and fire it up. I let the flame go out and light it again, and again. The flame feels hot on my hand and it warms my soul like mother's milk.

"Fire! Fire!" says the Town Crier. "Burn! Burn!" says Goody Stern. "Burn her! Burn him!"

When Miller finds out that Olga lived down the road from Lisa, he'll put two and two together. He will order forensic pathologists to examine her body, and the duct tape I wrapped around her, for prints and anything else that will link her directly to the spot in which she was burned. He will also order an emergency autopsy. Once the forensic exam and autopsy are complete, all evidence will lead not only to Lisa's house, but directly to me. The forensic unit he'll send to the house to scour the backyard will find all the evidence they need to prove I am the killer. Once the work of the forensic experts is complete, he will arrest me for murder one. Bourenhem's setup will be finished, his revenge complete.

Or will it?

What if I were to have one more face-to-face with him at his apartment? Maybe with that .38 aimed for the sweet spot between his eyes, I can get him to admit the truth: That he has been setting me up all along. That he himself is the killer. And if I can record the confession on my smartphone, I can at least get started on clearing my name. I know the confession won't stand up in court, but at the very least it'll convince Miller that I'm not a bad guy bent on acting out scenes from my own novel. That the real bad guy has been David Bourenhem all along.

Throwing the tranny back in drive, I fire up a cigarette and then pull away from the curb, headed for the steel bridge that will take me across the Hudson River back into downtown Troy.

Chapter 57

First Street is quiet on this Monday night as I drive slowly, keeping an eye out not only for Bourenhem but also the police, both Troy and Albany divisions. I'm not sure why I feel so surprised when I see that his toy-like Honda 4x4 is parked outside the front door to his building. But I am. Pulling to a stop behind it, I peer up through the passenger-side window at the second-floor window of his apartment.

The lights are on.

The shade is partially drawn, but it isn't long before I see the figure of a tall, thin man walking past it. I can't make out the face from down inside the Escape, but I know it's got to be Bourenhem. He's pacing back and forth past the window, moving his hands up and down rapidly, like he might be upset about something. For a moment I think he might be on the phone. But then, how can that be when he's waving both hands around like that?

That's when I see he's not alone.

I make out the figure of another person now positioned in front of the window. The person is shorter than Bourenhem, but also slim. I'm seeing his or her backside, which looks to be packed into a tight pair of blue jeans. It tells me the person is a woman. She too is waving her hands in the air like they're arguing about something.

Maybe he's got a new girlfriend, or perhaps that's just wishful thinking. But then, Lisa never mentioned his having a new girlfriend. Or maybe that's something she doesn't want to think about. But even if he did have a new woman in his life, it wouldn't negate the fact that he's still in love and obsessed with my significant other.

Reaching down, I pick up the revolver, set it between my legs.

I feel the cold, hard metal and its heaviness. I feel the essence of its killing power. If Bourenhem were all alone right now, I might stick to my original plan. I might head up to his apartment, gun in one hand, smartphone in the other, its voice-recording app engaged. I'd demand a little face time with him in which I would extract a full confession. Once the confession was recorded, I'd contact Miller and demand that he listen to it. He'd have no choice but to haul David in for questioning. Maybe he'd even arrest him. Maybe I'd be off the hook, once and for all.

But now that I can see he's not alone, there's no way I can follow through with any of it.

My cell phone vibrates and chimes. A new text has arrived. My spirits lift a little at the thought of Lisa returning my earlier text. I pull out the phone and glance at the text. My spirit crashes. The text is from Blood. I open it. It says, *Meant what I said. One call, I'm there.*

The plot thickens, but I'm OK, I thumb-tap in reply. *Chill out and take a na—*

I'll be dipped. Instead of thumbing in the "p" at the end of "nap," I stupidly hit "Send." I might be a writer, but I'll never amount to much of a texter. I'm about to retype the complete word "nap" when suddenly, twin headlights appear in my rearview mirror. Bright white halogens, half a block back. Even with the ceiling-mounted flashers not lit up like a Christmas tree, I can still make out their colorful reflection in the light that spills down from the streetlamps.

Stuffing the cell phone back in my jacket pocket, I lean over the center console, open the glove box, shove the revolver inside, then pull away from the curb. Keeping one eye on the rearview, I watch as the cop comes to a stop in the same spot I just occupied with my Escape. Maybe he suspects me of littering. Or maybe he thinks I'm a creepy Peeping Tom. Whatever the case, I'm not about to wait around to find out just what the hell he's thinking.

As I approach the street corner where I spotted Rachael earlier today, I can't help but wonder if she's presently at home, occupying an apartment located just mere yards away. I wonder what she's doing and who she might be doing it with. But then I quickly remind myself that it would be better just to erase her from my memory. Keep the past in the past.

Our breakup was that bad.

For Rachael, when it comes to our shattered relationship, a cauldron of hatred is surely brewing. As I tap the gas on the Escape and hook a right, I once more see the figure of a woman standing before Bourenhem's street-side window. I feel a cold chill fill my body. Because what if the woman standing in front of David's window is named Rachael, and if she is my former lover?

"You're making shit up again, Reece," I say aloud. "Making crazy shit up."

Chapter 58

I breathe a sigh of relief when I pull onto Lisa's street and see that, so far, anyway, the APD forensics pros are staying away from the house. But that doesn't mean they aren't on their way. Parking at the top of the driveway, I retrieve the revolver from the glove box and head inside. Frankie comes running immediately up to me. I wonder if she's eaten yet. Before I look into it, I go about the business of giving the entire interior, up and down, the once-over. Despite the threat of cop intrusion, I'm slow and meticulous with my search.

When I'm certain the coast is perfectly clear, I check on Frankie's food and water bowls and see that they're still full. As if reading my mind, she comes running back into the kitchen, stuffing her snout into the dry dog food.

"Where you been, Reecey Pieces," she says, her mouth full.

"Been a day for the ages, Frankie," I say. "Wanna hear about it?"

"Not at all. Besides, I was witness to the whole dog and pony show. Pun intended. Now I just wanna eat and go back to sleep."

"Can't blame you there," I say, grabbing a beer from the fridge, popping it open.

Stealing a quick swig, I take the beer with me out onto the back deck. The air is cool but crisp. I eye the backyard and find it almost impossible to conceive of the fact that a grown woman was murdered by fire on the back lawn today. In my head I see her body laid out on the grass and I see the fire consuming her. Tears fill my eyes. I'm not sure if what I'm feeling is profound sadness for Olga or sheer blistering anger at Bourenhem over what he's done.

Both.

I drink more beer and feel my head spin. The night is still young, which means this thing ain't over. Not by a long shot. What the hell does David have up his sleeve now? What's his next move? Who was he arguing with inside his apartment? Has the person partnered up with him? Is that person a woman, and is the woman Rachael?

I shake my head and do my best to convince myself that my imagination is running away with itself.

"What do you think, Dad?" I say aloud.

Be prepared for anything, Son, he says. *This guy David might not be a successful author, but he's a slick operator and he'll do anything to split you and Lisa up. Maybe even kill her, if that's what it takes.*

I feel ice water shoot up and down my spine.

"Why would he kill her if he loves her, Dad?"

Because if he can't have her, then nobody can have her.

After a time, I glance at my watch. I'm surprised to see that it's going on ten o'clock already. Time flies when you're being set up for crimes you did not commit. I know that with Olga being examined by forensic pathologists, it's only a matter of minutes until Miller and his team show up with a warrant to search the entire property, inside and out. That means I've got to pack up my shit and get the hell out. Do it ASAP. I should already be gone by now.

Finishing my beer, I head back inside. At the dining room table, I open up my laptop. The message is still there.

THE BESTSELLER IS A HERETIC AND LIKE ALL HERETICS HE
WILL BURN FOR HIS SINS.

Why the hell would Bourenhem think of me as a heretic when
it was Lisa who broke up with his ass? I go into the screen-saver control and delete the message. I don't bother with adding a new one.
Time is of the essence. I would rather just pack up the laptop, gather
up my things, and leave. I would do it immediately if the laptop's
Skype videophone doesn't start to ring.

Rarely do I use my Skype account. It comes in handy for communicating with Anna and Lisa when I'm travelling to a writers' conference or a foreign country for research, but that's about it. Too much
social media makes me insane.

So I might be surprised to simply be receiving this incoming
video call at all, but I'm rocked back in my seat to see that it's coming from Alexander Reynolds.

My heart begins to beat rapidly. My brain heats up as my plot-
building imagination takes over. Has something gone wrong with
Lisa's recovery? Did she suffer a bad reaction to the sedatives or the
anesthesia? Has she suffered an allergic reaction? Or are her wounds
becoming infected and now she's spiking a high fever? Or maybe
Anna is sick. My creative mind races with the ugly possibilities.

I stare at the ringing Skype page and the name "Alexander"
flashing on and off.

"Why the hell not just call me on my cell phone?" I ask aloud.

The caption on the Skype page asks me if I want to answer the
video call. Like I have a choice. I hit "Answer."

The face that pops up on the computer screen tells me that the
horrors of this day *and* night have only just begun.

246

Chapter 59

I see a close-up of Alex's face.

It's as if the camera on his laptop were positioned only a half inch from the tip of his nose. His face is chalk white. His bottom lip is swelled to twice its size. It's become black and purple, and there's a string of blood and drool hanging down from it. Whoever or whatever did this to him just got finished.

His eyes have been blindfolded by a strip of gray duct tape. There are words written on the tape in blood-red Sharpie marker. The words are penned in uppercase letters, just like they were on my computer. Like they were beneath the drawing of my head being blown off on the chalkboard wall. Like they were on the back of the author photo tacked to the bulletin board in Lisa's office.

THE HERETICS WILL BURN!

The sentence is lifted right out of *The Damned*. Pyromaniac Drew Brennen paints the walls of his victims with blood: THE HERETICS WILL BURN!

"Alex," I say into the laptop screen. "Alex, can you hear me? What the hell is happening?"

"The heretics will burn," he whispers.

But then something pokes him against the side of the head.

Something long, hard, and made of plastic. But I can't be sure of what exactly it is.

"Louder," comes a voice belonging to someone hidden from the computer camera's view. "Louder. Like your life depends upon it."

"The heretics will burn," Alex repeats.

"Where is Lisa?" I shout. "Where is Anna?"

I'm trying to look beyond Alexander's distressed and damaged face. Look behind it, catch a glimpse of Lisa, Anna, or Vickie. But I can't make out anything other than Alex's beat-up face.

The plastic object knocks against his head a second time.

"Say it again," demands the voice. The voice. The voice of David Bourenhem? Am I sure that it's his voice? Not entirely. But in my gut I know that it is. That it can only be his voice.

"The heretics will burn," Alexander repeats, the blood from the wound in his bottom lip running thicker and thicker. His head is bobbing, chin against chest, like he's drunk. But he's not drunk. He's beat to a pulp. He looks like he's about to pass out. But that's when he raises up his head and, looking at me as if he can see my face through the duct tape, shouts, "Reece, call the police now before they kill us all!"

"Before who kills you all?"

The plastic object appears in the laptop screen once more. A liquid of some sort is being squirted through the object. It comes to me then. I know precisely what the object is and what's being squirted from it. It's a kid's toy. A high-powered Super Soaker squirt gun. And the liquid being squirted from it onto Alex's face and head is gasoline. It's one of the ways Drew Brennen kills in *The Damned*. One of the ways he rids the world of heretics.

It's then that I begin to make out the sound of crying.

More than one woman crying.

"No, please don't," someone shouts. It's Victoria. "He's going to light Alex on fire. For the love of God."

He's going to burn them all. Just like in *The Damned*. Mother, father, daughter, granddaughter . . . he's going to soak them in gasoline and he's going to torch them all to death. Some will die outside like a pile of burning cordwood, while others will be burned alive inside pine caskets. Others, like Alex, will die while simply strapped to a chair.

The Super Soaker disappears from view. In its place comes a lit match. The fire slowly approaches Alex's gasoline-soaked head.

His mouth opens wide and he issues a scream that I hear and feel like a swift punch to my sternum.

The lit match comes closer.

"Nooooo!" Victoria screams and the video feed disappears like black smoke into thin air.

Chapter 60

My heart races while my eyes fill with tears of rage.

I can hardly catch a breath.

Maybe Alex and I never got along. But to see him about to be burned to death is too impossible to contemplate. Not even a diagnosed pyromaniac would wish such a death on his worst enemy. That kind of crime happens only in books. In movies. In war atrocities.

I pull out my cell phone from my bush jacket and it drops from my sweaty hand. I retrieve it, thumb the command that will connect me with "Recent Calls." I see Miller's number. But just as I'm about to make the call, a multimedia text chimes in. It's from a local number I do not recognize.

I open the message.

It's a photo of Lisa and Anna. They are both seated on the bed in Lisa's old upstairs bedroom. Duct tape covers Anna's eyes and mouth. Her wrists and ankles have also been duct-taped together. Lisa's mouth is covered in the thick gray tape and, like Anna, her wrists and ankles are bound. But her eyes have not been covered, as though whoever did this doesn't want to risk damaging her surgical wounds.

Bourenhem.

A second message chimes in.

Don't call the cops, bro. Or fire burns the ones we both love.

Using my thumbs I frantically type in a reply, letter by letter.

What do you want?

I wait for a reply.

I want to hear your voice. I want to feel your fear.

The phone rings and nearly startles me to death. I hit the green "Answer" button that appears on the glass screen.

"I'm here," I say.

"Not even a hello?" Bourenhem says. "If that's how you treat a friend, how do you treat your enemies?"

I try to swallow, but my mouth and throat are so dry it's almost impossible. How is it possible that I just saw Bourenhem standing in the window of his apartment almost an hour ago? How is it possible he was able to invade the Reynoldses' house, take the entire family hostage, beat up Alex, and Skype me in that short amount of time? The only answer is that he either had this whole thing planned minute to minute. Or he has help. Maybe both.

"Hello, David. Why are you doing this?"

"That's better."

"What did you do to my father-in-law?"

"Ex-father-in-law, bro."

"Did you burn him? Just like you burned Olga on my back lawn and set me up for the blame?"

"Let's just say that Drew Brennen would be proud of me. I mean, it smells like a fucking steak house in here. I love the aroma of charred meat. You of all people can dig that. Isn't that right, pyro boy? Makes me wet."

I can hear his smile.

"Come on," he continues, "you've got to admit that was some crazy shit, burning old man Reynolds with gasoline squirted out of a Super Soaker. *The Damned* comes alive for reals." He says "reals" like all the kids say it these days. Realzzzzz. "Even you have to be proud of me, Reecey Pieces. See, I meant it when I said I want to be just like you. You and I, we're two of a kind. We both burn with the devil's flame."

"David," I say.

"Yes, Reece?"

"Before this night ends, I'm going to kill you."

He laughs aloud.

"Really?" he says. "That's the best line you can come up with? I know for a fact that your now-roasted ex-father-in-law hated your guts and you weren't particularly fond of his. Lisa and I used to talk about it all the time in bed. You should be thanking me. I wonder how many times you secretly imagined his flesh burning over an open flame. Bet it gave you a nice juicy hard-on."

"If you touch my daughter, if you touch Lisa, or my mother-in-law, I will make it painful when I kill you."

"Sticks and stones, bro. Their fate lies in your hot little hands."

"Tell me how."

"First, I would like you to apologize for coming back into Lisa's life and fucking everything up for me. For destroying my family right before my eyes."

"They weren't your family and I make no apologies for something beyond my control."

"Gee, I wonder what Anna's scalp will look like when I burn her hair off?"

I exhale.

"David," I say. "I'm sorry."

"Okay, good. Apology accepted. Don't forget, we're friends, Reece. And friends forgive. It's important in a relationship, don't you think?"

"Then let Anna and Lisa go. It's me you want dead."

"I don't want you dead. I want to punish you for what you've done. I need Lisa and Anna to suffer because in their suffering, you suffer."

"Please, just stop now."

"We're not done yet, Reecey Pieces. What did Churchill say? This isn't the end. It's not even the beginning of the end. But it is the end of the beginning."

"What do you want from me?"

"Honestly?"

"Yes, David."

"A little humility and honesty on your part."

"What are you getting at?"

"I want you to think back a few years. Back when you were writing *The Damned*. You know, the one that finally put you on the map. The novel that broke you out of the desperation, your financial sinkhole, your depression, and your need to burn things up, like Lisa's house for instance. The novel that made you who you are now, Reecey Pieces Johnston, best-selling tool-a-mundo. I want you to try and recall sitting down at the keyboard and, in the immortal words of Ernesto Hemingway, bleeding from your fingertips."

My blood boils. If I could reach into the phone and gouge his eyes out, I would.

"You're insane."

More laughing. Mocking.

"In truth, Reece, and I mean this as a friend and a fan, you're the insane one. I mean, who decides to dump the body of a young woman savagely burned in Lisa's backyard in the river? Why not alert the authorities? Crazy shit, Reece, and you're going to pay for your crime against humanity. Did you know that the poor Russian girl had come around the house only to borrow a couple of Lisa's condoms? What a sad way to go."

He's right. I should have called Miller. I should have exposed the murder to him as soon as I was exposed to it. But I didn't. I panicked, thinking I would assume the blame.

"Tell me what you want now," I say.

"I want you to recall when you were putting typed words on a page back in the fall of 2006. Think about where you were and how you were. What was the weather like? What color were the walls painted? What were you eating back then? Drinking? Did you work on a laptop, or a typewriter? Did you write the first draft out by hand? Did you listen to music while you wrote it? Did you take breaks to masturbate in front of the mirror? Did you think about Lisa when you did it? Lisa, who had only recently become your ex-wife and who was fucking her new boyfriend so hard night in and night out? Think, Reece, think."

No choice but to do it. Think back to the time when I was writing *The Damned*. It's a disturbing exercise because I can't actually picture myself sitting at the writing table in what was then my brand-new downtown studio, pounding out the words, sentences, and paragraphs. I can picture myself as a writer actually performing the act of writing by hand or on my laptop, but in this case, I can't come up with writing anything specific. But then, I'm more than a little panicked right now. I can't think of anything other than getting Lisa and Anna out of that house and away from Bourenhem.

"What's the matter, bro? The truth burning a hole in your tongue? Those treatments with electroconvulsive shock therapy erase your desire for fire *and* your memory?"

The blood is speeding through my veins. Heart pounding up against my rib cage. I'm entering into a state of rage so profound, I am seeing through a filter of red.

"Think, Reece, think. Are you thinking?"

"Yes," I lie.

"But nothing comes to mind, bro. And nothing is going to come to mind."

"I write every day. Unlike you, creep, I'm a professional. A real writer. Why should I recall the exact events and moments of writing one single book?"

"That's because you can't possibly remember writing *The Damned.*"

"What the hell are you getting at?"

"You ready for a shocker, my bro? It's impossible for you to remember writing your first book because you didn't write it at all."

Now it's my turn to laugh. I'm laughing, but nothing is funny.

"Now that's a riot, Bourenhem. If I didn't write it, who did?"

"Taa daaa," he sings. "*I* wrote it. And guess what? You are going to tell the entire world about it right now. Or else your family and mine becomes burnt toast."

Chapter 61

"I don't believe a word of this," I say.

"Believe it," Bourenhem says. "In fact, I owe you a great debt. I never would have written *The Damned* without you. Or, without Lisa telling me all about your pyromania, that is, back when she and I first got reacquainted on the mighty Facebook. Let me see, that had to be around the summer of 2005. What a story you had. I had to write it before you did."

"You're crazy, Bourenhem. Obsessed with Lisa. You're trying to impress her in your own psychotic little way by acting out *The Damned*."

"Nothing could be more false," he says. "It's you I'm obsessed with."

His words hit me like a slap to the head. Because it sounds all too true.

He says, "It's because of you that I'm making *The Damned* become a reality. Because when the Reynoldses' estate burns to the ground, all evidence will point to you, Reece. After all, you took the credit as the author of *The Damned*. Now you're going to pay for it. It will make sense to the police. You tried to burn your boyhood home and, later on in life, you tried to burn down Lisa's home with me and Anna inside it.

Now you're already suspected of staging the break-in and ransacking of Lisa's new home along with the assault and battery of yours truly. And let's not forget poor Olga. And to think all she wanted was a condom. Poor lonely girl. You are a known alcohol abuser, and rumor has it the police confiscated your unlicensed handgun. Once the charred remains of your loved ones are tagged and bagged and when your prints are discovered all over the remains of the Reynoldses' estate, including the back fence, you will be the one who goes to prison for the rest of his life. Am I making sense, my friend?"

In my mind I'm trying to figure out how it's possible for him to be spreading my fingerprints all over Lisa's parents' house. Or maybe he's just bluffing. But can I afford to call his bluff? Bourenhem is obviously the crazy one here. He's already beat himself up to make it look like I did it. He murdered Olga by fire. By the looks of things, he's burned Alex to death. Who's to say he wouldn't burn Anna or Lisa? What if he literally loves them to death?

"What do you want me to do, Bourenhem?"

"I want you to record a video confession. A confession that declares the absolute truth directly from your own pieholio: that you stole my novel and published it as your own. Then, I want you to post it on YouTube, Facebook, Twitter, you name it, until it goes viral."

"And when exactly would you like me to make this false confession, you fuck?"

"See, that's exactly the attitude we don't need right now, Reece."

"Okay, confession. Not *false* confession. When would you like me to make it?"

"You have until eleven o'clock to get it done and make it viral, or else I resort to 'burning down the house . . .'" He sings the last words to the tune of the famous Talking Heads pop song.

"You really think you're going to get away with this scam?" I say, gripping the cell phone so tightly I feel like it might explode in my hand.

"I'm already getting away with it, precisely because it isn't a scam. I also know that once it's done it will destroy your career forever, and I know that you know it too. No reputable publisher or agent will touch you once you admit the terrible, evil truth. You betrayed us all, Reece Johnston. You went against the writers' code so firmly established by Hemingway, Faulkner, hell, even Stephen King. In their eyes you are a heretic. You betrayed Lisa, Anna, and yes, Rachael. You remember Rachael, don't you? But most of all, you betrayed yourself and your gift by resorting to the lowest act a writer can possibly engage in. You did it because you craved fame more than anything else in the world."

It's not his speaking of Rachael by name that raises the hairs up on the back of my neck. Naturally he's heard the name Rachael before, having spent so much time with Lisa. But how is it that he believes I betrayed *Rachael*? Sure, Rachael certainly thinks I betrayed her by my not letting go of my love for Lisa. But where in hell would Bourenhem get that idea? It's like Rachael fed him that line.

Once more I see the silhouette of Bourenhem up in the window of his Troy apartment. I see him arguing with someone. A woman. My instinct keeps trying to tell me that maybe the woman was Rachael, but that I'm over-imagining things due to the close proximity of Rachael's apartment to his. But perhaps it's all too true. Maybe she's in on it with him.

I feel the floor shift out from under my feet, feel myself falling into a black, bottomless pit, my body spinning clockwise, spinning down and down and down and never hitting ground.

"Reece, my friend," Bourenhem goes on, "the source of the fire that burns in you so ferociously is the devil, and you have sold your soul to him, lock, stock, and two smoking barrels. If I were you, I'd take another look at the message that was left for you on the back of the author photo tacked to the bulletin board in Lisa's office.

The one about becoming a *posthumous* best seller. The message isn't accidental. Like a good sentence, it's entirely thought out. Entirely deliberate. Or take another gaze at the chalkboard. What's there isn't just a cute drawing rendered out of anger or jealousy. It was a way of speaking the truth to you. Do the honorable thing and take the Hemingway way out. Do it as soon as you post the video. It's the only way to save Lisa and Anna."

"What if I just call the police?" I say, the words feeling like they're peeling themselves from the back of my throat.

"Of course you could call the police. Though the sound of a police siren will only result in instant death to Lisa and Anna. Or you could choose to do nothing at all and simply take the chance that I'm bluffing. But I assure you, I am not bluffing. This thing we've got going tonight is as serious as a heart attack. Just ask Alexander—errrr, well, scratch that. He's looking terribly fried right now and I'm not so sure he's up to answering questions from the likes of you or me.

"So what will it be, Reece Johnston, best seller? Which do you wish to save more? Your literary career, or the lives of your precious loved ones? You have until eleven to decide."

He hangs up.

My brain once more fills with the chalkboard drawing of the back of my head being blown away with a double-barrel shotgun. He's crazy. Of course I wrote *The Damned*. He's just setting me up for the ultimate fall. First he wants to destroy my career, and then he's going to destroy my family and I'm going to take the blame for it all. The police will testify that I had been acting irrationally and even violently all day. I'm a certifiable pyromaniac who was detained on two separate occasions by the APD, and even arrested. Then came the strange occurrence of a badly burned young woman being fished out of the Hudson River. A woman who lived down the street from Lisa. It's all culminated in a confession on Facebook and then the murder of my family. Naturally, all that will be left is for me to commit suicide.

I see my dad standing in the living room. This time he's accompanied by my big brothers Patrick, who's wearing a loose black T-shirt that says "Led Zeppelin" across the chest, and Tommy, who's dressed in a white wifebeater that shows off his muscles.

You can't let this shit happen to you, Reece, Tommy says.

Yeah, you can't let that Bourenhem dick get away with it, Patrick adds.

Your brothers are right, Son, says Dad. *You need to fight for what's right. You need to fight for Anna and Lisa's lives, Reece. You can't imagine the horror fire would do to their pretty faces. I saw your mother's face when they pulled her out. It was a horror, Son. A horror. That's why I didn't want you to name Anna after her. Too many memories. Bad memories.* He pauses for a moment, fighting with himself to keep it together. *But there's something else you have to do, Son. You also have to ask yourself something. Why can't you remember writing* The Damned?

I stare down at the cell. I know all it would take is a simple phone call to Miller and he will send his troops to the Reynoldses' estate. I could beg them to do so quietly, stealthily . . .

You can't take that chance, Reece, Dad insists. *What if that dumb ox Burly Cop hits his siren or engages the flashers on the cruiser? Bourenhem will set the house on fire and they'll all die.*

I have no choice but to make the video. No choice but to make it go viral. Do it now. Even if it ruins everything I've worked so hard and so long for.

Everything I hold dearest to my heart.

Chapter 62

I sit and stare at the computer screen knowing that I should be making the video immediately. The video will save my family. Instead, I once more stare into the living room. But I don't see my dad or my big brothers. I see something else. I see my past. Late October 2006, to be precise.

I see the white lab-coated anesthesiologist getting up from his stool. See him standing behind me, pressing a black plastic mask against my mouth, telling me to "slowly inhale."

I inhale a sour, plastic-like odor. When he releases the mask, he sits back down and begins making some adjustments to the airflow by typing in some commands on his laptop. The whole time, I've been watching his inverted reflection in the stainless steel ceiling-mounted surgical lamp.

The attractive presiding doctor gently brushes back her lush black hair behind her left ear, tells me to open my mouth. She slides a smooth but rigid plastic device onto my tongue so I don't choke on it during the procedure. It's the part of the process I hated the most as a boy, so that Dad had to hold my hand tightly when the doctor slid it onto my tongue. I recall holding his thick, cold hand, while trying hard not to cry.

"Lie back," says the doctor. "Chill out. Think of a song; maybe that will relax you."

"We're caught in a trap . . . I can't walk out . . . Because I love you too much, baby."

Through my sedated haze I focus on her dark hair as it drapes her face like a dark veil. I concentrate on her smile and her deep brown eyes. I suddenly have this enormous urge to sit up and kiss her mouth, as if that were physically possible.

But just then a young black man enters the room. Dressed in black scrubs, he's as wide as he is tall, with gigantic hands.

"Armando is going to prepare you," *the doctor says while typing more commands into her laptop, which causes some of the illuminated red and green lines on the display screen it's wired to to fly up and down, like on an old-fashioned radar readout.*

Armando doesn't smile. Nor is his tight, meaty face a pleasure to look at. Armando goes right to work, reaching for a thick belt that's attached to the lowest end of the table. Bringing it across my lower legs, he secures it to the other side of the table. He abruptly tightens the belt so that there is little or no slack against my shins. He then pulls a second belt tightly around my thighs and, following that, a third belt around my chest.

Shifting himself further up the table, he reaches under it and pulls out a narrow, hidden panel. Taking hold of my right arm, he sets it onto the panel, palm up, strapping it down tightly at the wrist. He goes around the table, pulls a second hidden panel out, and straps the left arm down tight at the wrist, palm up. His final task is to place a kind of hollowed-out block under my neck so that I can't jerk it during the procedure and injure my spine.

When his job is done, he shoots me a wide-eyed look like I'm insane and he knows it. Which isn't too far from the truth, given my circumstances. I tried to burn my wife's house down. To him, I must be the devil.

"Are you at peace?" *asks the doctor with a reassuring smile.*

I try to nod, but I can't move. I've never known peace. Not since my mother and brothers burned to death . . . my mother in her bed, my brother Tommy while trying to climb out his second-floor bedroom window, my brother Patrick on the floor curled up fetal by his locked bedroom door. We were told that the smoke made them pass out long before the fire burned them, but that never made me feel any more at ease.

Once more the doctor takes hold of the pump that sends air into the blood pressure device wrapped around my right bicep. I feel the device filling with air, getting tighter and tighter as the doctor records my pressure one final time. When she's satisfied with the results, she lets the air out of the device and the pressure on my bicep is released.

"Armando, the electrodes, please," she says.

Armando takes hold of a translucent plastic bottle that might hold ketchup or mustard in a diner and squirts some thick clear liquid onto two spongy pads that are attached to a long fabric strap. When he places a set of electrodes over each of my temples and tightens the strap around my skull, I feel the cold liquid against my scalp like a crown of thorns, only cold as ice.

Losing her smile, the doctor turns to the anesthesiologist to her left.

"Let's do this," she says. Then, to me, "Let's free the demon inside, Mr. Johnston."

Once more I eye eight identical versions of the anesthesiologist in the overhead lamp reflector panels, but in my head I see the faces of Tommy, Patrick, and my mother reflected in the square glass panes. I see the way the faces were before the fire got to them. The anesthesiologist reaches over my face with that black, bad-tasting mask and again sets it over my mouth and nostrils. This time for keeps.

The doctor turns, places her manicured hands onto the laptop keyboard.

"Initiating," she says.

I'm staring into a burning white spotlight as the first rush of electric shocks bombard my brain.

Chapter 63

With a quick shake of my head, I return to the present.

Front and fucking center.

My eyes glued to the laptop screen, I search for a place on the menu called "Media Center." If I click on it, it will bring up the built-in camera that's located at the top of the laptop screen. All it will take for me to film this so-called confession and save my family is to click on the button and make the recording. It should be easy peasy. A no-brainer. Just double-click on "Record" and recite the following words:

"I, Reece Johnston, of Albany, New York, do solemnly swear that I did not write the best-selling novel *The Damned*. That I stole it from its true author, David Bourenhem, and published it as my own."

That's all I have to say before I click on "Stop." From there I can upload the video onto YouTube and then copy the video's link and hope it goes viral via the many social networks. Accomplishing the task should take no more than ten or fifteen minutes if I'm expeditious about it.

Ten minutes to ruin my life. But ten minutes that will save my family.

Inhaling deeply, I click on the Media Center. I see the link for "Video Camera." Positioning my thumb and index finger on the keypad, I stare into the camera and double-click. A bright white light turns on at the very top center of the computer screen's hard plastic frame. It doesn't shine onto my face so much as attract my eyes like insects to a flame.

The camera is filming. I try to speak, but something happens. I can't do it. This is one fiction I'm not capable of. I can't lie about stealing Bourenhem's manuscript. It didn't happen. He wants me to lie not to save my family, but so that he can ruin my career. He might be envious of my renewed relationship with Lisa, but he's pathologically jealous of my success as a novelist, and for that, he wants to see me crash and burn. That's what this is all about.

What if I were to go public with a fiction about stealing *The Damned* from Bourenhem and he doesn't honor his end of the bargain and let my family go?

The damage will have been done. My career will be finished, and it will all have been for nothing. Even if I somehow manage to prove that I made the statement under duress, I will always be suspected of having plagiarized and that will make me untouchable to all publishers and readers.

I finger the command for "Stop," sit back in my chair, and glance at my watch. I have fifteen minutes to make the video or else risk my family's murder.

But here's the deal: I don't believe Bourenhem is going to burn my family. I think it's all a bluff. It's possible he hasn't even burned Alex and that the whole thing has been a charade designed to manipulate me. I never saw proof of a burned body on Skype. So here's what I'm going to do instead: He's ordered me to make a video and that's exactly what I'm going to do. As it's going viral, I will already have arrived at the Reynoldses' estate, totally undetected by Bourenhem.

My plan?

I'm going to bring terror to the terrorist. If he wants to play with fire, then so be it. Fire is my lover and I will bring him a fire that he will never forget. Pulling the lighter from my jacket pocket, I thumb a high, hot flame. I smell the burning fuel, feel the calming heat. In my head I see Bourenhem's face. See it melting as the flame consumes it.

Burn Bourenhem!

Chapter 64

It takes only eight and a half minutes for me to make the video and set up an auto-scheduler to air it on the social media networks at the top of the eleven o'clock hour, leaving me a half hour to get myself to the Reynoldses' house. With the distance being only one mile, all I need is five minutes. That gives me plenty of time to prepare for what it is I'm about to do.

I head into Lisa's bedroom, go to my one allotted drawer, pull out a pair of black jeans and a navy blue long-sleeved sweatshirt. I undress and change into the clothing, then step into a pair of black cross-training shoes.

Frankie is asleep on the edge of the bed, but the commotion wakes her.

"Where you going dressed like that?" she says. "You look like a cat burglar. You know how I feel about cats."

"Go back to sleep, Frank. Tomorrow, I'll bring Mommy and Anna back home with me, and we'll all live happily ever after."

"Ain't no such thing."

"I'm gonna make it happen. For all of us."

"That's what David used to say," she says before licking her chops, laying her chin back down on her paws, falling back to sleep.

In the medicine cabinet over the sink I find Lisa's black mascara and brush some of it onto my forehead and the parts of my face not already shaded by scruffy growth. I find a black watch cap in her walk-in closet in a box where she stores winter mittens and hats. Out in the vestibule, I find my black leather coat. Inside one of the pockets is a pair of black leather gloves that used to belong to Dad.

"Mind if I use your gloves, Dad?" I say.

Since when did you start asking if you could use my stuff?

Down in the basement I locate a full can of Raid wasp and hornet insecticide, which I take back upstairs with me. Out in the garage I find a can of gasoline, three old dish towels that are now used as rags, and some empty Budweiser bottles sitting idle inside the blue recycling bin. Back in the house, I empty out my writing satchel and add the can of Raid, the empty beer bottles, and the rags. Then, in the kitchen, I locate the long Bic butane barbecue lighter and stuff it into the right-hand pocket of my leather coat. In the drawer beside the stove, I find a stainless steel paring knife, which I attach to my right ankle with two separate strips of duct tape. Last, but not least, I stuff the .38 snub-nose into my coat pocket.

A text arrives.

I pull the phone from the interior pocket of my coat.

How did the video go, Bestseller?

I reply, *It's ready, and it should go viral at the appointed hour.*

Gee, thanks for complying. I hope we're still BWFF (Best Writing Friends Forever). Not to get technical, but if the video doesn't show up, our family broils. Are you going to take my advice and blow your brains out now? You might want to videotape that too. Could be useful when it comes to selling books posthumously. A violent suicide caught on YouTube vid is sure to go mad viral. One must always think about marketing.

Bourenhem is able to text so rapidly I can only assume he's using the voice recording option on his iPhone.

You're right, I type in as a reply. *Time for me to die. Just like when Brennen pours gasoline all over himself and lights the final match.*

Oh yes, Bourenhem types. *I know it by heart . . .*

"Sliding the matchbook cover up, Brennen found one final match inside. It would be this match or nothing. He pulled the match from the cardboard and struck it. The flame sparked to life.

"'Father,'" he said, 'into thy filthy hands I commend my spirit to the damned.'

"A single tear fell from his eye as he dropped the lit match onto his head."

Reading the final lines transcribed for me, I can't help but grow teary-eyed. I lived with Drew Brennen, the hopeless pyromaniac, for a long time before handing the manuscript in to my agent. The fictional Brennen wasn't a bad guy so much as he was sad, misunderstood. A man who suffered the death of his family when he was just a boy. And he was my friend, even if I did make him up.

I thumb "End" and slip the cell phone back into the interior pocket of my leather coat. Slipping on Dad's leather gloves, I grab the satchel and the keys to the Escape and I exit the house by way of the front door.

The next time I come back through that door, David Bourenhem will occupy a place of honor in hell.

Chapter 65

I don't park in the Reynoldses' driveway but instead pull off onto the soft shoulder maybe a quarter of a mile down the road. I pull the snubby from my coat pocket and tuck it into the waistband of my pants, easy access. Then, reaching back inside, I grab my writing satchel and pull the strap over my head and neck so it won't slip off my shoulder during my raid on the property.

Closing the Escape door, I pull out my cell phone and switch the volume to vibrate mode. That done, I make my way around to the hatchback and pull out the empty beer bottles from the satchel, fill each one with gasoline from the can in the back of the car. Tearing long, wide strips of rag, I stuff them three-quarters of the way into each of the bottle necks, sealing them up.

When I've prepared all three bottles to my satisfaction, I place them carefully back inside the satchel so that they're standing upright inside one of the interior pockets. I then begin power-walking my way along the dark road toward the Reynoldses' estate.

The Reynoldses' property is just up ahead. The five-acre estate is accessed by a long driveway that, surprisingly, is not gated. The woods horseshoe the property on three sides, minus the large front lawn that faces the road. It's the back lawn that is secured with the black iron, deer-impaling fence, which was constructed along the interior of the wood line. The purpose of the fence is not only security, but also to keep little kids from wandering onto the expansive property and accidentally drowning in the swimming pool. The only access into and out of the iron fence is through a single gate that is located at the very end of the driveway, and maybe twenty-five feet away from a back door off the kitchen. My guess is that the gate has been padlocked.

As I make my way up the long curved driveway, I can see that just about every light is on in the mansion. With the acres of woodland surrounding the back and sides of the property, Bourenhem might as well strike up a full orchestra while he's at it.

Moving at a crouch, I make my way to the back gate. I can see now that for certain, the gate entry is secured with the padlock. Bourenhem must have simply walked in the front door using Lisa's keys, then disengaged the alarm using the code penned on the supermarket membership card.

But I've come prepared, like a good pyromaniac should.

Reaching into my satchel, I take hold of the can of Raid, then find the butane barbecue lighter with the special extended flame nozzle. Take it from one who knows: Raid, when ignited, will produce a flame hot enough to melt most metals. Placing the can's nozzle about three inches from the U-shaped padlock shackle, I depress the nozzle, releasing the toxic propellant. With my other hand, I position the business end of the elongated lighter directly into the spray and, using both my thumb and index finger, depress the child safety trigger. Instantly, the spray ignites in a puff of white, red, and orange flame. The initial explosive cloud comes dangerously close to my face before settling into a concentrated stream of flame that goes to work melting the metal.

Within a few seconds, the metal is bubbling, and within a few more seconds after that, I've burnt a hole through it the width of my index finger. Dropping the can and returning the lighter to my black satchel, I remove the lock from the gate by lifting it from the still cool bottom. Then, lifting the latch on the gate, I swing it open and step inside.

That's when I feel my cell phone vibrating in my coat pocket.

Chapter 66

Standing inside the now-open gate on the brick paver pathway, I pull the phone from my pocket. Three texts from Blood have piled up without me noticing. This last one just reads *Answer*.

I want to answer him, but first I check my watch. It's straight-up eleven o'clock. If everything went as it should, the video has just gone viral.

As I shift my attention back to my cell phone, I'm startled by a voice that breaks the silence of the night. A man's shrieking voice.

Bourenhem's voice.

"Heretic!" he shouts. "Backstabbing heretic. He's betrayed me again. Betrayed you and me again."

The voice is coming from the house, but very close by. Not from the upstairs. The kitchen, maybe, just yards away. The voice travels through the plate-glass picture window. It's accompanied by a second voice.

"Calm down, David. What did you expect? Reece Johnston destroying his literary career just because you ask him to? You don't know him like I do. He'd gladly deliver his firstborn to the devil if it would guarantee him a best-selling novel."

The voice is most definitely female, and even though muffled and distorted through the kitchen window, it's somewhat familiar. My heart sinks into my stomach and my pulse beats in my temples. Could the voice be Rachael's? Is the voice the final proof I need to know that my ex-girlfriend has conspired with David to fuck up my life?

Or is the voice Lisa's? Now that I'm actually analyzing it, Lisa's and Rachael's voices...their manner of speaking...aren't all that different. Could Bourenhem and Lisa be working on this horrible plan not only to set me up for crimes I did not commit, including murder, but to ruin my writing career? But the last I saw of Lisa, she was bound with duct tape on her bed. However, maybe the whole scene was playacted for the purposes of luring me into a trap.

Blood boils while the heart pounds.

Pocketing my cell phone, I reach into my satchel, pull out one of the Molotov cocktails, then retrieve the long-necked butane lighter. Why in the world would I set the house ablaze with my family still inside? Why do the very same thing Bourenhem has threatened to do?

The answer has to do with control.

I wrote the book on the subject, not him. I can only assume that he does not want to suffer the agony of burning alive and that he will have no choice but to try to put the fire out once I start it. Soon as that happens, his guard will be down and I will pounce on his ugly head like a hungry lion on raw meat. By tossing the Molotov cocktail through the plate glass window of my out-laws' house, I am fighting fire with fire.

I fire up the lighter, bring the flame to the gasoline-soaked rag. It ignites in a waft of torch-like flame. Then, bending at the knees, I pull up a brick paver from out of the soft soil. Taking a few steps toward the big glass window, I cock back my throwing arm and heave the brick through the plate-glass, shattering it all to hell. I immediately toss in the Molotov cocktail. The explosion of fire that results robs me of my breath.

Reece Johnston, 1.

David Bourenhem, 0.

Chapter 67

A woman screams. Like her life is in danger.

"He's coming after us with fire!" Bourenhem shouts. "It's exactly what I expected."

Pulling another brick from out of the soil, I stand up straight, step back into the darkness.

"Call the fire department," the woman shouts.

"Let's call the police while we're at it," Bourenhem answers sarcastically. Then, "Get me a blanket. We need water. Pots and pans. Big pots. Fill them."

Bourenhem isn't panicking. He's going to attempt to put out the fire, like I knew he would. It means Lisa and Anna will be safe upstairs, that is, if Lisa isn't the woman who is working with him. Shoving the brick into my coat pocket, I begin making my way around to the front of the house. I pull the second Molotov cocktail from the satchel as I go. Standing outside the big floor-to-ceiling glass window wall, I light the rag. As the gas-soaked rag ignites, I pull out the brick, heave it against the center of the glass wall. The brick causes the glass to shatter on contact. Next comes the Molotov cocktail. The big, theater-like drapes behind the shattered glass immediately catch fire as the homemade bomb explodes.

I make a mad dash across the front yard to the home's north side, where the garages are located. It's possible the security-minded Alex changed the code sequence that will open the three overhead garage doors upon my split with his daughter, but it's just as likely it slipped his aging mind. Sliding open the narrow protective steel panel over the keypad embedded into the red brick wall, I punch in 3-18-41. Alex's birthday. The house trembles as all three overhead doors begin to roll up in unison.

That's my cue to pull the third and final gasoline bomb from my satchel.

Lighting it up, I toss it into the center garage bay, listen for the shattering of glass and the explosive spray of ignited liquid. The heat from the explosion slaps me in the face when Victoria's Volvo ignites in the white-hot fire. There's a Mercedes convertible to the left of it and to its right, a red pickup truck. If memory serves me correctly, there will be several cans of gasoline stored inside the garage, plus paint cans, paint thinner, and a dozen cans of aerosol insecticides. It will only be a matter of a few precious minutes before the entire garage explodes.

Punching in the code to lower the overhead doors, I then make my way the few feet to the end of the driveway and back through the open fence gate to the sounds of screams.

Chapter 68

Maybe the last thing Bourenhem wants right now is for the police and the fire department to show up. But their sudden appearance is a distinct possibility. I can only guess that he somehow disengaged the alarm once he had Alex tied and bound. He would have threatened to hurt Anna, Lisa, or even Victoria if Alex didn't provide the code. What I can't be sure of, however, is if the fire department will be alerted to the fire no matter what security channels have been disconnected or disengaged.

All I want to do now is free all three girls and get them to safety—and Alex, too, if he's still alive. Once that mission is accomplished, I'm going to finally have my come-to-Jesus with Bourenhem.

But again it strikes me like a roundhouse to the head, staggers me: What if Lisa has joined up with her former lover?

What if *she's* the source of the female voice I heard coming from the kitchen? What if I walk into that house through the flame and find the two of them together? Do I steal Anna away along with Victoria and Alex and let Lisa and Bourenhem fend for themselves? Or do I save them all and allow the cops to sort it all out later?

But what the hell am I saying?

Bourenhem himself spoke of Rachael. The two lived within a few yards of one another. I saw the shadow of a slim woman up in his apartment window. A small, well-built woman whose proportions would match Rachael's. The woman has got to be her.

The entire house is going up, the heat from the ever-intensifying flames slapping at my face. Maybe starting the place on fire wasn't the smartest of moves. But it was the only move for me.

I know fire.

Fire is my revenge and my weapon of choice. I feel the heat of the flames as it spreads, as it grows, as it feeds on the oxygen. I see the colors change as the materials and chemicals it comes into contact with burn, sizzle, and evaporate. I smell the fumes and I choke, but somehow I feel at peace and in total control. All along I've known precisely where Anna, Lisa, and Vickie are, holed up inside Lisa's second-floor bedroom. By lighting fire to the areas I have chosen on the first floor of the mansion, the flames are unlikely to creep up to their position. At least, not right away.

But then, fire has a nasty habit of getting away from you if you allow it to.

My daughter is inside that burning house and no matter how calculated my moves, it's only a matter of time until things become too dangerous for her. I'm a child of fire, and because I've lived with fire my entire life, I also know this: there isn't a whole lot of time left before a first-floor flash point is achieved and the entire house goes up in flame.

Pulling the .38 from my waist, I ascend the short flight of steps to the kitchen door, throw it open, step into the inferno.

Chapter 69

Half the kitchen area to my right is already consumed with fire, and only a few feet beyond it is the wood door that accesses the garage. I know that at any minute, the gas tanks on the vehicles and the portable gas cans will ignite, setting that portion of the structure ablaze. I make my way through the kitchen and into the attached dining room.

That's when I see Alex.

Bourenhem wasn't bluffing after all. The old man is duct-taped to the far chair at the head of the table, the usual place he occupies as the head of the family during the holiday and family dinners. His entire head and face are burned away, leaving only charred flesh and patches of hair. The lower half of his facial skeleton is exposed, his jaw clamped so tightly his visible white teeth appear to be crushing one another. In the place of eyes are now dark, empty holes.

I try to turn away from him, but I feel sick and my knees go weak. Dizziness sets in and I fear I might faint. The fog of toxic smoke doesn't help. But I have to move. I must get to my family before the garage explodes and my plan backfires and no one makes it out of here alive.

I turn and, covering my eyes with my forearms, sprint out of the dining room, through the burning living room to the vestibule and the wraparound staircase that leads to the second floor. As I take my first step up the stairs, my boot sole never touches the tread before I feel the explosion against the back of my head, and the burning world that surrounds me goes black.

Chapter 70

I awake to smoke and fire.

My world has gone black. I'm certain of the fire that surrounds me only because of the heat and the noise. The roar and the hiss.

My immediate reaction is to reach out with both hands, as if it's possible to clutch fresh air in my grip. Instead I feel nothing but empty space. But then, that's not right, either. My arms can't extend themselves without my hands crashing into something. They crash into wood. No matter how or where I thrust out my hands, they hit wood.

I try to turn myself around, but I can't.

I'm surrounded on all sides by wood.

Then it dawns on me. I'm trapped inside a wood coffin. Bourenhem's coffin.

"Remind you of anything?" comes a voice from outside the box. "It's straight out of *The Damned*. I remember writing the scene. You know, the one where Drew Brennen traps each member of that poor abducted family inside their own personal pine box before setting them ablaze. You remember their names. The Grahams. He stood there and listened to the screams of the Grahams as the boxes went up in glorious flame. Sick scene, even I have to admit, but a fun one to write . . . if I do say so myself."

"David," I shout. "Please. Open this thing up and let's talk this out like men."

"We *are* talking like men, bro. Talking amidst a house fire that's growing quite bad. Dangerously bad. Poor Lisa and Anna."

Something is being poured onto the casket. A liquid. It seeps into the casket through the slim spaces where the wood panels are joined together. It drips onto my face, into my eyes, burning them.

Gasoline.

"Now doesn't this just burn you up, bro?" Bourenhem says with a laugh.

I can barely hear his voice coming through the wood over the roar of the fire, getting louder by the second. Louder and hotter. But I can somehow make out the unmistakable flick of a switch. It's the starter on a lighter. I hear the *poof* sound that accompanies gasoline being ignited with open flame and, quite suddenly, the interior of the casket takes on an eerie red-orange glow.

I'm on fire.

"Catch me by surprise?" Bourenhem shouts. "Let me tell you something. I knew you'd come. And I'm ready for you. Me and the casket from *The Damned*."

I make out the sound of his footsteps. They are moving away from me, ascending the big vestibule staircase. The fire is beginning to consume the pine casket as if it were dry kindling. The heat the casket fire is giving off is almost unbearable. I have maybe a minute before the fire penetrates the interior and starts cooking me like a piece of meat in a broiler.

I push up on the lid. Hard.

It barely budges.

Bourenhem has nailed or maybe even screwed the coffin lid shut. I kick with my legs and feet. But it's the same story. I'm packed into this box tighter than a sardine in a can.

Then it dawns on me that I have a gun. Maybe it will be possible to shoot my way out. Or, at the very least, blow a few holes through the pine. If I can manage that, I can make the fire work for me, rather than against me. Maybe between the fire and the bullets, the wood will weaken enough for me to punch and kick my way through it.

It isn't easy, but I manage to wrest the pistol from the waistband of my pants. Cocking my wrist so that the barrel is pointed up at the casket lid, I fire a three-shot volley. The bullets blast three big holes in the wood. Big enough for me to make out the fire on the other side.

I have maybe a few seconds left before I burn. Stuffing the pistol back into my pants, I begin punching the burning lid. I punch hard and fast against the weakened wood, and it begins to break and bulge. Then it shatters into so much scrap. Brushing the burning embers from my face, I gather up all the strength I have left and leap out of the burning coffin.

Chapter 71

Heart pumping, brain on fire, I take the stairs two at a time, until I arrive at the top of the landing.

"Lisa!" I shout. "Anna!"

The upper floor isn't burning yet, but the smoke is getting thick, telling me the fire is creeping its way up the walls, and just a moment away from consuming the bedrooms. The revolver poised before me, I pass by the bathroom and then enter Lisa's bedroom, where I release a breath and lower the .38, try to comprehend what it is I'm looking at.

I don't see three people sitting on Lisa's bed. I see four.

Lisa, Anna, Victoria, and one more.

David Bourenhem.

An unbound and unconcerned Bourenhem peers up at me with wide eyes framed in rectangular lenses, his gasoline-filled Super Soaker resting in his lap. The three females laid out beside him are bound at the wrists and ankles with duct tape. They aren't reacting to my sudden presence. They seem to be out cold. Dead to the world that burns all around them.

My beating heart despairs.

"What the hell have you done to them?" I say, once more raising up the .38, aiming the short black barrel at Bourenhem's smiling face.

"Easy does it, bro," he says without showing even the slightest sign of fear. "First of all, allow me to congratulate you on your heroic escape from the burning-coffin portion of tonight's program. What a great circus act we are. Second, as for the girls, I've injected them with a sedative so that they won't feel the pain when the flames come for them." He smiles brightly. "Least I can do."

He's wearing black leather gloves that look similar to my own. The gloves explain why Bourenhem keeps swearing that it won't be his prints that are found all over the house once the police begin to investigate, but my own. I was here just a few hours ago. My fingerprints can be found downstairs and up.

Reaching into the breast pocket of his short-sleeve button-down, Lisa's ex produces an iPhone. He thumbs several commands, then turns the phone around so that I can see what he's playing. It's the video I made a short while ago. The video that apparently has just gone viral. I see my face and I hear the words that come from my mouth. I'm talking about David Bourenhem and I'm calling him a criminal. I'm telling the world how he has kidnapped my family, how he's holding them hostage in Lisa's parents' house, how it's possible he's already killed my ex-father-in-law with fire and how he could very well kill my daughter. I'm talking about his obsession with Lisa and how all he wants now is to destroy me.

"You went and did it," he says with a smile. "You betrayed us all again and, like the true heretic that you are, told the world a pack of lies. Now the police will be here at any moment."

"And they're going to bust your sorry ass."

"But don't you see, my bro? It's you they will be arresting. When they discover the truth about what you've done, what you've stolen from me, and how in the end you went crazy because of it, they won't have any choice but to lock you up forever. Hell, they might even slap you with the death penalty. If only they still burned heretics at the stake."

The fire is getting thicker as the flames rising up from the downstairs intensify with each passing second. In the back and front of my mind, I know the garage on the other side of the house is eventually going to ignite and perhaps even blow sky high. But when?

Burn him! Burn him! Burn Bourenhem!

Bourenhem pockets his phone, then sets his free hand on top of Anna's head. He pets her gently.

"Gonna be a shame to see her burn," he says, taking on a frown. "You know, I consider her my one and only daughter. I was twice the father you could ever hope to be. You were off half-drunk, or half-crazy, or staring at a blank screen while incessantly flicking your Bic lighter."

I thumb back the revolver hammer. "Shut up," I say. "Shut up or you're dead."

"Sure, shoot me, Reecey Pieces. But you don't want to shoot me. You want to see me burn so badly you can feel it. Taste it. Burning things is like sex to you. Either way, it won't change a thing. You stole my book and now you're going to steal the lives of these precious people. And for what? Your career? Your fortune and fame?"

"If I stole your story, then why not go public with it years ago? Why go through all this madness?"

"Who would have believed me? By the time the damage was done, you were the great Reece Johnston, best-selling author of *The Damned*, and I would have been just another crazy wannabe spreading a false story about how *you* plagiarized from *me*. You know how many famous authors have had to appear in court to defend the originality of their precious gems? Even the great one, Papa Hemingway, had to show up in court once."

"So you resort to murder."

"Not me, cowboy. You." Cupping his right hand behind one ear. "In fact, what's that I'm hearing right now? Could that be the sound of police sirens? I think it is." He slides off the side of the bed, that Super Soaker still gripped in his hand. "Darling artist!" he calls out. "Maybe it's time we took our leave before this place burns to the ground and the police pull in the driveway. Whichever comes first."

Darling artist?

I hear boot steps on the hallway floor. Turning, I recognize the face and body of a woman I once knew intimately. Rachael, my ex-girlfriend. The woman who broke up with me over my unceasing love for Lisa. Over my burning obsession.

The question has finally been answered.

Rachael and David have teamed up to kill me and my family.

Chapter 72

"Hello, Heretic," Rachael says.

She's staring into me with piercing blue eyes. Eyes I fell in love with, once upon a time, when getting back together with Lisa seemed like a long-lost dream. Her blonde, shoulder-length hair drapes her narrow face, and the thick gray turtleneck she wears with her jeans makes her already tight, pale face even tighter. Like it's about to implode at any moment.

"How's it feel to be paying for your sins?" she adds.

"Never took you for the religious type, Rache," I say, my .38 still aimed at Bourenhem, the heat, smoke, and noise from the fire creeping its way up the walls from the first floor and growing stronger by the second. She raises her red-gloved left hand and points an automatic at me. Another surprise, since Rachael abhors guns of all kinds. But like an old firearms pro, she keeps the muzzle leveled at my torso as she brushes past me on her way to the spot where Bourenhem sits beside my girls. "And would you look at that?" I go on. "A proud new member of the NRA. Wow, you've really changed, Rache. You still painting? Or you give that up for target shooting at the gun club?"

"On the contrary, Heretic. I've been painting lots and lots, now that you aren't around to suck the life from me."

Rachael never could get used to balancing a love affair with her desire to make art. She always felt that by spending too much time in her studio, she would be leaving me alone to my devices, which, in her mind, had to include my seeing other women. But nothing could have been further from the truth.

Rachael the artist.

It hits me then. The chalkboard drawing at Lisa's house.

"That was your work on Lisa's chalkboard," I say, recalling the earring I found stuck inside Anna's piano lesson book. Rachael's earring. "My head getting blown to smithereens. My God, Rachael, you haven't lost your touch. Christ, I should have recognized your style."

"Cut the chatter, Reece," she says. "Case you haven't noticed, the house is burning down all around us."

"Fire doesn't bother me. Remember?"

"Yes, how could I forget? Fire gives you a major hard-on."

My eyes shift in turn from Bourenhem to my family laid out on the bed to Rachael.

"What is it you want," I ask her, "besides being convicted of multiple first-degree homicides like your psycho friend, David, here?"

She laughs bitterly. "Psycho? That's turning the tables just a little now, isn't it?"

"My psychosis is entirely under control. Unlike yours, apparently. So how are your hands feeling after beating the crap out of him this afternoon so that it looked like I went ballistic on him?"

She lifts up her free hand, makes an arcing, sweeping gesture with it.

"My hands are just fine," she says. "Brass knuckles will do wonders when utilized properly. But this burning house proves that your pyromania is alive and well and not so fine."

I could argue that the equally pyromaniacal Bourenhem just torched Alex to death, but the war of words is getting old and the fire is growing deadly.

"I'll say it again, Rachael. What the fuck do you want from me? Quickly. Before we all die in a particularly uncomfortable way."

"I want an apology."

Jesus, not again. Not another apology. Have she and Bourenhem scripted their dialogue together? Maybe that's what they were doing up inside his apartment earlier this evening.

The sirens are in the near distance now. The smoke that's been rising up from the downstairs is growing so thick it's getting nearly impossible to breathe. Lying on the bed unconscious are three generations of Reynolds women. If they breathe in enough of the toxic smoke and fumes, they will die in their sleep, just like Bourenhem said they would.

"That's what you want? An apology?" I say. "That's what your friend wanted."

I shoot David another glance. He smiles, runs the tips of his fingers up and down the smooth plastic of the Super Soaker, like it's his little baby. Turning back to Rachael, I see that she's staring at me, unblinking. Staring into me.

"Apologize for betraying me," she insists. "You already apologized to him. Now it's my turn."

"We're all going to die together inside this house," I say.

Sirens. Sirens, smoke, and now flames rising up the wall to my left, which tells me the fire has crept up the vestibule staircase and entered the second-floor hallway.

"Then we all die in this house," she says. "Apologize for betraying me, Heretic. Betraying us all."

I steal another glance at Bourenhem, my gun trained on him while Rachael's is trained on me, that big smile still planted on his face like he's looking forward to burning to death. I feel the sweat running down my forehead into my eyes along with the smoke, making them sting. The smoke invading my mouth and nostrils is causing the back of my throat to feel like it's disintegrating in acid. Behind me, out in the hall, the fire is rumbling, sizzling, singing, getting ready to roar. What the hell choice do I have?

"I'm sorry, Rachael. I never meant to hurt you."

That's when the garage explodes.

Chapter 73

The entire Reynolds mansion shudders.

Rachael falls backward into a giant fissure that's suddenly appeared in the portion of floor directly behind her as the wooden bearing beam underneath splits in two across its center. My feet slip out from under me and I go down onto my back, the .38 dropping out of my hand on impact. The entire garage side of the house disappears like a giant claw has ripped it away. Rachael vanishes into the smoke-filled, burning rubble while the bedroom floor assumes a sharp angle downward. Bourenhem rolls out of the bed, but somehow the three girls are still planted on the mattress.

Bourenhem is down on his knees. He lunges for the gun, grabs it with his left hand. Reaching out with my right, I grab hold of his left wrist. But it's all wrong because the muzzle is pointing at me, its blackness filled with death. I shift my head sharply to the left at the precise moment he triggers off a shot.

Rising up onto my knees, fighting for balance against the severe angle of the floor, I slam his hand and the gun it holds onto the floor. The gun pops out. He lunges forward, head-butts me in the face. I rear back, spin around, and drop down onto my chest, my head pounding and spinning, electric-white stars flashing before my eyes. He's on me then, sticking two fingers up into my nostrils, yanking my head around and punching me in the face. One driving punch after the other. His hands must be breaking as his fisted, gloved knuckles make contact with the bones in my face and head. I never would have guessed he had so much fight in him.

"My book!" he screams. "My book. The one thing that was mine." Another slam to my face. "You stole it from me. You stole my fucking life!" Another. "So I took Lisa. So you'd suffer whenever you thought of me fucking her." Another.

He keeps on hitting me; he'll beat me to death before I burn him to kingdom come. Or maybe not. Out of the corner of my eye, I see the fire creeping up what's left of the bedroom wall. It's spreading along the now-angled bedroom floor, the carpeting catching fire. The room is going to flash and when it does, all of us are dead. I need to get Bourenhem off of me, but I can't move myself. He's beaten me. He's exacted his revenge, even if that revenge will result in his own suicide.

But then suddenly he stops punching me. Heaving out a breath, he reaches down with his bloody hand for the .38. I'm paralyzed and powerless to do anything about it as he picks the piece up off the angled floor and presses the short, hot barrel against my forehead.

"Own it," he whispers, his voice almost inaudible against the roar of the fire that is now consuming the entire bedroom floor, walls, and ceiling. "Just say it. You stole my manuscript."

I look into his black, eyeglass-covered eyes. Eyes that reflect the fire. His thick black hair is sticking up in two separate waves above each earlobe, his mouth gaping open, exposing two sharp incisors. I know he is going to kill me. But I don't intend on meeting my maker having lied as my final act on earth.

"Go to hell," I say, at the exact moment David Bourenhem bursts into flames.

Chapter 74

His scream comes from a place buried so deep inside his tortured soul that it sounds almost inhuman. His eyeglasses melt off his face, the black plastic running down his nose and lips. Then his facial skin shrivels and shrinks as it burns and melts from his skull. The gun drops from his hand, the black glove and the skin that covers the bones on his hand still grasping it. His arms retract, his still intact hand forming a fist as he falls to the side and assumes a fetal position while the fire consumes his flesh entirely.

Leaning up, I gaze upon the bed, and I see that Lisa has somehow sat herself up. She's got Bourenhem's Super Soaker gripped in both her hands. The effects of the sedation must have worn off. She must have then somehow come free of the duct tape and fired the gasoline spray directly at her ex's back.

The fire surrounds us.

If we don't all exit the bedroom right now, we'll all burn up just like David.

"We need to go!" I shout above the roar of the encroaching flames, my energy and will to live suddenly restored.

"Where?" Lisa screams, looking wildly around us. "The flames!" She's right. They're surrounding us. We're trapped inside a broiler oven.

"We have to try," I shout while ripping away the duct tape that binds Anna's ankles and wrists. "Try and wake your mother, Lisa," I add, grabbing Anna in my arms and then placing her in a fireman's hold over my right shoulder so that her chin rests against my back.

Lisa tosses the Super Soaker to the floor and tears away the duct tape that binds her mother. Using my free hand, I grab hold of Victoria's left hand and pull her up and off the bed. She's so unsteady from the toxic fumes and the sedative that she would fall back onto the bed if not for me holding on to her.

"Grab her other hand, Leese," I say, "and do what I do." That's when I pull us all through the curtain of flame in the bedroom doorway.

The hallway is burning, but it's not entirely engulfed in flame.

"The staircase is on fire," Lisa cries. "We won't make it."

Like the hallway we've just entered, only one side of the staircase is on fire.

"Hug the right-hand railing and go down fast," I insist, letting go of Victoria's hand. "You can make it. You hear me, Lisa? You and your mother can make it. You have to make it. No choice." Then, sliding Anna off my shoulder and settling her into both my arms, I cradle her like she's still a baby. She's semiconscious now and agitated, trying to free herself from my tight hold. "Listen, Anna, we have to make a run through the fire. I do not want you to breathe. You understand? When I give you the order, I want you to close your mouth and your eyes, and don't breathe in. You got it? Do not take a breath."

Something miraculous happens then. A hard tubular spray of water shoots against the staircase, temporarily dousing some of the flames, but not all of them. Looking down onto the vestibule floor I see an oxygen-masked fireman manning the hose and another holding a fireman's axe.

"Go!" I shout. "Go now, Lisa! While you have the chance!"

Clutching her mother with both her arms, Lisa manages to guide Victoria down the stairs. As soon as they hit the landing, I see the fireman with the axe pull the two women out of the burning mansion and to safety.

From where I'm standing at the top of the landing, I feel the heat from the hallway fire growing more intense as the entire space fills with flame. I see the two-story interior wall behind the remaining fireman become entirely engulfed, the fire spreading up onto the ceiling.

Despite the spray of the water against the staircase, the fire is still growing. Still getting hotter. Still spreading. I know precisely what the immediate future holds.

"Get out!" I shout out to the fireman below. "It's going to flash!"

Before I can get the words out of my mouth, the entire vestibule explodes in a blaze of white-hot heat, blowing the fireman out through the shattered wall onto his back, and then I see nothing at all.

Chapter 75

I see myself driving. I'm driving the highway south to New York City for NoirExpo 2006, when suddenly the sensation hits me over the head like the fat end of a baseball bat. A cold wind blows through my body.

"Lisa," I whisper aloud. "You're not alone."

Up ahead is an exit. I take it, then sweep over the overpass and accelerate back onto the highway going the opposite direction. I make the fifty miles back home in less than an hour, all the time my head filled with visions of Lisa and her new friend, David, together. I push the Jeep and I smoke cigarette after cigarette and I trigger a tall flame on my lighter until the fuel is gone.

When I arrive in the driveway of the house, his Honda 4x4 is there, just like I knew it would be. Before getting out of the Jeep, I grab my 9mm from the glove box, and I carry it with me to the back door off the kitchen. I ease open the door, step into the kitchen, and hear the noise coming from all the way upstairs in the bedroom. Moans and groans of pleasure. I hear voices. Passionate voices. Quietly racking a round into the chamber, I take the stairs slowly, one at a time, until I reach the landing. Then, I walk the length of the empty hall until I come to the master bedroom. The bedroom I share with my wife.

I throw open the door, aim the weapon dead center at the man and woman locked in an embrace on my bed . . .

When I come to, I see that Anna and I are down on the floor of the landing. Anna's big brown eyes are wide, glazed with shock. I must have been knocked out for only a few short seconds. Precious seconds. The fire rages all around us in a white-hot, red glow. For a brief moment, I'm convinced we are about to suffer the same death as my mother and brothers. But I can't let that happen to us. Can't allow it to happen to Anna. I have to at least try to save her, even if it means burning my entire body while doing it.

Getting myself back up onto my knees, I once more pick her up and toss her over my shoulder. Her blouse has caught fire, and I pat it out with my free hand. Looking down, I can see that the staircase is aflame, but the very center of the treads is free of fire. It's our only hope.

"Anna, close your eyes! Close your mouth! Do not breathe! You hear me? Do not breathe!"

The roar of the fire might be deafening, but her sobs are louder. She's squirming now, as though trying to free herself from my hold. But where the hell would she go? There's nowhere to go. We're trapped inside this house ablaze. We have no choice but to make a run through the fire. It's either that, or stand here and die.

"Please, baby, please!" I shout. "Close your eyes and do not breathe!"

With Anna over my shoulder, I begin to descend the stairs, on our way down through the fire. Through hell on earth.

Chapter 76

At the bottom of the stairs, I sprint outside and hand off Anna to a fireman who immediately slaps an oxygen mask on her face and wraps a fire-resistant blanket around her torso. A second fireman puts a mask on my face, strapping it to my head while wrapping a blanket around my shoulders.

"You damned fool," he barks through his own mask. "You're lucky you didn't light up like a matchstick. You should have waited for us to come get you."

"We would have burned alive," I want to say, if only I can work up the words through my tar- and smoke-clogged throat. I might be in pain, but I feel a wave of relief wash over me knowing that Anna hasn't suffered any serious burns and neither have I. I have known fire all my life and now, I no longer want anything to do with it.

Sucking in a deep breath of the fresh oxygen, I cough the smoke from my lungs like a rescued drowning man purges water. Eyes tearing, lungs feeling scraped and fried, it takes me a few minutes to get my breath back. But when I do, I pull off the mask and wipe the smoke-induced tears from my eyes with the backs of my soot-covered gloves and I make out the many police cruisers, EMS vans, and fire trucks that occupy the front lawn. In the near distance I can see an EMT crew bathed in bright white spotlight working on Lisa, Victoria, and Anna. There's also a crowd of reporters who have set up a perimeter just in front of the tall trees at the far edge of the property's north end.

A hand comes down on my right shoulder. Detective Miller.

"You okay?" he says.

"It's all right. I . . . my family . . . I think we're okay now."

The lean, trench-coated detective purses his lips, nods. "Listen, I know this is a hell of a time to ask," he says. "But I need to have a word with you. Alone."

"I understand. Alone."

"My car is up there," he says, walking on toward the top of the estate's private drive.

Following him, I see Lisa, Anna, and Victoria drenched in the light pouring out of the many portable lamps that have been set up all along the property. Lisa is clutching Anna in her arms, the two of them sitting on the back bumper of an EMS van. Anna might be crying, but she appears to be unharmed. I see Victoria seated beside them on the same bumper. She's cradling her head in her hands, sobbing over the loss of her husband. I never did get along very well with Alex, but right now I feel her pain like I feel the pounding of my heart inside my chest. If it weren't for Miller wanting to see me up close and personal right now, I would go to my wife and daughter, wrap my arms around them, and never let go.

Set beside a second EMS van are two gurneys, each of them supporting a single body. I can only assume that the gurney furthest from me contains Alex's body. The black rubber sheet that hides the body glistens in both the stark artificial lamplight and the warm, almost pleasant orange glow of the house fire. The second gurney, closer to me, holds Rachael's body. I know this for certain because her right foot is exposed under the rubber sheet. She's wearing the brown leather boots I bought her in New York during a beautiful fall weekend we spent there together not all that long ago. Back when I loved her and she loved me and I was trying to put my love for Lisa behind me, but not succeeding.

My love for Lisa would kill my relationship with Rachael, and it would die a very ugly death. A death so ugly it somehow drove her to partner up with David Bourenhem, and together they would have killed my family by fire if only I hadn't brought the fire to them first. Yet somehow, I look at the booted foot and, for some reason unexplained, I feel my eyes well up with tears. The sad fact of the matter is this: Rachael chose the wrong man. And I chose the wrong woman. But then, any woman I could have chosen after Lisa and I broke up would have been wrong. You can't give your love over entirely when you are still in love with another.

Pulling my eyes away from Rachael, I close in on Miller's car, then sense something happening behind me. Turning around, I see yet another gurney being wheeled out of the still-burning house. This one no doubt contains Bourenhem's body. Unlike my reaction with Rachael, I feel no remorse over his death.

Only profound relief.

———⌣———

Miller holds the car's rear passenger-side door open for me, and as I sit myself down inside, I realize for the first time that night how exhausted I am. He comes around the back of the vehicle, opens the other rear door, and settles down across from me with a profound exhale. Aside from his gray trench coat, he's wearing a blue blazer and, as usual, the knot on his necktie is perfect. He doesn't look at me, but straight ahead, over the front seat and out through the windshield at the organized chaos that is presently orbiting the hopelessly burning mansion.

"This might sound strange," he says after a time, "but fire can really be a beautiful thing."

"Beauty and the killer beast," I say.

"I apologize for suspecting you all along."

"I was set up. Or better yet, caught in a trap. You see the truth now, don't you, Detective Miller? See it in the fire?"

"Yes," he says. "Your prints were all over everything at Lisa's house. There was no sign of forced entry, Reece. Later on, when that woman showed up in the river, most of her body burned beyond recognition, her home address just a few doors down from your ex-wife's and a nice little burn spot on the back lawn, well . . ." He lets the thought trail off, then turns to face me. "Well, I assumed wrong, and you paid the price. Your family has paid the price."

"The woman laid out on that gurney," I say, after a beat. "It's Rachael. My ex-girlfriend. You remember I told you about her? Our breakup? That's her. She was working with Bourenhem all along, it turns out, and together they nearly succeeded in destroying me, my art, and my girls."

Miller nods, taking this in.

"This might sound strange," Miller says a bit under his breath. "But in a small way, I can't blame her for being so upset with you. If you loved Lisa so much, then why hang on to Rachael for so long? Why not just let her go before you caused her too much pain?"

The tears once more press themselves against the backs of my eyeballs. Miller is right, and he knows it. There might be no forgiving Rachael for what she did to my family today and tonight, but the entirety of the blame does not rest upon her soul.

"Why didn't I leave her before I caused her too much pain?" I say. "Maybe I just didn't want to be alone."

"Maybe after you and Lisa got back together you should have left town, picked up somewhere else."

We sit and watch the fire for a minute like we're Boy Scouts gathered 'round the campfire. But we're not Boy Scouts. We're not that good. But there was a time when watching fire, any fire, would have had the effect of calming me down. Now, I'm watching the last remnants of the Reynoldses' house burn to the ground and I don't feel the least bit good about it or myself. I don't feel good inside. I feel only sadness. Maybe what I had inside me for so many years, the burning desire for fire, has finally been doused. Maybe in facing down Bourenhem and Rachael, I've somehow come to terms with the deaths of my mother and my two older brothers. Maybe I will be able to finally erase the sadness that I automatically feel for my dad whenever I recall his desolate face on the morning he lost his family to fire.

"Bourenhem would have gotten to me . . . to *us* . . . one way or another," I say. "So would have Rachael."

In my head, I once more see the shadowy figure of a woman standing before Bourenhem's First Street apartment window in Troy, the two of them arguing. Arguing about precisely how they were going to exact their ultimate revenge on me, the heretic.

"Did either of them show any signs of violence before today? Tonight?" Miller poses.

"I can't speak for Bourenhem. As for Rachael, she had her bouts of jealousy. If I even looked at another woman, she'd get upset. Like you said, I was causing her pain. More pain than I realized."

"She ever hit you? Threaten you with a weapon?"

I shake my head. "Not at all."

"In the end, did you break up with her?"

"No, she broke up with me."

"Doesn't make sense. If she broke up with you, why all this?"

"Like I told you, she broke up with me because I was still in love with Lisa. Not because she didn't love me anymore."

He nods. "She couldn't compete with your love for your ex, so she ditched you, thinking that would solve everything." He cocks his head at me. "Bad breakup?"

"Thought she'd kill me. Tear my eyeballs out."

There's a beat, and then both of us laugh. But nothing's funny.

"Well, there you go," Miller says. "That only made her angrier, and her frustrations festered."

Both of us look off at the inferno, the flashing fire department and EMS vehicle lights lighting up the smoke. "So this was all because of a bad breakup," I say.

"Bad breakups. Plural. I'll say it again. You, Lisa, and Anna should have left town."

"Right," I say. "Too late now."

"But Bourenhem was angry with you for something else. He called you a heretic."

I clear my throat of some lingering smoke and look at him. "He claims, or claimed, that I stole his manuscript, *The Damned*."

"My favorite Reece Johnston novel," he says with a grin.

"I've written four others that have seen print."

"None of them as good as that one, Reece. My humble opinion, of course."

My stomach tightens. He's right, and everyone knows it. And I still can't picture myself actually sitting down and writing that first book.

"*The Damned* is crazy and violent as all hell," he says. "Stays with you, whether you want it to or not, like a bad dream. Totally different animal from your other books." He's eyeing me. "If books had fingerprints . . ." He trails off.

"You're not suggesting . . . " I never finish the sentence because he knows full well what I'm getting at. I breathe in, smell the stale, smoky odor of the car. Exhale.

Reaching out, Miller pats my leg, shoots me a wink. It's like he's trying to tell me he believes I'm not capable of plagiarism. But on the other hand, he's not entirely convinced.

"Listen," he says, "it's been a day we'd all rather forget. Your family needs you and in the end, you're lucky to have them back. Go to them."

In my brain I see Bourenhem on fire in Lisa's bedroom, and I see Rachael falling off the side of the destroyed house into the fire and the rubble. Still, I'm having trouble believing they are both dead.

I open the door, get out.

"Reece," Miller calls out, leaning over the seat toward the open door. "Remember, don't go anywhere. We'll need you and Lisa for statements."

"Sure thing," I say, closing the door behind me. I lean down and say through the open window, "I have nowhere to go now other than home."

"Where's your home?"

"With Lisa and Anna."

"Couldn't have written it better myself."

I walk on toward my family as the fire within me and the fire that consumes Lisa's childhood home finally begin to burn out.

Chapter 77

Victoria is sedated and taken away in an ambulance to the Albany Medical Center, where she will remain for observation until cleared to return home by her doctor. Problem is, she won't have a home to come to when she's cleared.

I find Lisa seated in the back of an EMS van, where a medical tech is placing a gauze bandage on a small burn on her left forearm. Anna occupies a piece of empty lawn just ten or so feet away from us. She's wearing a fireman's helmet that one of the firefighters has let her borrow, and now she's running around with it on, running in and out of the white spotlight.

"Now you see me," she sings, while jumping in front of the light, "and now you don't." Then she jumps out and away from the light, into the darkness.

Just moments ago, Anna was facing down a death by fire, and now she's playing, like her immediate past occurred a century or more ago. The power of little kids' minds. The power of innocence, youth, and the ability to forget. If only I could have forgotten about the fire. If only I could have let it go.

"Does it hurt, Leese?" I say to my ex-wife while standing outside the EMS van.

She turns slowly, purses her lips. "Only when I laugh," she says. "Well, after today, I'm sure it won't hurt a bit. For a little while, anyway."

Lisa thanks the EMT and climbs out of the vehicle. Without saying a single word, she approaches me, wraps her arms around me. She holds me tightly.

"I'm so sorry," she says.

"For what? You're the one who lost her father."

She lets loose with a sob and holds me tight. I hold her just as tight and let her cry it out. Finally, she pulls back just a little, says into my ear, "I'm sorry for everything. I never should have allowed David back into my life like that. I thought we could be friends. And yes, before you ask me, I gave him a key to the place in a moment of weakness. I trust him, or trusted him. I saw no reason not to go on trusting him as a friend and as someone who was very, very close to Anna. But I was wrong. I never realized just how sick he was and what a threat he had become. I just never saw it coming. Will you ever forgive me?"

I feel her tears. They're running down her cheek and my cheek where they are joined together. It's not hard to see that she is truly sorry for what's happened. But something dawns on me at the same time.

Gently I break away from her so I can look her directly in the eyes.

"You knew David was having trouble? That he was sick?"

She wipes the tears from her face with the backs of her hands. She nods, regretfully.

"Yes, I knew," she admits. "You writers. You will literally drive yourselves to the edge of sanity to get what you want. David went too far with his obsession over your success. Now this." With an open hand she gestures at the smoldering fire. A fire that was begun not by Bourenhem but by me, fighting fire with fire. "I wonder what my attraction to writers is all about?" she adds, not without a bitter laugh.

"Had he been diagnosed with pyromania or something like it?"

She shakes her head. "Not officially, like in your case. I'm not even sure his problem was fire, necessarily. But it doesn't take a rocket scientist to spot depression, obsession, anger, and psychosis. He was seeing someone. A professional. I even paid for the sessions for a while. Then he stopped going. Soon after that, you came back into my life and I broke up with him for good."

"But you knew he was mentally unstable and still you gave him a key after having the locks changed?" It's a question I pose while recalling the many books of mine stacked on his apartment shelves, the pine casket lifted right out of *The Damned*.

"Yes, I knew he was growing unstable. But not dangerously so. Or maybe I just didn't want to believe it."

"He seemed so sweet," I say, putting her own words back in her mouth. "He wouldn't hurt a fly."

"Yes, I truly believed that. The last thing I ever thought David was capable of was hurting another human being. And I mean that with all my heart, Reece."

She's tearing up again. Now is not the time to keep on pushing her about Bourenhem's psychosis and her decision to grant him access to her keys. What difference does any of it make at this point anyway? He's dead.

Once more I look into her wet eyes. Eyes that are swelled, the sockets slightly black and blue from the tear duct surgery.

"They look better," I say. "They really do."

"What looks better?"

"Your eyes. The doc did a good job. No more excessive tearing."

"Oh damn," she says, placing both hands to her cheeks. "I've forgotten about my eyes. I'm supposed to be on my back icing them."

"Don't worry. Now that this is all over, we'll get you home and get you some ice cubes. Your eyes aren't the only thing that needs healing right now."

I pull her back into me and once more hold her tightly. Over her shoulder, I look at the EMS vans, at the cop cruisers, at the gathering of reporters and nosy neighbors. I look at the dark woods off in the distance. That's when a wave of ice-cold water washes over me.

I pull away from Lisa.

"For the love of God," I say. "Anna . . . Anna is gone."

Chapter 78

Lisa turns in the direction of the EMS vans. She looks one way and then the other. Anna is nowhere to be seen.

"I told her to sit right there and not move an inch," she says, pointing to the back of the first van, the doors to which are wide open, the interior light shining down on the now-empty back bumper. "But then she ran off to play with the firemen."

"Anna!" I shout.

But I get nothing in return.

I take a step forward, toward the second van that's parked further away in the semidarkness. I spot three gurneys set beside it. Two of the gurneys still support bodies. The third one, however, is empty.

"Rachael," I say. "Rachael took Anna."

I'm running toward the burning house and the police who are still working the exterior scene. I find Burly Cop standing beside Miller while the detective talks into his cell phone pressed up against his right ear.

"Anna's gone," I bark. "So is Rachael."

Miller tells whoever he's talking to that he's got to call them back.

"That's impossible. Rachael's dead," he says, pocketing his cell phone.

"No she's not and she's got Anna." I'm shouting now. "Look at the gurney."

He does, then turns to Burly Cop. "Round up your men and search the property perimeter. We have a possible abduction and murder suspect fleeing the scene. A very *alive* suspect."

Weapons and Maglites drawn, a team of cops begin searching for my daughter in the woods that create the private perimeter beyond the iron fence around both sides and the back of the Reynoldses' estate. A second team of officers enter through the open back gate to start searching the big backyard and pool area. Pulling his cell phone back out, Miller calls in an official AMBER Alert to APD dispatch.

"Go to your wife," he insists. "She needs you." It's the first time he hasn't referred to Lisa as my ex-wife.

I see Lisa standing there all alone, her arms tightly crossed over her chest, the tears streaming from her tender eyes. Part of me wants to go to her, comfort her. But another part of me wants to head into the woods along with the cops. I want to put this thing with Rachael right, once and for all. To do that, I will steal back my daughter first, then I will take hold of Rachael's neck with my two bare hands and break it.

I'm about to head into the dark woods beyond the southern perimeter of the front lawn when I hear her ravaged voice.

"Don't come any closer," Rachael insists. "Or I swear I'll slice her open."

Chapter 79

All time stops dead as Rachael appears from out of the woods, holding on to my little girl.

Rachael has Anna in a choke hold with one arm and with the other she's holding something up against Anna's frightened, tearstrewn face. Miller shines his Maglite onto them and in the bright white beam I can plainly see that the object is a gleaming silver carving knife.

Fire has reduced Rachael's clothing to charred and tattered rags. Her hair is completely burned away. The left side of her face is burned almost beyond recognition, while the other side appears to be untouched. Her black bikini underwear is visible, and from the way she's limping, she's suffered a break in her left foot or ankle. How she was mistaken for dead is beyond me, but I suppose the firemen had no choice but to work swiftly. Unconscious and as badly burned as she is, it would've been easy enough to mistake her for dead. She still looks dead, like a zombie with a death grip on my daughter.

I can see Rachael's one remaining blue eye peering not at me, but into me. Into my heart and soul.

"You took something from me, Reece," she says. "You stole my life and now I'm going to steal something from you. Do you understand me? I'm going to cut your daughter's neck and I'm going to paint the earth with her blood. It will be my dying masterpiece, and I will dedicate it to you."

She positions the knife so that it's pointed directly at Anna's neck. She's about to plunge the knife through it.

"No!" Lisa screams.

I lunge forward, as if it's possible to tackle her from a distance of twenty or more feet away.

Then a gunshot rings out.

Chapter 80

An exit wound almost magically appears close to the center of Rachael's forehead. It's about the size of a charcoal briquette. She wobbles for a moment, her one eye still locked on mine. The knife falls from her hand as she issues me the slightest of smiles on the portion of mouth that still functions. Her lips move in a way that says *I still love you* only an instant before she collapses onto her face.

Anna screams and runs for her mother, who is already running toward her.

"I'm coming out," comes the deep voice of a man.

It's Blood stepping from the woods.

Dressed entirely in black, he blended perfectly into the woods' darkness. He's holding high over his head the automatic he just used to kill Rachael, surrendering.

Blood is one hell of a shot.

Miller jogs over to him, gesturing at the other cops to stand down and hold their fire. "I've got this," he insists. He retrieves the automatic from Blood, whose hands are still held high.

I take a few steps forward, so that I'm standing only a few feet away from the Sentinel of Sherman Street. "How will I ever thank you, Blood?" I say.

"You don't," he says. "We got one another's backs, you know that. But you might answer your text messages now and then."

"I've got to book you, Blood," Miller says. "You know that, right?"

"You got a job to do, Detective," Blood says, now lowering his hands and positioning them behind his back so that Miller can cuff him. "So by all means, proceed. Bail cash will be no problem and by then the charges will be dropped. Can't say I'm comfortable with shooting a woman in the back of the head. But it had to be done."

Miller cuffs him, then turns to Burly Cop. "Take him downtown and put him in my office," he instructs.

Burly Cop nods. "Come on, Blood. Looks like I'm giving you a lift."

"We stop for coffee on the way? Me being a hero and all."

"You buying?"

"You cops all the same," Blood says, throwing me a wink. "Don't worry 'bout nothing, Reece," he adds. "You all safe now."

I feel hot blood rushing through my veins, my heart throbbing. It's been the longest day and night of my life. Sad to say, as guilty as Rachael and David were, I know I'm not without my own guilt. Bourenhem was right. I did want to see him burn, and I did get pleasure out of seeing it happen. Real, physical pleasure. That's also how the world works. How it sadly and tragically works.

That's a fact that will burn in my soul for the rest of my days.

Chapter 81

Four days later the three of us return to Lisa's house. We've just buried her father at the Albany Rural Cemetery and returned Victoria to the new apartment we've secured her at one of those brand-new high-end senior living communities that are springing up all over upstate New York these days.

While Anna cradles Frankie in her arms and immediately proceeds to her bedroom along with her headphones and iPod, Lisa kisses me gently on the cheek, tells me she's going to take a very long and sweet nap. "No calls," she insists with a smile. "No interruptions. Not even from God."

"I'll try and control myself," I say.

I stand in the middle of the kitchen floor. The house is quiet but not silent as the familiar sounds of the girls tending to their various relaxing habits in their separate bedrooms fill the warm indoor spaces. The place has been cleaned from top to bottom since the break-in Bourenhem and Rachael partnered up on more than half a week ago. The break-in in which Rachael drew my image on the chalkboard wall, the barrels of a double-barreled shotgun shoved into my mouth and discharged, the back of my head blowing off in a spray of brain, blood, and bone. I should have known then that Rachael had to be involved. The artwork was just too good.

I go to the refrigerator, find a cold beer, and take a deep drink, then wipe the foam from my mouth with the back of my hand and set the can onto the counter. Looking off into the living room, I see a line of paperback novels on the metal bookshelf against the far wall. All five of them are mine. *Drop Dead, Action/Reaction, Death Do Us Part, Killer Be Mine,* and of course, my all-time best seller— the novel that outsells them all combined—*The Damned.*

As my eyes lock on to the spine of the book, the dark background and gray block lettering spelling out *"The Damned"* and "Reece Johnston," I don't feel the small surge of pride I normally do when I eye one of my books. I feel only fear. Like the book no longer belongs to me. Like the book has become a stranger, and a malevolent one at that.

I go to grab hold of my beer again and nearly tip it over. My hand is shaking. In fact, both my hands are trembling. Drawing a deep breath, I try to calm myself down. But then, knowing exactly what it is I have to do, I exhale and walk the few steps to the basement door, like a condemned killer on his way to face a firing squad.

―――――――

Flicking on the light, I descend the stairs into the basement. I go left, make my way over the carpeted floor of Anna's playroom to the laundry room. Stored on the aluminum shelves pushed up against the concrete-block wall beside the washer and dryer are the dozen or so white banker's boxes containing drafts of my manuscripts, each box dated and labeled under both working and final titles.

Swallowing something dry and bitter, I cross the room and stand before the boxes. The banker's box that's set on the very top shelf to the immediate left contains all the drafts of my very first novel. Written not while Lisa and I were married, but after we'd finally separated. How the words suddenly came to me after having been blocked for so long is still a mystery to me. I have absolutely no memory of how I managed my miraculous escape from the writer's-block prison where I would sit down at my keyboard and stare into an eternal whiteness that screamed, "Nada!"

Looking around the room, I locate one of the little wooden chairs that goes to an old tea set Anna used to play with back when she was in kindergarten and I was living somewhere else. I carry the chair over to the shelf and step up onto it, praying it can hold me. It does, long enough for me to pull down the first white box. I step down off the chair, set the heavy, dusty box onto the naked concrete floor, take a knee, and open the lid.

At the very top of the box are several early drafts of *The Damned*, including a copy of the clean "final" version I sent on to my agent who, in turn, sold it to the big publisher in New York for two hundred fifty thousand dollars. I push the final version to one side and pull the top title sheet off one of the early drafts.

There's a sheet of blank white paper underneath it. And a sheet of blank white paper under that, and under that. I pull out a chunk of manuscript from the middle of the book and it, too, is blank.

Shifting my hand to another early draft, I yank off the title sheet and once again find nothing but a stack of white paper. My head spins, and my mouth goes dry. I pull out the final manuscript version, set it onto the floor. Reaching back into the box, I dig through several more sets of blank drafts until I come to yet another, smaller box that's buried at the very bottom. It's a box that houses nearly a full ream of paper. My hands trembling, I pull the lid off the box and stare at the title of the novel and the name of the writer who authored it.

The Damned

by

David Bourenhem

My heart sinks, my eyes fill with tears.

He was right all along. I did betray him. I did betray them all. Most of all, I betrayed myself.

Heretic . . .

"It was the shock treatment," Lisa says from the open laundry room door, sending a shot of hot adrenaline up and down my backbone. "The shock treatment makes you forget. That's why you don't remember stealing the novel. That's why you don't remember any of it, Reece. Your rages, your threats, your power over us both."

I shake my head.

"I don't understand," I whisper, my brain buzzing, burning.

"Of course you don't understand. The shock treatments made you forget so much about the past, you even forgot that you couldn't write anymore." She laughs. But it's a sad, cold laugh. "You did, however, find yourself fully capable of authoring a best seller like *The Damned*, even if you aren't really the man who wrote it."

A single tear runs down my face, falls off my chin onto the manuscript.

"But I did write those other novels, didn't I? Tell me I wrote those other books, Lisa."

"You did, Reece. You did write them."

I nod, expecting a rush of relief that doesn't come. Because it's *The Damned* that matters. "Leese, tell me I wrote it too. Tell me I wrote *The Damned*. That what I'm looking at in this box is all a mistake. Tell me you're lying."

"Think, Reece," she says. "Think real hard. Do you have any recollection at all of writing it?"

I struggle to stand on weakened knees. Grab the dryer for sta-
bility. I try to think. In my head, I see myself writing. But what
I can't see are the fingers on my two hands creating *The Damned*
on the keyboard. It's impossible to relive the experience. I can see
myself writing the novels that followed. But not *The Damned*.
When I attempt to recollect the process, I don't see a man sitting at
his laptop, his fingers pushing the keys that create words and sentences. Instead I see a man pushing the keys on a laptop that copy
exactly the words already typed out on a thick manuscript set beside
him. Maybe that's why I don't recall writing *The Damned*. Maybe I
don't want to remember writing . . . *copying* it. Maybe I've tried to
erase the memory from my mind.

"David wrote *The Damned*," I say.

In my head I see his apartment, the floor littered with manuscripts. Stacks of them. I see his shelves covered with editions of my
novels and no one else's.

I shake my head again, as if the action will help me to accept
the truth.

"That's right, Reece. David wrote *The Damned*, based on the
information I fed him about your pyromania," she goes on. "He
sent it to me to read months after we got reacquainted on Facebook.
You were immediately jealous of him, not because he was falling in
love with me, but because I was reading someone else's novel when
you couldn't write one of your own."

Me, just shaking my head. Still not believing what I'm hearing,
but somehow believing it too.

"I don't remember."

"I know you don't, Reece. The memory has been erased. Either
by the shock treatments, or because you've done your best to erase it."

"But why would he allow me to steal it?"

She exhales, looks down at the floor. "You caught us in an
affair," she says, her voice so low I can barely hear her. She forces

herself to look up at me, to look into my eyes. "You broke into the bedroom. You were supposed to be at a mystery conference in New York City. But halfway there you turned around. You couldn't get yourself to attend because you were ashamed about your writer's block. You came home unannounced and you caught us together. You pointed a gun at us. For a brief second, I thought you were actually going to kill us. But instead, you lowered the gun and began to cry. Then, you simply turned, walked out, and drove away. The next day you pulled up with a van, and you moved out. "

I'm still shaking my head, the buzzing in my head growing louder and louder. "Had I already taken the manuscript?"

"You knew where the manuscript was, but you hadn't yet made the decision to steal it. It wasn't until you caught us together that you decided to take it for your own. Before you left that day, you went back downstairs, stole the manuscript out of my closet, and took it with you to your new studio, where you proceeded to copy it, word for word. And when you were done, you sent it to your agent, and there was nothing either David or I could do about it."

"Why?"

"Because if he made even the slightest stink, you were going to spring news of our affair on David's wife."

"He was married?"

She nods. "A divorce would have crushed him financially. Back when he was writing *The Damned*, he wasn't much better off money-wise than you were." She raises her hand, wipes the tears from both cheeks. "Turns out his wife divorced him later on anyway when she finally did find out about me, but that was months after you and I broke apart."

"So I took the book and he never did anything about it?"

"What the hell could he do? *The Damned* became a big success. He would have just appeared to be some crazy man crying plagiarism. Finally there was the matter of the story itself. The pyromaniac, Drew Brennen. He was based on you, what you went through. You might not have written *The Damned*, but in many ways, it was still your book."

"You deliberately gave him my story."

"Yes, I confided in him about your troubles like anyone would confide in a good friend or a lover. But I didn't know he was going to write a novel based on them."

"But you told me he wanted me to look at it while it was still in progress. Why would he do that? Surely I'd recognize the character as me."

She nods her head like she's been anticipating the question all along.

"He was goading you. Baiting you. Asserting some kind of weird power over you that must have come in part from his sleeping with Reece Johnston's wife. He knew deep down that you would never really look at the book. He knew that if it was indeed a good book, you would hate him even more."

"I didn't look at it until I stole it?" I say like a question.

"That's right, Reece. You never did look at it, even though you had plenty of opportunities over the many months we conducted our affair right under your nose." She starts to cry. "An affair I so deeply regret now."

"David had talent," I say, working up a bitter smile. "He should have moved on and written more books."

"That's true, of course. But something strange happened along the way. After the shock therapy, your writer's block ended, and you were able to write four more novels. As for David, he found that as hard as he tried, he simply could not write another after *The Damned*. You destroyed his career, Reece. You betrayed him and he wanted nothing more than to destroy you. In his eyes, you were a heretic. You had betrayed the solemn oath he claims every author takes, whether he's even aware of it or not. You must never steal another man's words. Ever."

"So why did he wait so long to try and kill me?"

"Because . . ." Her voice trails off and she begins to quietly weep.

"Because why, Lisa?"

I'm not sure how it happens, but the answer comes to me without her having to say the words. Comes to me not from my brain, but from my gut.

"Anna," I say.

"Yes," she cries. "Anna is David's daughter."

"He was your lover while we were married. He fathered our daughter. Now I know why you gave him a key to the place, even after you split up and changed the locks."

In my head, I once more see myself holding little Anna only moments after she was born. I see her full head of hair and her face that bore a smile. But it can't be a real memory. It has to be a fabricated memory. A figment of an overactive imagination. The imagination of a fiction writer. But then, that's not exactly right either. I was there holding the newborn Anna. My dad was there too.

"You led me to believe that Anna was my own," I say, then start in on the awful math. "Anna was born in July of 2006, and I left that September after I caught you and David in bed. That means for the three months the three of us lived in this house, I naturally assumed Anna was my own, but in fact, she was David's."

Lisa's sobs fill the basement spaces. Until I work up the courage to ask her the only question left to ask.

"Why did you take me back?"

"I loved David. But I loved you more. That's all there is to it."

"I've had some success, even with my own books. That kind of success eluded David."

"Yes, the successful part of you is attractive, I will admit. But I do love you with or without it. You must believe me."

"Even knowing what I've done? Even knowing my relationship with fire? You still loved me more than David?"

She exhales, once again wipes her face dry of the tears that fall from red, swollen eyes.

"You're a writer, Reece. David was a writer. I can't begin to understand what happens inside your head, inside your soul. All I know is that I have loved you both. Eventually I had to make a choice. I chose you. Fire and all. Craziness and all."

"And David died because of it. Because of me."

"No, Reece. David was a hair's breadth from dying even before you and I got back together. He couldn't go on if he couldn't write. I would have left him even if you hadn't come back into my life when your dad died. He'd become a tale of two men. On one hand he was still the sweet, quiet man who would lie down on the floor and play games with Anna for hours on end. But then there was the man who was starting to live out the storyline of *The Damned*, buying caskets, experimenting with fire, reading and rereading all your books." She exhales, bitterly. "For Christ's sakes, Reece, you saw what he did to my father."

"But still you gave him a key to the house, you still answered his calls, still texted with him, still Facebooked with him. You did it behind my back, because even though you love me and wanted to try again, you still couldn't shake your feelings for him entirely, no matter how nuts he'd become. After all, you shared a strong bond, you two. Your daughter, Anna."

"Yes. It was a mistake I'll regret for the rest of my days."

For a moment more we just stand there inside the basement, the manuscript of *The Damned* set out on the floor, every word on every page a lie connected to another lie. But also a lie based on the truth. My truth and my past.

Lifting my head, I go to Lisa and face her. In my head I see her and David together, sitting in some nondescript restaurant, the room dark and candlelit. I see them sipping wine and I hear Lisa telling him everything about my obsession with fire, about how it came to be, and how it took control of me.

Looking at her teary-eyed face, I don't feel love for her, so much as sadness. Suddenly our second chance at being together, the prospect of spending my life with her, no longer seems as real as it did only four days ago when she left the house for tear duct surgery.

I slip on past her.

"Where are you going?" she asks.

I stop, turn myself around to face her. "I'm going to do something I should have done years ago."

"And what is that exactly, Reece?"

"I'm going to do what David asked me to do just before he burned your father to death. I'm going to tell the world the truth about *The Damned.*"

Chapter 82

Upstairs in the dining room, I boot up my laptop. I trigger the command that initiates the laptop video camera. As soon as I'm ready, I press "Play." For a few seconds I just stare into the camera, as though I'm incapable of making words. But then, just like that, the words come to me. They come out of me like a heated flood of emotions that have been building up for nearly an entire decade.

"My name is Reece Johnston. I'm a best-selling author and I have a confession to make . . ."

While the first viral video I made paints a picture of an evil David Bourenhem who was about to kill my family, this one is entirely different. In this video I tell the truth about *The Damned*, spilling it all out, and in doing so, I feel my body grow lighter than it's felt in years. I admit to everything. About the writer's block, about the desperation that resulted from it, about turning to the dark side, as it were, about becoming a heretic. I also reassure those who care that the four books that followed are indeed my own. However, even I must admit, the novels aren't as good as *The Damned* and for that I have David Bourenhem to thank, even if he did steal my personal story of fire. Maybe I had no choice but to kill him in the defense of my family, but he is the father of my daughter. And while I still consider Anna my daughter as if she were my own, he will always be as much her biological creator as he was the true creator of *The Damned*.

When the filming is done, I save the digitally videotaped message and post it on all the social media networks. I have no idea what will come of it. Or, if my career, such as it is, is now entirely ruined, and if . . . God forbid . . . I might actually have to seek out traditional employment. You know, get a real job. But in the end, I have come clean, and that's what matters most.

David Bourenhem was right.

I did wrong when I took his manuscript and published it as my own. It's a shame I killed his ability to write, and it's a shame he had to die over it all in the end. But that's what happened. In writing *The Damned*, that's exactly what he became. And when Lisa became his illicit lover, and spilled my story to him, that's what she, too, became.

Maybe I am now also damned. Maybe one day I will burn in hellfire as my punishment. Maybe an eternal fire pit awaits us all. Or maybe Jesus wasn't preaching fictions when, dying on the cross, he said, "Father, forgive them, for they know not what they do."

That's what I prefer to believe. That in the very end, we will all be forgiven our trespasses.

I look around the room. It occurs to me I haven't seen my dad since the fire at the Reynoldses' estate.

"How'd I do, Dad?" I say to the empty dining room.

The only response I get is the pitter-patter of paws on the floor. It's Frankie. She looks up at me, her tail wagging, as if happy to see me sitting before my laptop. As she lowers herself comfortably onto the floor by my feet, her head resting on her paws, I place my hands on the keyboard, click open the word processor, and bring up a blank page.

"Here we go, Frank," I say.

Staring into the infinite white space, I begin to type the opening words to a brand-new novel.

The boy wakes to smoke and fire . . .

Acknowledgments

I write all my books by myself. Nobody helps me. Well, I'm lying, but then, that's what I do for a living. That said, I've had a tremendous amount of help along the way on this novel. It's impossible to name everyone who helped, but for sure I want to thank my editors at Thomas & Mercer, Kjersti Egerdahl and Alan Turkus, and also my marketing genius and undying supporter and friend, Jacque Ben-Zekry (you are the title master!). A big debt of gratitude goes to creative editor David Downing for working his magic on the manuscript and making me see not only the possibilities in my words but also in myself as a writer. I need to thank my Janey-on-the-spot editor Holly Lorincz for going through several drafts of this manuscript prior to my white-knuckled submission to my publisher. Also deserving of a major man-hug is my agent, Chip MacGregor. You've escaped New York, but somehow you still manage to seal the deal. Now comes the gray area where I'm going to forget a few people, but I would certainly be remiss without thanking Laura Roth, without whom this novel would not have been written (or *The Remains,* for that matter). I also want to thank my kids, Ava, Harrison, and Jack, for not being too upset with my long absences both when I'm home and away. Love you guys. Finally, I'm not going to name names, but I want to thank a few special people who have been there for me over the past nine years. You were a source of undying support, and you are not forgotten. Like I said, I'm not going to name names, but I'm quite certain you know who you are.

About the Author

Photo © 2013 Jessica Painter

Vincent Zandri is the *New York Times* and *USA Today* bestselling author of more than sixteen novels, including *The Innocent, Godchild, The Remains, Moonlight Falls,* and *The Shroud Key*. A freelance photojournalist and traveler, he is also the author of the blog *The Vincent Zandri Vox*. He lives in New York and Florence, Italy. For more, go to http://www.vincentzandri.com/.